"Lafayette! My boy, you've repented! You've come to me to make a clean breast of it, to tell me where you've hidden her! I'll go to His Majesty—"

"Hold it!" O'Leary sank down on a wobbly stool. "I haven't repented of anything, Nicodaeus! I told you, somebody came to my room, told me Adoranne was in trouble and led me into a secret passage. Then the double-crosser gave me a push and shoved some junk into my hand, and the lights went on."

"Certainly, lad, and now you've decided to throw yourself on His Majesty's mercy."

"You mean apologize for not letting him cut me into slices for something I didn't do? Ha! Look here, Nicodaeus, there's something funny going on around here. I want to see Adoranne and explain what happened. She thinks I stole her crown jewels or . . ." He broke off, seeing the expression on the other's face. "What's the matter?" He came to his feet in sudden alarm. "She hasn't been hurt?"

"You mean—you really don't know?" Nicodaeus blinked through his rimless glasses.

"Don't know what?" O'Leary yelled. "Where's Adoranne?"

Nicodaeus' shoulders slumped. "I had hoped you could tell *me* that, Lafayette. She's been missing since some time before dawn. And everyone thinks you, my boy, are the one who stole her."

THE TIME BENDER

KEITH LAUMER

ace books
A Division of Charter Communications Inc.
A GROSSET & DUNLAP COMPANY
51 Madison Avenue
New York, New York 10010

An ACE Book

First Ace printing: March 1981
Published Simultaneously in Canada
2 4 6 8 0 9 7 5 3 1
Manufactured in the United States of America

CHAPTER I

Lafayette O'Leary came briskly up the cracked walk leading to Mrs. MacGlint's Clean Rooms and Board, reflecting on his plans for the evening: First, he'd grab a quick bite, then check to see how his plastics experiment was coming along; after that, a look in on his *penicillium notatum* NRRL 1249.B21 culture, and then. . . . He hefted the weighty book under his arm. Professor Hans Joseph Schimmerkopf's book on mesmerism ought to be good for at least a week of evenings.

As O'Leary put foot on the sagging veranda, the front screen door popped wide open. A square figure five feet eleven in height confronted him, a heavy-duty broom held at port arms.

"Mr. O'Leary! What's that mess you've got percolating on my hot plate back in my third-best western exposure?"

Lafayette retreated a step. "Did I leave my polymers cooking, Mrs. MacGlint? I thought I turned them off——"

"Them fumes has faded the colors right out of the wallpaper! Not to say nothing about running up the electric bill! I'll put it on your bill, Mr. O'Leary!"

"But——"

"And all this reading at night! Burning light bulbs like they was free! My other boarders don't set up all hours, studying Lord knows what in them un-Christian books you got!" She eyed the volume under O'Leary's arm with unmistakable hostility.

"Say, Mrs. MacGlint," O'Leary edged back up on the porch, "a funny thing happened last night. I was running a little statistical study, using ball bearings, and I happened to drop a couple of them—three-quarter-inchers—and they all rolled right to the northwest corner of the room——"

"Prob'ly marked up my linoleum, too! And——"

"I knew the floors slanted but I hadn't noticed how much," Lafayette gained another foot. "So I made a few measurements. I'd say there's a two-inch discrepancy from wall to wall. I knew you'd want to know, because Section Four, Article 19 of the Building Code—the part that covers Hazardous Conditions Due to Settlement of Foundations—is pretty clear. Now, the inspector will have to check it, of course, and after the house is condemned and the roomers find other quarters, then maybe they can save the place by pumping in concrete. That's pretty expensive, but it's better than breaking the law, eh, Mrs. MacGlint?"

"Law?" The landlady's voice squeaked. "Building Code? Why, I never heard such nonsense . . ."

"Do you want to report it, or shall I? I know you're awfully busy, keeping everybody's affairs in order, so . . ."

"Now, Mr. O'Leary, don't go to no trouble . . ." Mrs. MacGlint backed through the door; Lafayette followed into the gloom and cabbage aroma of the hall. "I know you got your science work you want to get to, so I won't keep you." She turned and puffed off along the hall. O'Leary let out a long breath and headed up the stairs.

On the shelf behind the curtain in the former broom closet which served Lafayette as kitchen alcove were a two-pound tin of salt-water taffy, a cardboard salt shaker, a ketchup bottle, a can of soup and two tins of preserved fish. He didn't really like sardines, he confessed to himself, unwrapping a succulent taffy. Too bad they didn't can *consommé au beurre blanc Hermitage*. Tend-R Nood-L Soup would have to do. He started warming a saucepan of soup, took a beer from the foot-square icebox and punched a triangular hole in the lid. He finished off the candy, then the beer, waiting for the pot to boil, then set out a bowl, poured the soup and put two sardines on a cracker. Munching, he picked up his book. It was a thick, dusty volume, bound in faded dark blue leather, the cramped gilt letters on the spine almost illegible. He blew the dust away and opened it with care; the old binding crackled. The title page announced:

Mesmerism, Its Proper Study and Practice; or The Secrets of the Ancients Unlocked.
By Herr Professor Doktor Hans Joseph Schimmerkopf, D.D., Ph.D., Litt. D., M. A., B. Sc., Associate Professor of Mental Sciences and Natural Philosophy, Homeopathic Institute of Vienna. 1888.

O'Leary riffled through the tissue-thin pages of fine print; pretty dry stuff, really. Still, it was the only book on hypnotism in the library that he hadn't already read, and what else was there to do? O'Leary looked out the narrow window at the sad late-afternoon light, yellowing into evening. He could go out and buy a newspaper; he might even stroll around the block. He could stop by the Elite Bar and Grill and have a cold beer. There were any number of ways a young, healthy, penniless draftsman in a town like Colby Corners could spend an evening in the sunshine of his happy youth.

A rattle of knuckles at the door announced a narrow-faced man with thin hair and a toothbrush mustache slid into the room.

"Hi, Laff, howza boy?" the newcomer rubbed knuckly hands together. He wore a purple shirt and white suspenders supporting trousers cut high above bony hips.

"Hello, Spender," O'Leary greeted him without enthusiasm.

"Say, Laff, you couldn't slip me five until Tuesday?"

"I'm busted, Spender. Besides which, you owe me five."

"Hey, what's the book?" Spender edged in beside him and poked at the pages. "When do you get time to read all this stuff? Pretty deep, huh? You're a funny guy; always like studying."

"This is a racy one," O'Leary said. "The press it was printed on was smashed with crowbars by a crowd of aroused peasants. Then they ran the author down and gave him the full werewolf treatment—silver bullet, stake through the heart—the works."

"Wow!" Spender recoiled. "You studying to be a werewolf, O'Leary?"

"No, I'm more interested in the vampire angle. That's the one where you turn into a bat——"

"Look, Laff, that ain't funny. You know I'm kind of like superstitious. You shouldn't ought to read them books."

O'Leary looked at the other speculatively. "What I need now is some practical experience——"

"Yeah, well, I'll see you, boy." Spender backed out the door.

O'Leary finished his repast, then stretched out on the lumpy bed. The water stains on the ceiling hadn't changed since yesterday, he noted. The opalescent globe shielding the sixty-watt bulb dangling on its kinked cord still contained the same number of dead flies. The oleander bush still scraped restlessly on the screen.

He flipped open Schimmerkopf's book at random and skimmed the print-packed pages. The sections on mesmerism were routine stuff, but a passage on autohypnosis caught his eye:

> ". . . this state may readily be induced by the adept practitioner of the art of Mesmeric influence, or of hypnotism, as it is latterly termed, requiring only a schooled effort of Will, supported by a concentration of Psychical Energies. Mastery of this Force not only offers instantaneous relief from sleeplessness, night sweats, poor memory, sour bile, high chest, salivation, inner conflict, and

other ills both of the flesh and of the spirit, but offers as well a veritable treasurehouse of rich sensation; for it is a commonplace of the auto-Mesmerist's art that such scenes of remembered or imagined Delight as must be most highly esteemed by persons sensible of the lamentable drabness of Modern Life can in this fashion be evoked most freely for the delectation and adornment of the idle hour.

"This phenomenon may be likened to the hypnogogic state, that condition of semi-awareness sometimes achieved by a sleeping person who, partially awakened, is capable of perceiving dream-state images, whilst at the same time enjoying consciousness of their illusory nature. Thus, he is rendered capable of examining the surface texture and detail of an imagined object as acutely as one might study the page of an actual book, throughout maintaining knowledge of the distinction between hallucinatory experience and real experience. . . ."

That part made sense, O'Leary nodded. It had happened to him just a few nights ago. It was almost as though his awareness had been attuned to a different channel of existence; as though he had emerged from half-sleep at the wrong floor, so to speak, and stepped off the elevator into a strange world, not totally different, but subtly rearranged—until the shock of realization had jarred him back to the familiar level of stained wallpaper and the lingering memory of brussels sprouts boiled long ago. And if you could produce the effect at will. . . .

O'Leary read on, looking for precise instructions. Three pages further on he found a line or two of specifics:

> ". . . use of a bright object, such as a highly polished gem, as an aid to the Powers of Concentration, may, with profitable results, be employed by the earnest student of these pages. . . ."

Lafayette considered. He owned no gems——not even glass ones. Perhaps a spoon would work. But no——his ring; just the thing. He tugged at the heavy silver ornament on the middle finger of his left hand. No use; the knuckle was too big. After all, he'd been wearing it for years now. But he didn't need to remove the ring; he could stare at it just as well where it was, on his hand.

Lying on his back in the twilit room, he looked up at ancient floral-patterned paper, faded now to an off-white. This would be a good place to start. Now, suppose the ceiling were high, spacious, painted a pale gold color . . .

O'Leary persevered, whispering persuasively to himself. It was easy, the professor had said; just a matter of focusing the Psychical Energies and attuning the Will . . .

Lafayette sighed, blinked through the gloom at the blotched nongolden ceiling; he rose and went to the icebox for another warm beer. The bed squeaked as he sat on its edge. He might have known it wouldn't work. Old Professor Schimmerkopf was a quack, after all. Nothing as delightful as what the old boy had described could have gone unnoticed all these years.

He lay back against the pillows at the head of the bed. It would have been nice if it *had* worked. He could have redecorated his shabby quarters and told himself that the room was twice as large, with a view of a skyline of towers and distant mountains. Music, too; with total recall, he could play back every piece of music he'd ever heard.

Not that any of it really mattered. He slept all right on the sagging bed—and taffy and sardines might get boring, but they went right on nourishing you. The room was dreary, but it kept off the rain and snow, and when the weather got cold, the radiator, with many thumps and wheezes, kept the temperature within the bearable range. The furniture wasn't fancy, but it was adequate. There was the bed, of course, and the table built from an orange crate and painted white, and the dresser, and the oval rag rug Miss Flinders at the library had given him.

And, oh yes, the tall locked cabinet in the corner. Funny he hadn't gotten around to opening it yet. It had been there ever since he had moved in, and he hadn't even wondered about it. Strange. But he could open it now. There was something wonderful in it, he remembered that much; but somehow he couldn't quite recall what.

He was standing in front of the cabinet, looking at the black-varnished door. A rich-grained wood showed faintly through the cracked glaze; the key hole was brass lined, and there were little scratches around it. Now, where was the key? Oh, yes . . .

Lafayette crossed the room to the closet and stepped inside. The light was dim here. He pulled a large box into position, stepped up on it, lifted the trapdoor in the ceiling, climbed up and emerged in an attic. Late afternoon sun gleamed through a dusty window. There was a faded rug on the floor, and large, brass-bound trunks were stacked everywhere. Lafayette tried the lids; all locked.

He remembered the keys. That was what he had come for. They were hanging on a nail, behind the door. He plucked them down, started for the trap-door.

But why not take the stairs? Out in the hall, a white-painted bannister gleamed. He went down, walked along a hall, found his room and stepped inside. The French windows were open, and a fresh breeze blew in. The curtains, billowy white, gleamed in the sun. Outside, a wide lawn, noble trees, a path leading somewhere.

But he had to open the cabinet, to see what was inside. He selected a key—a large, brassy one—and tried it in the keyhole. Too large. He tried another; also too big. There was only one more key, a long, thin one of black iron. It didn't fit. Then he noticed more keys, hidden under the last one, somehow. He tried them, one by one. None fitted. He eyed the keyhole, bright brass against the dark wood, scarred by near misses. He had to get the cabinet open. Inside there were treasures, marvelous things, stacked on shelves, waiting for him. He tried another key. It fit. He turned it carefully and heard a soft click!

A violent pounding shattered the stillness. The cabinet door glimmered, fading; only the keyhole was still visible. He tried to hold it——

"Mr. O'Leary, you open up this door this minute!" Mrs. MacGlint's voice cut through the dream like an ax. Lafayette sat up, hearing a buzzing in his head, still groping after something almost grasped, but lost forever now.

The door rattled in its frame. "You open this, you hear me?" Lafayette could hear voices, the scrape of feet from the neighboring rooms. He reached, pulled the string that switched on the ceiling light, went across to the door and jerked it open. The vengeful bulk of Mrs. MacGlint quivered before him.

"I heard voices, whispering like, and I wondered," she shrilled. "In there in the dark. Then I heard them bedsprings creak and then everything got quiet!" She thrust her head past Lafayette, scanning the room's interior.

"All right, where's she hid?" Behind her, Spender, from next door, and Mrs. Potts, in wrapper and curlers, hovered, trying for a glimpse of the source of the excitement.

"Where is who hid?" O'Leary oofed as the landlady's massive elbow took him in the short ribs. She bellied past him, stooped to stare under the spindle-legged bed, whirled, jerked the alcove curtain aside. She shot an accusing look at O'Leary, bustled to the window and dug at the hook holding the screen shut.

"Must of got her out the window," she puffed, whirling to confront Lafayette. "Fast on your feet, ain't you?"

"What are you looking for? That screen hasn't been opened for years——"

"You know well as I do, young Mr. O'Leary—that I give house space to for nigh to a year——"

"Laff, you got a *gal* in here?" Spender inquired, sidling into the room.

"A girl?" Lafayette shook his head. "No, there's no girl here, and not much of anything else."

"Well!" Mrs. MacGlint stared around the room.

Her expression twitched to blankness. Then she tucked in her chins. "Anybody would've thought the same thing," she declared. "There's not a soul'd blame me . . ."

Mrs. Potts sniffed and withdrew. Spender snickered and sauntered out. Mrs. MacGlint moved past O'Leary, not quite looking at him.

"Respectable house," she muttered. "Setting in here in the dark, talking to hisself, *alone* . . ."

Lafayette closed the door behind her, feeling empty, cheated. He had almost gotten that cabinet door open, discovered what was inside that had promised such excitement. Ruefully he eyed the blank place beside the door where he had dreamed the mysterious locker. He hadn't had much luck with the professor's recipes for self-hypnosis, but his dreaming abilities were still impressive. If Mrs. MacGlint hadn't chosen that moment to burst in . . .

But the trunks upstairs! Lafayette thought with sudden excitement. He half-rose——

And sank back, with a weak smile. He had dreamed those, too; there was nothing upstairs but old Mr. Dinder's shabby room. But it had all seemed so real! As real as anything in the wide-awake world; more real, maybe.

But it was only a dream—a typical escape wish. Crawl through a trapdoor into another world. Too bad it wasn't really that easy. And the cabinet—obvious symbolism. The locked door represented all the excitement in life that he'd never been able to find. And all that fumbling with keys—that was a reflection of life's frustrations.

And yet that other world—the dim attic crowded with relics, the locked cabinet—had held a promise of things rich and strange. If only this humdrum world could be that way, with the feel of adventure in the air.

But it couldn't. Real life wasn't like that. Real life was getting up in the morning, working all day on the board, then the evening's chores, and sleep. Now it was time for the latter.

Lafayette lay in bed, aware of the gleam of light under the door, tiny night sounds, the distant stutter of an engine. It must be after midnight, and here he was, lying awake. He had to be up in six hours, hurrying off to the foundry in the gray morning light. Better get to sleep. And no more time wasted on dreams.

Lafayette opened his eyes, looked at a brick wall a yard or two away, warm and red in the late orange sunlight. The bricks were tarnished and chipped, and there was moss growing along one edge of each, and between them the mortar was crumbling and porous. At the base of the wall there was grass, vivid green, and little yellow flowers, hardly bigger than forget-me-nots. A small gray insect appeared over the curve of a petal, feelers waving, and then hurried away on important business. O'Leary had never seen a bug quite like it—or flowers like those, either. Or for that matter, a brick wall like this one . . .

Where was he, anyway? He groped for recollection, remembering Mrs. MacGlint's, the book he'd been reading, the landlady's invasion; then going to bed, lying awake . . . But how did he get *here*—and where was *here*?

Quite suddenly, O'Leary was aware of what was happening: he was asleep—or half-asleep—and he was dreaming the wall, each separate brick with its pattern of moss—a perfect example of hypnogogic illusion!

With an effort of will, Lafayette blanked out other thoughts; excitement thumped in his chest. *Concentrate!* the professor had said. *Focus the Psychic Energies!*

The bricks became clearer, gaining in solidity. Lafayette brushed aside vagrant wisps of distracting thought, giving his full attention to the image of the wall, holding it, building it, *believing* it. He had known dreams were vivid; they always seemed real as they happened. But this was perfect!

Carefully he worked on extending the range of the scene. He could see a flagstone path lying between him and the wall. The flat stones were grayish tan, flaking in flat laminae, almost buried in the soil, with tiny green blades sprouting between them. He followed the path with his eyes; it led away along the wall into the shadow of giant trees. Amazing how the mind supplied details; the trees were flawless conceptualizations, every branch and twig and leaf, every shaggy curl of bark as true as life. If he had a canvas now, he could paint them . . .

But suppose, instead of letting his subconscious supply the details, he filled them in himself? Suppose, for example, there were a rosebush, growing there beside the three. He concentrated, trying to picture the blossoms.

The scene remained unchanged—and then abruptly began to fade, like water soaking into a blotter; the trees blurred and all around dim walls seemed to close in——

Dismayed, Lafayette grabbed for the illusion, fighting to hold the fading image intact. He switched his gaze back to the brick wall directly before him; it had shrunk to a patch of masonry a yard in diameter, thin and unconvincing. He fought, gradually rebuilding the solidity of the wall. These hypnogogic phenomena were fragile, it seemed; they couldn't stand much manipulation.

The wall was solidly back in place now, but, strangely, the flowers were gone. In their place was a cobbled pavement. There was a window in the wall now, shuttered by warped, unpainted boards. Above it, an expanse of white-washed plaster crisscrossed by heavy timbers extended up to an uneven eave line silhouetted against an evening sky of deep electric blue in which an early moon gleamed. It was a realistic enough scene, Lafayette thought, but a bit drab. It needed something to brighten it up; a drugstore, say, its windows cheery with neon and hearty laxative ads; something to lend a note of gaiety.

But he wasn't going to make the mistake of tampering, this time. He'd let well enough alone, and see what there was to see. Cautiously, Lafayette extended his field of vision. The narrow street—almost an alley—wound off into darkness, closed in by tall, overhanging houses. He noted the glisten of wet cobbles, a puddle of oily water, a scattering of rubbish. His subconscious, it appeared, lacked an instinct for neatness.

There was a sudden jar—a sense of an instant's

discontinuity, like a bad splice in a movie film. O'Leary looked around for the source, but saw nothing. And yet, somehow, everything seemed subtly changed—more *convincing*, in some subtle way.

He shook off the faint feeling of uneasiness. It was a swell hallucination and he'd better enjoy it to the fullest, while it lasted.

The house across the way, he saw, was a squeezed-in, half-timbered structure like the one in front of which he was standing, with two windows at ground-floor level made from the round bottoms of bottles set in lead strips, glowing amber and green and gold from a light within. There was a low, wide door, iron-bound, with massive hinges; over it a wooden sign hung from an iron rod. It bore a crudely painted representation of the prow of a Viking ship and a two-handed battle-ax. Lafayette smiled; his subconscious had seized on the device from his ring: the ax and dragon. Probably everything in the scene went back to something he had seen, or heard of, or read about. It was a fine illusion, no doubt about that: but what was it that was changed?

Odors, that was it. Lafayette sniffed, caught a scent of mold, spilled wine, garbage—a rich, moist aroma, with undertones of passing horses.

Now, what about sound? There should be the honking of horns, the clashing of gears—motor-scooter gears, probably; the street was too narrow for any except midget cars. And there ought to be a few voices hallooing somewhere, and, judging from the smell, the clash of garbage can lids. But all was silent. Except—Lafayette cupped a hand to his ear . . .

Somewhere, hooves clattered on pavement, retreating into the distance. A bell tolled far away, nine times. A door slammed. Faintly, Lafayette heard whistling, the clump of heavy footsteps. *People!* Lafayette thought with surprise. Well, why not? They should be as easy to imagine as anything else. It might be interesting to confront his creations face to face, engage them in conversation, discover all sorts of hidden aspects of his personality. Would they think they were real? Would they remember a yesterday?

Quite abruptly, O'Leary was aware of his bare feet against the cold paving stones. He looked down, saw that he was wearing nothing but his purple pajamas with the yellow spots. Hardly suitable for meeting people; he'd better equip himself with an outfit a little more appropriate to a city street. He closed his eyes, picturing a nifty navy-blue trench coat with raglan sleeves, a conservative dark gray suit of expensive cut, a black homburg—might as well go first class—and a cane—an ebony one with a silver head, for that man-about-town touch . . .

Something clanked against his leg. He looked down. He was wearing a coat of claret velvet, breeches of brown doeskin, gleaming, soft leather boots that came up to his thigh, a pair of jeweled pistols and an elaborate rapier with a worn hilt. Wonderingly, he gripped it, drew it halfway from the sheath; the sleek steel glittered in the light from the windows across the way.

Not quite what he'd ordered; he looked as though he were on his way to a fancy-dress ball. He still had a lot to learn about this business of self-hypnosis.

There was a startled yell from the dark street to O'Leary's right, then a string of curses. A man darted into view, clad in dingy white tights with a flap seat, no shoes. He shied as he saw O'Leary, turned and dashed off in the opposite direction. O'Leary gaped. A man! Rather an eccentric specimen, but still . . .

Other footsteps were approaching now. It was a boy, in wooden shoes and leather apron, a wool cap on his head. He wore tattered knee pants, and carried a basket from which the neck of a plucked goose dangled, and he was whistling *Alexander's Ragtime Band*.

Without a glance at O'Leary, the lad hurried by; the sound of the shoes and the whistling receded. O'Leary grinned. It seemed to be a sort of medieval scene he had cooked up, except for the anachronistic popular tune; somehow it was comforting to know that his subconscious wasn't above making a slip now and then.

From behind the tavern windows, he heard voices raised in song, a clash of crockery; he sniffed, caught the odors of wood smoke, candle wax, ale, roast fowl. He was hungry, he realized with a pang. Taffy and sardines weren't enough.

There was a new noise now: a snorting, huffing sound, accompanied by a grumbling, like a boulder rolling slowly over a pebbled beach. A bell dinged. A dark shape trundled into view, lanterns slung from its prow casting long shadows that fled along the street. A tall stack belched smoke; steam puffed from a massive piston at the side of the cumbersome vehicle. It moved past, its iron-bound wooden wheels thudding on the uneven stones. Lafayette caught a glimpse of a red-faced man in a tricorn hat, perched high up above the riveted boiler. The steam car rumbled on its way, a red lantern bobbing at its tail gate. O'Leary shook his head; he hadn't gotten *that* out of a history book. Grinning, he hitched up his belt.

The door of the Ax and Dragon swung open, spilling light on the cobbles. A fat man tottered out, waved an arm, staggered off up the narrow street, warbling tunelessly. Before the door shut, Lafayette caught a glimpse of a warm interior, a glowing fire, low beams, the gleam of polished copper and brass, heard the clamor of voices, the thump of beer mugs banged on plank tables.

He was cold, and he was hungry. Over there was warmth and food—to say nothing of beer.

In four steps he crossed the street. He paused for a moment to settle his French cocked hat on his forehead, adjust the bunch of lace at his chin; then he hauled open the door and stepped into the smoky interior of the Ax and Dragon.

CHAPTER II

In the sudden warmth and rich odors of the room, O'Leary paused, blinking against the light shed by the lanterns pegged to the wooden posts supporting the sagging celing. Heads turned to stare; voices trailed off into silence as Lafayette looked around the room. There were wine and ale barrels ranked along one side; to their right was a vast fireplace in which a whole hog, a goose, and half a dozen chickens turned on a spit over a bed of red coals. Lafayette sniffed; the odors were delightful!

The texture and solidity of the scene were absolutely convincing—even better than Professor Schimmerkopf had described—full tactile, auditory, visual and olfactory stimulation. And coming inside hadn't disturbed things in the least; after all, why should it? He often dreamed of wandering through buildings; the only difference was that this time he *knew* he was dreaming, while a small part of his mind stayed awake, watching the show.

There was a vacant seat at the rear of the long

room; O'Leary started toward it, nodding pleasantly at staring faces. A thin man in a patched tabard scrambled from his path; a fat woman with red cheeks muttered and drew a circle in the air. Those seated at the table toward which he was moving edged away. He sat down, put his hat beside him, looked around, smiled encouragingly at his creations.

"Uh, please, go right ahead with what you were doing," he said in the silence. "Oh, bartender . . ." He signaled to a short, thick-necked man hovering behind a trestle between the beer kegs. "A bottle of the best in the house, please. Ale or wine, it doesn't matter."

The bartender said something; O'Leary cupped his ear.

"Eh? Speak up, I didn't get that."

"I says all we got is small beer and *vin ordinaire,*" the man muttered. There was something odd about the way he spoke . . . Still, O'Leary reminded himself, he couldn't expect to get everything perfect the first time out.

"That'll do," he said, automatically making an effort to match the other's speech pattern.

The man gaped, closed his mouth with an audible gulp, stooped and plucked a dusty flagon from a stack on the floor, which, Lafayette noted idly, seemed to be of hardpacked dirt. A nice detail, he approved. Practical, too; it would soak up spilled booze.

Someone was muttering at the far end of the room. A barrel-shaped ruffian rose slowly, stepped out into the clear, flexed massive shoulders, then sauntered forward. He had a wild mop of unkempt red hair, a flattened nose, one cauliflowered ear, and huge, hairy fists, the thumbs of which were hooked in the rope tied around his waist. O'Leary noted the striped stockings below the patched knee breeches, the clumsy shoes, like loafers which large iron buckles. The man's shirt was a soiled white, open at the neck, with floppy sleeves. A foot-long sheath knife was strapped to his hip. He came up to Lafayette's table, planted himself and stared down at him.

"He don't look so tough," he announced to the silent room in a growl like a Kodiak bear.

Lafayette stared into the man's face, studying the mean, red-rimmed eyes, the white scar tissue marking the cheek bones, the massive jaw, the thick lips, lumpy from past batterings, the sprouting stubble. He smiled.

"Marvelous," he said. His eyes went to the barman. "Hubba hubba with that wine," he called cheerily. "And I'll have a chicken sandwich on rye; I'm hungry. All I had for dinner was a couple of sardines." He smiled encouragingly at his table mates, who crouched back, eyeing him fearfully. The redhead was still standing before him.

"Sit down," Lafayette invited. "How about a sandwich?"

The lout's small eyes narrowed. "I say he's some kind of a Nance," the rumbling voice stated.

Lafayette chuckled, shaking his head. This was as good as a psychoanalysis! This oaf, a personification of a subconscious virility symbol, had stated an opinion doubtless heretofore suppressed somewhere deep in the id or superego, where it had probably been causing all sorts of neuroses. Now, by getting it out in the open, he could face it, observe for himself the ludicrousness of it and thereafter dismiss it.

"Come on, sit down," he ordered. "Tell me just what you meant by that remark."

"Nuts to youse," the heavyweight grated, looking around for approval. "Yer mudduh wears ankle socks."

"Tsk, tsk." Lafayette looked at the fellow reproachfully. "Better do as I say, or I'll turn you into a fat lady."

"Huh?" Big Red's rusty eyebrows crawled like caterpillars on his low forehead. His mouth opened, revealing a row of chipped teeth.

The landlord sidled nervously around the redhead and placed a dusty bottle on the table with a roast fowl beside it *sans* plate.

"That'll be a buck fifty," he muttered. Lafayette patted his hip pocket, took out his familiar wallet, remembering belatedly that there was only a dollar in it. Hmmm. But why couldn't it have fifty dollars in it, instead? He pictured the impressive bill, crisp and green and reassuring. And why just one? Why not a whole stack of fifties? And maybe a few hundreds thrown in for good measure. He might as well dream big. He squinted, concentrating . . .

There was an almost silent pop! as though a vast soap bubble had burst. O'Leary frowned. Funny sensation; still, it might be normal in hallucination; it seemed to happen every so often. He opened the wallet, revealed a stack of crisp bills, withdrew one with a grand gesture; it was a fifty, just as specified.

But the lettering . . . The hen-tracks across the top of the bill looked incomplete, barely legible—. The first letter was like an O with a small x on top, followed by an upside-down u, a squiggle, some dots . . .

Then suddenly the strangeness faded. The letters seemed to come into focus, like a perspective diagram shifting orientation. The words were perfectly readable, O'Leary saw. But the first letter: it *did* look like an O with an x on top of it. He frowned at it thoughtfully. There wasn't any such letter—was there? But there must be: he was reading it —

He smiled at himself as the explanation dawned. His dreaming mechanism, always consistent, had cooked up a foreign language to go with the foreign setting. Naturally, since he'd invented it himself, he could read it. The same probably applied to the spoken tongue. If he could wake up and hear his conversation here, it would all probably come out as gibberish, like the poems people dreamed and wrote down to look at in the morning. They never made sense. But the words on the bill were clear enough: the legend "Royal Treasury of Artesia" was lettered above the familiar picture of Grant—or was it Grant? Lafayette saw with some surprise that he was wearing a tiny peruke and a lacy ruff. Play money, after all.

But what did it matter? He smiled at himself. He couldn't take it with him when he woke up. He handed the bill over to the barman who gaped and scratched his head.

"Geez, I can't break no fifty, yer lordship," he muttered. As the man spoke, O'Leary listened carefully. Yes, it was a strange language—but his mind was interpreting it as modified Brooklynese.

"Keep it," Lafayette said grandly. "Just keep the wine flowing—and how about bringing over a couple of glasses, and possibly a knife and fork?"

The barman hurried off. The redhead was still standing, glowering.

"Down in front," Lafayette said, indicating the seat opposite him. "You're blocking the view."

The big man shot a glance at the customers watching him and then threw out his chest.

"Duh Red Bull don't drink wit' no ribbon-counter Fancy-Dan," he announced.

"Better change your mind," O'Leary cautioned, blowing dust from the lopsided green bottle the waiter had brought. "Or I may have to just shrink you down to where I can see over you."

The redhead blinked at him; his mouth puckered uncertainly. The barman was back with two heavy glass mugs. He darted a look at the Red Bull, quickly removed the cork from the bottle, slopped an inch or two of the wine in one cup and shoved it toward Lafayette. He picked it up and sniffed. It smelled like vinegar. He tasted it. It was thin and sour. He pushed the mug away.

"Don't you have something better——" he paused. Just suppose, he mused, there was a bottle of a rare vintage—Chateau Lafitte-Rothschilde, '29, say—over there under that heap of dusty bottles . . . He narrowed his eyes, picturing the color of the glass, the label, willing it to be there——

His eyes popped open at the abrupt flicker in the smooth flow of—of whatever it was that flowed when time passed. That strange little blink in the sequence of the seconds! It had happened before, just as he was providing the reserves in his wallet, and before that, out in the street. Each time he made a modification in things, he had felt the jar. A trifling flaw in his technique, no doubt. Nothing to worry about.

"——the best in the place, yer Lordship," the barman was protesting.

"Look under the other bottles," O'Leary said. "See if there isn't a big bottle there, shaped like this." He indicated the contours of a Burgundy bottle.

"We ain't got——"

"Ah—ah! Take a look first." Lafayette leaned back, smiling around at the others. My, what an inventive subconscious he had! Long faces, round ones, old men, young women, fat, thin, weathered, pink-and-white, bearded, clean-shaven, blonds, brunettes, baldies——

The barman was back, gaping at the bottle in his hand. He put it on the table, stepped back. "Is this here what yer lordship meant?"

O'Leary nodded complacently. The barman pulled the cork. This time a delicate aroma floated from the glass. O'Leary sampled it. The flavor was musty, rich, a symphony of summer sun and ancient cellars. He sighed contentedly. It might be imaginary wine, but the flavor was real enough. The redhead, watching open-mouthed, leaned forward slightly, sniffed. A thick tongue appeared, ran over the scarred lips. Lafayette poured the second glass half full.

"Sit down and drink up, Red," he said.

The big man hesitated, picked up the glass,

sniffed, then gulped the contents. An amazed smile spread over the rugged features. He threw a leg over the bench and sat, shoving the mug toward Lafayette.

"Bo, that's good stuff you got there! I'll go fer another shot o' that!" He looked around belligerently. Lafayette refilled both glasses. A turkey-necked gaffer down the table edged closer, eyeing the bottle.

"Garçon," Lafayette called, "more glasses!" The man complied. Lafayette filled one for the oldster and passed it along. The old man sipped, gaped, gulped, licked toothless gums and grinned.

"Hey!" he cackled. "We ain't seen wine like this since the old king died."

A round-faced woman in a starched wimple with a broken corner shushed him with a look and thrust out a pewter mug. Lafayette filled it.

"Everybody drink up!" he invited. Clay cups, topless bottles, copper mugs came at him. He poured, pausing now and then to take a healing draft from his own mug. This was more like it!

"Let's sing!" he suggested. Merry voices chimed in, on *Old MacDonald*. The words were a little different than the ones O'Leary was accustomed to, but he managed, adding a fair baritone to the din. A hand touched the back of his neck; a buxom wench in a tight-laced blouse and peasant skirt slid into his lap, nibbled at his ear, bringing with her, O'Leary noted, a disconcerting odor of goat. He snorted, twisted to get a better look at the girl. She was cute enough, with red cheeks, a saucily turned-up nose, corn-yellow hair and pouty lips—but it seemed nobody had told her about soap. Still, there might be a remedy for that. Lafayette narrowed his eyes, trying to remember the odor of the perfume he had smelled once when a bottle broke at the drugstore when he was sweeping up just before closing time . . .

There was the familiar jog in the machinery. He sniffed cautiously. Nothing. Again—and he caught a whiff of Ivory soap; a third time, and the scent of Chanel No. 22 wafted to his nostrils. He smiled at the girl. She smiled back, apparently noticing nothing unusual. More glasses were thrust out. Lafayette disengaged himself from the soft and eager lips, poured, paused to swallow, refilled the girl's glass, then Red's pint mug, and another, and another . . .

The old man sitting next to the big redhead was frowning thoughtfully at the bottle in O'Leary's hand. He said something to the skinny grandma beside him. More frowns were appearing now. The singing was faltering, fading off into silence. The merry drinkers at the next table fell silent. People began crossing themselves—or rather, describing circles over their chests.

"What's the matter?" he inquired genially, lifting the bottle invitingly. Everyone jumped. Those nearest were rising hastily, moving back. A babble was growing—not the gay chatter of a moment before, but a fearful muttering.

Lafayette shrugged, pouring his glass full. As he moved to place the bottle on the table, a thought struck him. He hefted the flask. It seemed as heavy as ever. He reached over and poured the Red Bull's glass full. The big man hiccupped, made a wobbly circle before him with a finger like a Polish sausage, lifted the glass and drank. Lafayette tilted the bottle, peered inside the neck; a dark surface of deep red liquid gleamed an inch from the top. No wonder they were spooked, he thought disgustedly. He had carelessly decanted several gallons of wine from a one-liter bottle.

"Ah . . . look," he started, "that was just a trick, sort of . . .

"Sorcerer!" someone yelled. "Warlock!" another charged. There was a general movement toward the door.

"Wait!" O'Leary called, rising. At that, there was a stampede. In thirty seconds the tavern was deserted—with the sole exception of the Red Bull. The big man—sweating heavily but still game, Lafayette observed approvingly—held his ground. He licked his lips, cleared his throat.

"Dem other slobs," he growled, "pantywaists."

"Sorry about the bottle," O'Leary said apologetically. "Just a slip on my part." He could hear the voices of a gathering mob outside. The word "sorcerer" seemed to ring out with distressing frequency.

"A little magic, that ain't nuttin'," Red said. "But they got a idear dat on account of you're a . . . like a phantom ya might stick a . . . you know, whammy, on 'em. er maybe split open duh ground and drag 'em down into duh Pit. Er——"

"That's enough," Lafayette cut in, noticing the increasing nervousness on the battered features as the man enumerated the possible fates of those who trafficked with spooks. "All I did was pour out a few drinks. Does that make me a ghost?"

Big Red smiled craftily, eyeing Lafayette's

clothes. "Don't rib me, mister," he grated. "I know duh Phantom Highwayman when I see him."

O'Leary smiled. "You don't really believe in phantoms, do you?"

The Red Bull nodded vigorously. Lafayette noticed that he smelled of Chanel No. 22; apparently he'd overdone the perfume a trifle.

"On nights when duh moon is like a ghostly galleon," Red stated, "dat's when yuh ride."

"Nonsense," Lafayette said briskly. "My name is Lafayette O'Leary, and——"

"Now, what I got in mind, Bo, you and me, we could make a great team," Red bored on. "Wit' dem neat tricks you can do, like riding tru duh sky an all, and wit' my brains——"

"I'm afraid you're on the wrong track, Red." O'Leary refilled his glass for the fourth—or was it the fifth time? Lovely wine—and the glow was just as nice as though he hadn't dreamed up the whole thing. Would he have a hangover, he wondered, when he woke up in the morning? He hiccupped and refilled Red's glass.

". . . cased a coupla joints dat I figger dey'll be a cinch to knock over," the rumbling voice was saying. "Duh way I got duh caper doped out, I keep duh eyeball peeled for duh city guardsmen. Dem guys is all over like fleas in a four-bit flop dese days. If youse ast me, duh country ain't no better'n a police state; it ain't like de old days when I was a nipper. Anyways, youse can pull duh job, an' pass duh swag to me, and while duh johns is busy tailing youse, I'll——"

"You're talking nonsense, Red," O'Leary interrupted. "Crime doesn't pay. I'm sure you're really an honest fellow at heart, but you've been influenced by evil companions. Why don't you get yourself a job—at a service station, maybe——"

The Red Bull's forehead furrowed ominously. "Youse try'na tell me I look like a grease monkey?"

Lafayette peered at his companion's rugged features through a light fog which seemed to have arisen. "Nooo," he said thoughtfully. "More of an ape, I think. An oil ape." He beamed, raising his glass. "Tha's pretty clever, don't ye agroo? I mean don't you agree?"

The Red Bull growled. "I gotta good mind tuh rip youse apart, spook er no spook—!"

"Ah—ah!" Lafayette wagged a finger at the other. "No threats, please."

The redhead was on his feet, swaying slightly. "I can bust a oak plank in two wit' one punch," he stated, displaying a fist like a flint ax.

"Sit down, Red," O'Leary ordered. "I want to talk to you. As a figment of my imagination, you should be able to tell me lots of interesting things about my psyche. Now, I've been wondering, what role has sibling rivalry played——"

"I can ben' a iron bar inta pretzel wit' one hand tied behind me," the Red Bull stated. "I can——"

"Red, if you don't sit down, I'll be forced to take steps," Lafayette warned. "Now tell me, how does it feel to start existing all of a sudden, just because I dreamed you——"

"I can tear duh head off a alligator," Red declaimed. "I can rip duh hind leg off a elephant . . ." As the redhead rambled on, Lafayette concentrated. Red's voice rose higher, from bass to baritone, through tenor to a high contralto. ". . . handle any ten guys at oncet," he shrilled, "wit' bot' hands tied behind me . . ."

Lafayette made a final effort, listened for the result:

". . . I'm thimply a brute, when arouthed," Red squeaked. "Thometimeth I jutht get tho mad I could thpit!" He broke off, an amazed look settling over his meaty features. "Thpit?" he chirped.

"Now, Red, drink your wine and pay attention," Lafayette said severely. "You're port of an impartent experiment. I mean you're pent of an apartment—you're portable part of—apart of port—an appointment of pit—ah, the hell with it!" He picked up his wine mug.

The door burst open. A tall man with long curls slammed into view, gorgeously arrayed in a floppy hat with feathers, a purple and blue striped jacket, a wide sash, baggy pants above sloppily rolled boots. He whipped out a slender épée and advanced on the lone occupied table. Another ornately outfitted swordsman crowded in behind him, and a third, and a fourth. They spread out and ringed the table, blades at the ready.

"Hi, fellas." Lafayette waved his heavy glass. "How about a little snort?"

"In the King's name," the leading dandy roared. "You're under arrest! Will you come along quietly, or have we got to run your through?" A fierce black mustache curled up on each side of his face like a steer's horns.

O'Leary eyed the nearest sword point, six inches from his throat. Rolling his eyes sideways, he could see two more blades poised, aimed at his heart. Across from him, the Red Bull gaped, his mouth hanging open.

"You, there!" the mustached officer bellowed, eyeing the redhead. "Who're you?"

"Me, offither?" the big man chirped. "Why, I wath jutht thitting here, thipping my therry and waiting for my thupper."

The cop blinked, then guffawed. "The bum looks enough like the Red Bull to be his twin."

"Beat it, you," another ordered. The redhead scrambled from his place and hurried unsteadily to the door. Lafayette caught a glimpse of faces peering in as it opened. The mob was still noisy outside.

"All right, on your feet," the man on his left commanded. O'Leary smiled negligently at the man, focusing his attention on the swords. *Salamis,* he thought. *Swords into salamis, kazam!*

A sharp point prodded his side; he jumped. The bright steel blade was set against his ribs, just above the kidney. "Salami!" O'Leary commanded aloud. "Turn into a salami, damn it!"

The blade—still stubbornly steel—poked harder. "No spells now, or you won't make it to a cell!"

"Hey!" Lafayette yelled. "Careful! You'll break the skin!"

"Look, Mac, have I got to slit your weasand to convince you this is a pinch? We're musketeers of the city guard, see? We're putting the sneeze on for disturbing the peace!"

"You mean about the wine bottle," O'Leary said. "I can explain——"

"Tell it to the executioner," a three-striper snarled. "On your feet, bub!"

Lafayette got up. "This is ridiculous," he started.

A hard hand gripped his arm and propelled him doorward. He shook it off, grabbed his hat from the table and settled it over his eyes. No need to get excited, he reminded himself. The salami gambit hadn't worked, but that was because he hadn't had time to concentrate properly and get his Psychic Energies attuned—besides which, he had already discovered it was tricky trying to change anything in plain view. He was a little woozy from the wine, but as soon as he had a quiet moment, he would handle these fellows . . .

He stumbled through the door, out into the frosty night air. A rank of frightened faces gaped at him. Fists shook. A vegetable came flying and bounced off his shoulder.

"All right, clear the way there!" the tallest musketeer roared. "Make way, in the King's name!" He and two of his men laid about them with the flats of their blades, opening a route to a waiting steamcar.

"Watch it, Mac," said the musketeer detailed to guard O'Leary, "Us police aren't what you'd call popular." He ducked as a ripe tomato whizzed past. "Can't say as I blame 'em much, the way his Majesty has got us putting the screws on lately. Everything that ain't compulsory is illegal."

"Sounds like a totalitarian regime," O'Leary commented. "Why don't you start a revolution?"

"You kidding? King Goruble's got a army that would——" he broke off. "Never mind that," he said. He looked at O'Leary curiously and edged closer.

"Say, is that the straight dope?" he said from the side of his mouth. "I mean about you being a sorcerer?"

O'Leary eyed the man. "You mean an intelligent fellow like you believes in magic?"

"Naw—but, well—they got you on a 902—that's a necromancy rap; o'course that's just a standard charge we use to hold suspicious characters for twenty-four hours. But I figure maybe where there's a frog there's a puddle——"

"Did you ever see anyone perform magic?" Lafayette demanded.

"No, but my wife's aunt's cousin claims he knew a fellow——"

"I'm no magician," Lafayette said. "As a matter of fact, I'm—but you wouldn't understand."

"Look, what I was wondering—well, my wife, she's kind of running to fat lately; stringy hair, no make-up; you know the routine. Only been married a year. Maybe you could give me something to slip into her martini to kind of like put the old zazzle back; warm her up a little, if you know what I mean . . ." He winked elaborately, and casually shoved an overeager spectator back into line.

"That's silly——" Lafayette started, then paused. Well, why not? Good practice. He squinted, pictured a popular movie starlet whose name he had forgotten, imagined her as married to the cop at his side, then pictured her hurrying along a street, attracted by the mob noise . . . The scene winked. O'Leary relaxed, feeling complacent. OK, now he could get back in command of the situation. . . .

"Roy!" a girlish voice called above the clamor. "Oh, Roy!" The cop beside O'Leary jumped, looked around. A lovely girl with huge dark eyes and soft brown hair was pushing through the crowd.

"Gertrude! Is it you?" the cop bleated, a look of delighted astonishment spreading across his face.

"Oh, Roy! I was so worried!" The girl hurled herself at the cop, staggering him. His sword dropped. O'Leary retrieved it and handed it back.

"I heard there was a dangerous arrest, and you were on it, and I know how brave you are, and I was afraid——"

"Now, now, Gertrude, I'm in the pink. Everything's jake."

"You mean it was a false alarm? Oh, I'm so relieved."

"False alarm? Yeah—I mean . . ." The musketeer turned to blink at Lafayette. He swallowed hard. "Cripes!" he muttered. "This guy is the McCoy!" He thrust the girl aside. "Excuse me, baby!" He cupped a hand beside his mouth. "Hey, Sarge!"

The large musketeer loomed up beside him. "Yeah?"

"This guy——" the cop jerked a thumb at O'Leary. "He's the goods! I mean, he's a sorcerer, like they said!"

"You lost your marbles, Shorty? Get your pris'ner and let's move out!"

"But look at Gertrude!" He pointed. The big cop

glanced, jumped, gaped. He swept his hat off, executed an elaborate bow.

"Holy Moses, Gertrude," he said, "you got a new hairdo or something?"

"Hairdo?" Shorty snorted. "She's lost fifty pound o' lard, stacked what's left in the right places, developed a curl in her hair, and remembered how to smile! And *he* done it!" He pointed at O'Leary.

"Oh, it was nothing," Lafayette said modestly. "And now, if you fellows don't mind——"

Abruptly, steel rasped. Four sharp blades jumped out, poised, ringing O'Leary in. The sergeant mopped sweat from his forehead with his free hand.

"I'm warning you, mister, don't try nothing! I'll have twelve inches of steel into you before you get past the first abracadabra!"

Lafayette snorted. "The whole thing is getting silly," he said. "That's the trouble with dreams; just when they begin to get interesting, things start to go wrong. I may as well just wake up and start over tomorrow night."

He squinted, concentrating; he was getting pretty good at the trick now, he thought complacently. Just picture what you wanted, build it up in the mind's eye——

Someone was jerking at his arm. Damned nuisance. Hard to concentrate. *Mrs. Mac Glint's; the old family wallpaper, the homey smells, the creaky floor* . . . He opened an eye and saw a ring of angry faces. He shut his eyes tight, seized on the fading visualization of his room, working to solidify it. *Wake up,* he commanded himself. *This is just a whacky dream* . . .

The sounds around were fading now; he could almost see the blotched walls, the curtained alcove, the orange-crate table——

The hand was hauling at his arm again. He stumbled, almost fell. His eyes snapped open. A voice yelled in his ear.

The mob sounds swelled back to normal. Lafayette's breath made a frosty cloud before his face. The musketeers were staring at him, mouths wide.

"Did you see that, Sarge?" Shorty choked. "Like he turned to smoke!" They were backing away. The three-striper stood his ground, swallowed hard.

"Look, pal," he said desperately, "be nice and come along quiet, huh? I mean, if you got to do a fade, do it in front of witnesses, you know what I mean? If I report in with a story like this—and no pinch—well, it's goodby retirement, and me with twenty-one years on the force."

For the moment, O'Leary saw, it seemed there was no help for it: he was stuck in the damned dream—at least until he could manage a moment of peace and quiet.

"Certainly, Sergeant," O'Leary said grandly, "I'll be glad to accompany you. Just keep it couth, if you don't mind."

"Sure, kid gloves all the way, buddy. Now, if you don't mind just stepping this way?" The sergeant indicated the lane to the waiting vehicle. O'Leary strolled to the car, stood by while one of the guardsmen opened the rear door and then clambered up, seating himself on the wooden bench.

"All clear," he said. "Button her up." As the

cops hurried to close the door, O'Leary caught a glimpse of four nervous faces looking oddly different . . .

Then he saw it: The big sergeant was now clean-shaven; somehow in the reshuffling of scenes, his immense mustachios had been inadvertently transferred to the upper lip of Shorty. O'Leary smiled, relaxed. There was really no need to be in a crashing hurry to get back to reality; why not stay with it a bit longer, and see what his subconscious came up with next? He could always wake up later.

O'Leary braced himself with one foot against the opposite bench and settled down for the ride.

CHAPTER III

It was a bumpy twenty-minute trip. Lafayette held on, feeling his teeth clack at each uneven cobble, regretting that he had neglected to provide padded seats and a window. The wagon swayed, mounted a slight incline and then halted with a jolt. Feet clattered; voices muttered. The door clanked and swung open. Lafayette stepped down, looked around interestedly at a wide, cobbled courtyard fronted on all four sides by elaborate façades of rusticated stone, ornate with columns, pilasters, niches with statues, bright-lit rows of high, Gothic-arched windows. Far above, the slopes of massive mansard roofs gleamed a dull green in the moonlight. There were flower beds and geometric shapes of manicured lawn; clumps of tall poplars shimmered their silvery leaves in the night breeze. Flaming lanterns atop tall poles lighted a cavernous colonnaded entry, beside which two brass-helmeted, ramrod-stiff guardsmen in baggy knickers of Bromo-Seltzer blue and puff-sleeved jackets in red and yellow stripes stood with arquebuses at order arms.

"Now, if you'll just step this way, ah, sir," the sergeant said nervously, "I'll turn you over to the household detachment. After that you can disappear any time you like, just so I get a receipt from the desk sergeant first, OK?"

"Be calm, Sergeant," O'Leary soothed. "I'm not going to vanish just yet." He shook his head admiringly. "This is the fanciest police station I ever saw."

"You kidding, mac? I mean," the noncom amended hastily, "uh, this is the palace. Where the King lives, you know. King Goruble the First."

"I didn't know," said Lafayette, starting in the indicated direction. He stumbled and grabbed for his hat. It was difficult, walking in unfamiliar boots across uneven paving stones, and the sword had a disconcerting way of attempting to get between his legs.

The rigid sentries snapped to as the detachment mounted the wide steps; one barked a challenge. The sergeant replied and urged O'Leary on into the well-lit interior of a high-vaulted, mirror-lined hall, with a floor of polished marble in red and black squares. Elaborate gilt chandeliers hung from the fretted ceiling; opposite the mirrors, vast, somber draperies reflected woodland scenes.

Lafayette followed his escort along to a desk where a man in a steel breastplate sat, picking his teeth with a daggar. He cocked an eyebrow at O'Leary as the party came up.

"Book this, uh, gentleman in, Sarge," Lafayette's escort said. "And give me a receipt."

"Gentleman?" The desk sergeant put the dagger away and picked up a quill. "What's the charge?"

"A 902." Lafayette's cop looked defiantly at the pained expression that appeared on the other's lined face.

"Are you kidding, Sarge?" the desk man growled. "Grow up! You can use a 902 to hold a drunk overnight, but you don't book 'em into Royal Court——"

"This one's the real article."

"That's right, Sarge," Shorty chimed in. "You oughta see what he done to Gertrude!"

"Gertrude? What is this, an assault?"

"Naw, Gertrude's the wife. He took fifty pounds off'n her and put the old shake back in her hips. Wow!" Shorty made lines in the air indicating Gertrude's new contours, then looked guiltily at O'Leary.

"Sorry, Bud," he whispered behind his hand. "I appreciate the favor, but——"

"You guys are nuts," the desk man said. "Get out of here before I lose my temper and have the lot of you clapped into irons!"

The musketeer sergeant's face darkened. He half-drew his sword with a rasp of steel. "Book him and give me a receipt, or I'll tickle your backbone from the front, you paper-pushing son of a——"

The desk sergeant was on his feet, whipping a saber from the sheath hung on the back of his chair, which fell over with a clatter. "Draw on a member of the Queen's Own Light Cavalry, will you, you flat-footed night watchman——"

"Quiet!" someone barked. Lafayette, who had

been watching the action open-mouthed, turned to see a dapper, gray-haired man in shirt sleeves frowning from an open doorway, surrounded by half a dozen elaborately garbed men in fantastic powdered wigs.

"What's the meaning of this altercation, right outside our gaming room?" The newcomer aggrievedly waved the playing cards clutched in a hand heavy with rings.

Everyong came to attention with a multiple clack of heels.

""Ah, Your Majesty, sir, this police officer," the desk sergeant stumbled, "he was wising off, sir, and——"

"I beg your Majesty's pardon, Your Majesty," the arresting sergeant cut in, "but if Your Majesty would——"

"See here, can't you go somewhere else to argue?" the king demanded. "Confound it, things are coming to a pretty pass when we can't play a few quiet hands of stud without some unseemly interruption!" The monarch turned to re-enter the room, his courtiers scattering from his path.

"If it please your Majesty," the formerly mustached musketeer persisted, "this prisoner is——"

"It doesn't please us in the least!" The king thrust out his mustached lip. "Scat, we say! Begone! And silently!"

The sergeant's face grew stubborn. "Your Majesty, I got to have a receipt for my prisoner. He's a dangerous sorcerer."

The king opened his mouth, then closed it.

"Sorcerer?" He eyed O'Leary with interest. At

close range, Lafayette noted, the king looked older, more careworn, but meticulously groomed, with fine lines around his eyes and mouth.

"Are you sure of this?" the king asked in a low voice.

"Absolutely, your Majesty," the arresting cop assured him.

The desk sergeant bustled around the desk. "Your Majesty, I'm sorry about this; these nut cases, we get 'em all the time——"

"Are you a magician?" The king pursed his mouth, raising one carefully arched eyebrow at Lafayette.

"Why does everyone ask the same question?" Lafayette shook his head. "It would all be lots more fun if you just accepted me as one of yourselves. Just consider me a . . . ah . . . scientist."

The king's frown returned. "You show less than proper respect for our person. And what in the name of the Sea-fiend is a—what did you call yourself?"

"A scientist. Someone who knows things," O'Leary explained. "You see, I'm engaged in an experiment. Now, none of you fellows realize it, but none of you actually exist."

The king was sniffing loudly. "The fellow reeks of wine," he said. He sniffed again. "Smells like good stuff," he remarked to a satin-coated dandy at his elbow.

"Phaugh, Majesty," the courtier said in a high nasal, waving a hanky under his nose. "Methinks the scoundrel is well and truly snockered. Didst hear him but now? None of us exist, quoth he—including your Majesty!"

"Sire, he's a warlock, take my word for it!" the sergeant burst out. "Any minute he's liable to poof! Disappear!"

"Yeah, yer Majesty," Shorty added, wagging his head, making his curls flop. "The guy is terrific!"

"How say you, knave?" The courtier fixed O'Leary with a slightly blood-shot eye. "Art a dabbler in the Black Arts?"

"Actually, it's all very simple," Lafayette said. His head was beginning to throb slightly as the glow of the wine faded. "I just—ah—have this slight ability to manipulate the environment."

The king's forehead wrinkled. "What does that mean?"

"Well . . ." Lafayette considered. "Take wine, for example." He squinted his eyes, concentrated on the upper right drawer of the desk beside him. He felt a slight, reassuring jar. "Look in the drawer," he said. "The top one."

The king gestured. "Do as he says."

One of the perfumed flunkeys minced forward, drew open the drawer, glanced inside, then, looking surprised, lifted out a bottle and held it up.

"Hey!" The desk sergeant started.

"Drinking on duty, eh?" The king beetled an eyebrow at the unfortunate fellow. "Ten days in the dungeon on canned soup."

"B-but, your Majesty, it's not mine!"

"That's right," Lafayette put in. "He didn't even know it was there."

"Then it's ten days for not knowing the contents of his own desk," the king said blandly. He took the bottle, looked at the label, held it up to the light and squinted at it.

"Good color," he stated. "Who has a corkscrew?"

Four manicured hands shot out with four elaborate corkscrews. The king handed over the bottle and watched as the cork was drawn with a loud *whok*!

He took the bottle, sniffed, then tilted it and took a healthy drag. A delighted expression lifted his rather sharp features.

"Zounds! We like it! Damned good vintage, that! Better than we find at our own table!" He looked at Lafayette approvingly.

"Still say you're not a magician, eh?"

"No, 'fraid not. After all, magic's impossible." O'Leary wagged an admonitory finger. "I suppose I seem a little unusual to you, but there's a perfectly simple explanation. Now, in this dream——"

"Enough!" The king held up a manicured hand. "This talk of dreams, we like it not—and yet, this wine we like right well. 'Tis a matter for our council to consider." He turned to a slight, pasty-faced man with a large moist nose, who was dressed in powder-blue silk with ruffles at the throat.

"Summon my councillors, we shall look into this affair. Mayhap the fellow has a simple explanation for these, ah, irregularities." He smacked his lips, looked fondly at the bottle and handed it to O'Leary. As the latter reached for it, the monarch seemed to start suddenly, half withdrew the bottle, then held it out again, staring at O'Leary's hand as he took the flask.

"We'll meet—immediately," the king said, sounding shaken.

"Tonight, Majesty?" a fat man in pink velvet squeaked.

"Certainly! In the High Chamber in a quarter of an hour!" King Goruble waved a hand at the musketeers. "Be there! And as for you——" he shot a sharp glance at O'Leary. "You come with us, lad. We have a few questions to put to you."

The king waved his retainers back and closed the heavy door behind himself and Lafayette, who stared around the richly decorated gaming room admiringly. There were huge gilt-framed pictures against the paneled walls, a well stocked bar, deep rugs, soft lights to supplement the bright luminaries hanging over the card and billiard tables.

"I see you have electric lights here," O'Leary commented. "I can't quite figure out just what sort of place this is I've wandered into."

"This is the kingdom of Artesia." The king pulled at his lower lip, watching O'Leary speculatively. "Have you lost your wits, boy? Perhaps, ah, forgotten your name, your station?"

"No; I'm Lafayette O'Leary. I don't have a station: It's just that I can't quite place the, ah, context. Swords, steam cars, knee breeches, electric lights . . ."

"O'Leary, eh? A curious name. You came from a far land, I wot; you know nothing of our fair realm of Artesia?"

"Ummm," said Lafayette. "I guess you could say that; but in another sense, I live here—or near here."

"Eh? What mean you?"

"Oh, nothing much. You wouldn't understand."

Goruble worried his lower lip with even, white, false-looking teeth. "What errand brought you hither?" he sounded worried, O'Leary thought.

"Oh, no errand. Just . . . looking around."

"Looking for what?"

"Nothing special. Just sight-seeing, you might say."

"You came not to, ah, crave audience with ourself, perchance?"

"No—not that I'm not honored."

"How came you here?" Goruble demanded abruptly.

"Well, it gets a little complicated. To tell you the truth, I don't really understand it myself."

"You have—friends in the capital?"

"Don't know a soul."

Goruble took three paces, turned, took three paces back. He stopped and eyed O'Leary's right hand.

"Your ring," he said. "An interesting bauble." His eyes cut to O'Leary's face. "You, ah, bought it here?"

"Oh, no, I've had it for years."

Goruble frowned. "Where did you get it?"

"I guess you could say it came with me. It was hanging around my neck on a string when they found me on the orphanage doorstep."

"Orphanage? A place for waifs and strays?"

O'Leary nodded.

Goruble became suddenly brisk. "Just slip it off, there's a good fellow; I'd fain have a look at it."

"Sorry; it's too small to get over the knuckle."

"Hmmm." The king looked at O'Leary sharply. "Yes, well, let us make a suggestion, my lad. Turn the ring so that the device is inward. Others, seeing the symbol of the ax and dragon, might place some bothersome interpretation on't."

"What kind of interpretation?"

Goruble spread his hands. "There's a tale, told in the taverns. A mystical hero, 'tis said, will appear one day bearing that symbol, to rid the land of, ah, certain encumbrances. Sheer balderdash, of course, but it might prove embarrassing to you to be taken for the warrior of the prophecy."

"Thanks for the tip." O'Leary twisted the ring on his finger. "Now, do you mind if *I* ask a few questions?"

"Ah, doubtless you're wondering why you were brought here to the palace, rather than being trussed in chains and cast into a dungeon along with the usual run of felons."

"No, I can't say that I am. Nothing around here seems to make any sense. But now that you mention it, why *am* I here?"

" 'Twas our royal command. We instructed the captain of the city garrison a fortnight since to comb the city and bring to us any person suspect of witchery."

Lafayette nodded, found himself yawning and patted his mouth. "Excuse me," he said. "Go on, I'm listening."

" 'Tis a most strange manner of deportment you affect," the king said snappishly. "Hast no respect for royalty?"

"Oh, sure, uh, your Majesty," O'Leary said. "I guess I'm just a little tired."

The monarch sat himself in a deep leather chair,

and watched open-mouthed as Lafayette settled himself in another, crossing his legs comfortably.

"Here!" the king barked, "we've given you no leave to sit!"

O'Leary was yawning again. "Look, let's skip all that," he suggested in a reasonable tone. "I'm pooped. You know, I have an idea these dream adventures are just as fatiguing as real ones. After all, your mind—part of it, anyway—thinks you're really awake, so it reacts——"

"Have done!" the king yelped. "Your prattle threatens to unhinge my wits!" He glared at O'Leary as though pondering a difficult decision. "Look here, young man, you are sure there isn't something you'd like to, well, tell us? A matter we might ah, discuss plainly?" He leaned forward, lowering his voice. "To our mutual advantage?"

"I'm afraid I don't know what you mean."

"Answer us plainly, yea or nay? Speak without fear; we offer you amnesty."

"Nay," Lafayette said flatly. "Absolutely nay."

"Nay?" the kings shoulders slumped. "Drat it, I was hoping . . . perhaps . . ."

"Look here," Lafayette said in a kindly tone, "why don't you tell me what your problem is? Maybe I can help you. I do have certain, ah, techniques——"

The king sat erect, looking wary. "We took you here aside to, ah, advise you privily that you'd have our royal pardon in advance for the practice of your forbidden arts in the service of the crown. You spurn our offer—and in the same breath hint at the possession of demonic powers. Almost it seems you ask to have your bones stretched!"

"I wonder," O'Leary said. "If I went to sleep

now, would I wake up here—or back at Mrs. MacGlint's house?"

"Bah!" the king exploded. "But for a certain mystery we sense about you, we'd banish you forthwith to the county jail on a charge of lunacy!" He eyed the wine bottle on the table. "Tell us, he said in a confidential tone, "how *did* the bottle get in the desk drawer?"

"It was always there," O'Leary said. "I just pointed it out."

"But how—" the king shook his head. "Enough." He went to a bell cord. "We'll hear your case in open court—if you're sure you have nothing to impart in confidence?" He looked at O'Leary expectantly.

"This is all nonsense," O'Leary protested. "Impart what? Why don't you tell me about yourself? I have an idea that you represent some sort of authority symbol."

"Symbol?" Goruble roared. "We'll show you whether we be symbol or sovereign!" He yanked the cord. The door opened; a squad of household troops stood waiting.

"Escort him to the bar of justice," Goruble ordered. "He stands accused of sorcery."

"Oh, well," O'Leary said airily, "I guess it's no use trying to be reasponable. It may be amusing at that. Lead on, my good man." He gestured sardonically at the bull-necked corporal as the squad moved to box him in.

It was a five-minute walk along echoing corridors to the chamber where the hearing was to be held. A crowd of gaudily clad men and a few women in full skirts and cleavage eyed O'Leary curiously as he came in under guard. The ceremonial sentries beside the double doors motioned him and his escort through into a domed chamber, a roccoco composition in red and green marble and heavy hangings of green velvet with gold fringes that reminded Lafayette of the lobby of the Colby opera house. At one side of the room a vast chair occupied a raised dais. A row of boys in baggy shorts, long stockings, pointed shoes, sailor's shirts and bangs raised long horns and blew a discordant fanfare. Through doors at the opposite side of the room the figure of the king appeared, wearing a scarlet robe now, followed by the usual retinue of hangers-on. Everyone bowed low, the women curtsying. Lafayette felt a smart kick in the shin.

"Bow, bumpkin!" hissed a bearded stranger in pea-green knickers. Lafayette bent over, rubbed the spot where the other's boot had bruised him. "How would you like a punch in the jaw?"

"Silence! Wouldst have me rub your nose on the floor, wittol!"

"You and what other six guys?" O'Leary came back. "Ever had a broken leg before?"

"Before what?"

"Before you had a broken arm. I may just cross your eyes, too, while I'm at it."

"Art daft, varlet?"

"Maybe you haven't heard. I'm here on a witchcraft rap."

"Ulp?" The man moved away hastily. The king was seated on his throne now, amid much bustling of courtiers stationing themselves in position according to an elaborate scheme of precedence, each elbowing for a spot a foot or two closer to the throne. There were more trumpetings; then an old dodderer in a long black robe stepped forward and pounded a heavy rod on the floor.

"The Court of Justice of His Majesty King Goruble is now in session," he quavered. "All those who crave boons, draw nigh." Then, without pausing: "Let those who have offended against the just laws of the realm be brought forward."

"That's you, bud," a black-haired guard muttered. "Let's go." O'Leary followed as the man pushed through the throng to a spot ten feet from the throne where King Goruble sat, nibbling a slice of orange.

"Well, how plead you, my man?"

"I don't know," O'Leary said. What's the charge?"

"Sorcery! Guilty or not guilty?"

"Oh, that again. I was hoping you'd thought up something more original, like loitering at the post office."

An effeminate-looking fellow in parakeet green stepped from the ranks of the retainers grouped around the throne, made an elaborate leg and waved a bit of lace from which an odor of dime store perfume wafted.

"An't please your Majesty," he said, "the fellow's insolence gives him away. 'Tis plain to see, he has a powerful protector. The villain is, I doubt not, a paid spy in the hire of the rebel Lod!"

"Lod?" Lafayette raised his eyebrows. "Who's he?"

"As is doubtless well known to you, this creature, thus y-clept is the fearsome giant, the bandit who impertinently presses a suit for the hand of her highness, the Princess Adoranne."

"And dreams of the day he will usurp our throne," Goruble added. He slapped the carved arm of the throne, looking angry.

"Well, fellow, do you deny it?" the green-clad exquisite persisted.

"I never heard of this Lod," Lafayette said impatiently. "And I've already told you the sorcery business was silly. There isn't any such thing!"

Goruble narrowed his eyes at O'Leary, pinched his chin between jeweled fingers.

"No such thing, eh?" He gestured. "Let Nicodaeus come forward!"

A tall, well muscled but slightly paunchy gray-haired man in yellow tights and a short cloak ornately appliquéed with stars and crescent moons stepped from the ranks, bowed medium low before the throne, took a pair of rimless glasses from a breast pocket, put them on, turned and studied Lafayette.

"You deny the existence of magic, eh?" he asked in a mellow baritone. "A skeptic." He wagged his head, smiling ruefully, reached up and took an egg from his mouth. A little murmur of wonder went through the crowd. The gray-haired man sauntered a few feet, paused before a plump lady-in-waiting, plucked a gaily-colored scarf from her well filled bodice, tossed it aside, drew out another, and another. The fat woman retreated, squealing and giggling as the onlookers tittered.

"Well done, Nicodaeus!" a fat man in pale purple puffed. "Oh, jolly well done!"

Nicodaeus strolled to the dais, and with a murmured apology took a mouse from the king's pocket. He dropped the tiny animal on the floor and it scurried away, amid dutiful squealing from the ladies. He plucked another from the king's shoe, a third from the royal ear. The monarch twitched, shot a sharp glance at O'Leary, waved the magician aside.

"Well, how say you now, O'Leary!" he demanded. "True, the feats of my faithful Nicodaeus are harmless white sorcery, blessed in the temple of Goop the Good and employed only in defense of our crown; but none can deny the ordinary laws of nature have here been set aside."

"Fooie," Lafayette said. "That's just sleight-of-hand. Any carnival sideshow prestidigitator has a better routine than that."

Nicodaeus looked thoughtfully at O'Leary, walked over to stand before him.

"Do you mind telling me," the magician said quietly, "just where you come from?"

"Well, I'm, ah, a traveler from a distant land, you might say," O'Leary improvised. Nicodaeus turned to face King Goruble.

"Majesty, when I heard your police had picked up a sorcerer, I looked over the report. The arrest was made in a tavern in the Street of the Alehouses, about eight P.M. All the witnesses agree that he performed some sort of hocus-pocus with a wine bottle. Then when the officers were taking him out to the wagon, he reportedly tried to vanish, but didn't quite have the skill to manage it. I also heard a story that he cast some sort of spell on a woman, the wife of one of the arresting officers; changed her appearance, it seems."

"Yes, yes, I know all that, Nicodaeus!"

"Your majesty, in my opinion all this is meaningless gossip, the product of wine-lubricated imaginations."

"Eh?" Goruble sat forward. "You're saying the man is innocent?"

"Not at all, Majesty! The really important point hasn't been mentioned yet. The accused was first seen, as I said, in the alehouse . . ." He paused dramatically. "Before that—no one had caught a glimpse of him!"

"So?"

"Your Majesty doesn't seem to get the point," Nicodaeus said patiently. "The city guards say he wasn't observed to approach the street where he was taken. The sentries at the city gates swear he never passed that way. He came from a far land, he says. Did he come on horse back? If so, where are the stains of travel—and where's the animal itself? Did he walk? Look at his boots; the soles show no more dust than a stroll in a garden might account for!"

"Are you saying he flew here?" Goruble shot a sharp look at Lafayette.

"Flew?" Nicodaeus looked annoyed. "Of course not. I'm suggesting that he obviously slipped into the city by stealth—and that he has confederates who housed and clothed him."

"So you agree he's a spy?" Goruble sounded pleased.

Lafayette sighed. "If I wanted to sneak into town, why would I suddenly walk into a tavern in plain sight of the cops?"

"I think the costume explains that," Nicodaeus said, nodding. "You've tricked out as the Phantom Outlaw, I believe. You intended to convince the gullible patrons of the dive that you were this mythical ghost, and then force them to do your bidding by threats of supernatural vengeance."

Lafayette folded his arms. "I'm getting tired of this nonsense." he stated loudly. "Starting now, this dream is going the way *I* want it to, or I'm just going to wake up and to hell with it!" He pointed at Nicodaeus. "This phony, now; if you'll detail a couple of men to hold him down while somebody goes through his pockets, and the trick compartments in the dizzy-looking cloak, you'd find out where all those mice come from! And——"

The magician caught O'Leary's eye, shook his head. "Play along," he whispered from the corner of his mouth.

Lafayette ignored him. ". . . I'm getting just about fed up with nonsense about magic and torture chambers," he went on. Nicodaeus stepped close. "Trust me, I'll get you out of this." He turned to the king and bowed his head smoothly. "The king is wise——"

"Nuts to all of you," O'Leary said. "This is just like a dream I had a couple of weeks ago. I was in a garden with nice green grass and a little stream and fruit trees, and all I wanted to do was relax and smell the flowers, but people kept coming along, bothering me. There was a fat bishop on a bicycle and a fireman playing a banjo, and then two midgets with a pet skunk——"

"Your Majesty, a moment!" Nicodaeus cried out. He threw a comradely arm about Lafayette's shoulders, led him closer to the throne. "It just came to me!" he announced. "This man is no criminal! We've been making a terrible mistake!

How stupid of me not to have realized sooner."

"What are you babbling about, Nicodaeus?" Goruble snapped. "One minute you're sewing up a watertight case, the next you're hugging the man like a long-lost brother!"

"My mistake, my liege!" Nicodaeus said hastily. "This is a fine young man, an upstanding subject of your Majesty, a model youth."

"What do you know about him?" Goruble's voice was sharp. "A moment since, you said you'd never seen him before!"

"Yes, well, as to that——"

There was a tinkle of bells, and a face like a gargoyle's appeared between the king's feet.

"What's afoot?" a deep bass voice rumbled. "Your patterings disturb my slumbers!"

"Be quiet, Yokabump!" King Goruble snapped. "We're conducting important business."

The face came farther out, a small body behind it. The dwarf, rising to bandy legs, looked around, scratching his chest.

"Solemn faces!" he bellowed. "Sour pusses! You're all a bunch of stick-in-the muds!" He whipped out a harmonica, tapped it on his oversized palm and started a lively tune.

"Sticks-in-the mud, you mean," Goruble corrected. "Go away now, Yokabump! We told you we're busy!" He glared at Nicodaeus. "Well, we're waiting! What do you know of the fellow that should prevent his hanging by his thumbs?"

Yokabump stopped playing.

"You mean," he boomed, pointing at O'Leary, "you don't recognize this hero?"

Goruble stared down at him. "Hero? Recognize? No, we don't."

Yokabump bounded forward and struck a pose.

"When the dragon came out of the west,
The worst ran away with the best;
But one man with an ax stopped the beast in his tracks
And came home with the hide of the pest."

King Goruble frowned darkly. "Nonsense!" he said flatly. He turned to the dwarf. "No interference from you, mannikin; this is a matter of deepest import. Don't distract us with foolish stories."

"But he is, in very truth, sire, the dragon slayer of the prophecy!"

"Why, ah, as a matter of fact . . ." Nicodaeus patted O'Leary heartily on the shoulder. "I was just about to make the announcement."

Yokabump waddled up to O'Leary, threw back his head and stared at him.

"He doesn't *look* like a hero," he announced in his subcellar bass. "But a hero he is!" He turned his heavy head, winked grotesquely at the magician, faced O'Leary again. "Tell us, Sir Knight, how you'll face the foul monster, how you'll overcome those mighty jaws, those awful talons!"

Goruble chewed at his lip, staring at O'Leary.

"Jaws and talons, eh," Lafayette said, smiling condescendingly. "No wings? No fiery breath? No——"

"Scales, yes—I think," Nicodaeus said. "I haven't seen him myself, of course, but the reports——"

A slender fellow in a pale yellow suit with a starched ruff came forward, sniffing a snuff box. He closed it with a click, tucked it in a sleeve and eyed O'Leary curiously.

"How say you, fellow? Wilt despatch the great beast that guards the approaches to the stronghold of Lod?"

There was a sudden silence. Goruble blinked at O'Leary, his lips thrust out.

"Well?" he demanded.

"Agree!" Nicodaeus muttered in O'Leary's ear.

"Certainly!" Lafayette made an expansive gesture. "I'll be only too pleased to attend to this little matter. My favorite sport, actually. I often kill half a dozen dragons before breakfast. I'll promise to annihiliate any number of mythical beasts, if that will make you happy."

"Very well." Goruble looked grim. "A celebration is in order, we suppose," he said sardonically. "We hereby decree a fete for tonight in honor of our valiant new friend, O'Leary." He broke off and shot Lafayette a fierce look. "And you'd better deliver the goods, young fellow," he added in an undertone, "or we'll have the hide off you in strips!"

CHAPTER IV

The room that O'Leary was shown to was forty feet long, thirty wide, carpeted, tapestried and gilt decorated. There was an immense four-poster bed, a vast, carved wardrobe, a gaily decorated chamber pot in a rosewood stand, a tall mirror in a frame, and a row of curtained windows with a view of lanterns strung in a garden where fountains played among moonlit statues of nymphs and satyrs. He tried a door, looked into a cedar-lined closet filled with elaborate costumes on satin-covered hangers. Another door opened into a tiny chapel, complete with a wheel of Goop and a fresh package of sacrificial incense sticks. There was one more door. O'Leary paused to give thought to what would be behind it, picturing the details of a cozy tiled bath with heated floor, glassed-in shower stall, plenty of hot water . . . He reached for the knob, swung the door wide, stepped through.

There was a loud squeal. Lafayette halted, staring. In the center of the small room was a long wooden tub containing soapy water and a girl. Her dark hair was piled high on her head, a few bubbles provided inadequate concealment for her charms. She stared back at him, amazement on her pretty features.

"Wha. . .?" Lafayette stammered. "Where- . . . but I was just . . ." He waved a hand vaguely toward the door.

The girl gazed at him wide-eyed. "You—you must be the new wizard, sir!" She took the towel from the rack attached to the side of the tub and stood up, wrapping it around herself.

"I—I'm sorry!" O'Leary blurted, his eyes straying to the expanse of white thigh revealed by the skimpy towel. "I was just—I mean——" He stared around at shelves stacked with clean sheets and towels.

"Something's wrong here," he said protestingly. "This was supposed to be a bathroom!"

The girl giggled. "You can have my bath, sir, I'd hardly started."

"But it wasn't supposed to be like this! I had in mind a nice tile bath, and a shower and plenty of hot water and soap and shaving cream——"

"This water's just right, sir," the girl stepped out onto the rug, loosened the towel and began modestly drying her neck, holding the towel more or less in front of her. "I'm Daphne; I'm the upstairs chambermaid."

"Gosh, miss, I didn't mean to disturb you. I was just——"

"I've never met a real magician before," Daphne said. "It was so exciting! One minute I was right there in my room, looking at the crack in the plaster, and the next—zip! Here I was!"

"You were somewhere else—taking a bath?" Lafayette frowned. "I must have made a mistake. Probably distracted by all the excitement."

"I heard about the fete," the girl said. "It *is* exciting. There hasn't been a real affair in the palace for months, not since that horrible ogre Lod came with his men under a truce flag to woo Princess Adoranne."

"Look, ah, Daphne, I have to get ready; after all, I'm sort of the guest of honor, so——"

"Oh." Daphne looked disappointed. "You didn't summon me on purpose?"

"No. Ah, I mean, I have to take a bath now."

"Would you like me to scrub your back?"

"No, thanks." O'Leary felt himself blushing. "I'm sort of used to bathing myself. But thanks just the same. But, uh, maybe I'll see you at the party."

"Me, sir? But I'm only a chambermaid! They won't even let me watch from the kitchen door!"

"Nonsense! You're as pretty as any of them! Come as my guest."

"I couldn't, sir! And besides, I haven't a thing to wear." She tucked the towel demurely about her slender figure, smiling shyly.

"Well, I think that can be fixed." Lafayette turned to the clothes closet, considering. "What size do you wear, Daphne?"

"Size? Why, as you see, sir . . ." She held her arms from her sides, twirled slowly around. Lafayette took a deep, calming breath, fixed his eye on the closet, concentrating. He opened the door, glanced over the array of finery, reached, pulled out a pink-and-gold-brocaded gown.

"How about this?"

She gasped. "It's lovely, sir! Is it really for me?"

"It certainly is. Now, just run along like a good girl; I'll be looking forward to seeing you at the party."

"I've never seen anything so pretty." She took the dress tenderly in her arms. "If you'll just lend me a robe, sir, I'll be off like a flash. I know just where I can borrow a pair of shoes to go with it, and . . ."

Lafayette found a terry-cloth robe, bundled it about her shoulders and saw her to the door.

"I'd like to apologize again about, ah, disturbing you in your bath," he said. "It was just an accident."

"Think nothing of it, sir." She smiled up at him. "This is the most exciting thing that ever happened to me. Who'd have ever thought magicians were so young—and so handsome?" She went to tiptoes, kissed him quickly on the end of the nose, then turned and darted away along the hall.

There was a rap at the door as Lafayette was buttoning the last gilt button on the dark blue coat he had selected from the dozens in the closet.

"Come in," he called. He heard the door open behind him.

"I hope you don't mind my barging in on you," a deep voice said. Lafayette turned. Nicodaeus, trim in a gray outfit, closed the door behind him. He took out a pack of cigarettes, offered them and lit up with what appeared to be a Ronson lighter.

"Say, you're the first one I've seen smoking cigarettes here," O'Leary said. "And that lighter——"

Nicodaeus fingered the lighter, looking at

O'Leary. "Plenty of time for explanations later, my young friend. I just wanted to take a few minutes before the festivities begin, to, er, have a little chat with you."

"I want to thank you for helping me out this evening." Lafayette buckled on his sword belt, paused to admire the cut of his new knee breeches in the mirror. "For a while there, it looked like old Goruble had his heart set on railroading me into the Iron Maiden. What's eating the old boy?"

"He had an idea that if you knew a little magic, you might be a big help in the upcoming war with Lod's rebels. He was a bit put out when you denied it. You must excuse him; he's rather naive in some ways. I was glad to help you out; but frankly, I'm a little curious about you myself. Ah . . . if you don't mind telling me, why are you here?" In the mirror O'Leary watched the magician, still fiddling with the lighter.

"Just a sight-seeing trip."

"You've never visited Artesia before?"

"Nope. Not that I know of. There was one dream I remember, about a glass house and a telescope—but there's probably no connection." He turned suddenly. Close behind him, Nicodaeus started and dropped the lighter in his pocket.

"What's that you had in your hand?" O'Leary demanded. "What are you creeping up behind me for?"

"Oh, that . . ." Nicodaeus blinked, smiling weakly. "Why, it's, ah, a little camera; you see I have a hobby—candid shots—and I just——"

"Let me see it."

Nicodaeus hesitated, then dipped into the

pocket of his weskit and fished it out. It was made in the shape of a lighter—even worked as one, O'Leary saw—but it was heavy. And there were tiny dials set in its back. He handed it back. "I guess I'm overly suspicious, after being threatened by a number of horrible fates in less than two hours."

"Think nothing of it, my dear O'Leary." Nicodaeus glanced at the other's hand. "Ah, I noticed your ring. Very interesting design. Mind if I have a closer look at it?"

O'Leary shook his head. "I can't take it off. What's so interesting about a ring?"

Nicodaeus looked grave. "The device of the ax and dragon happens to have a peculiar significance here in Artesia. It's the insignia of the old royal house. There's an old prophecy—you know how people pretend to believe in that sort of thing—to the effect that the kingdom will be saved in its darkest hour by a, ahem, hero, riding a dragon and wielding an ax. He was supposed to appear bearing a symbol of his identity. I suppose that annoying clown Yokabump spotted the ring—he has sharp eyes—and improvised the rest. Luckily for you, I might add. He *could* have set up a howl that it was an evil charm. Lod carries an ax, you see, and of course he owns a dragon."

Lafayette glanced sharply at Nicodaeus, then laughed. "You almost sound as though you believe in the monster yourself."

Nicodaeus chuckled comfortably. "A mere fable, of course. Still, I'd wear the ring reversed if I were you."

"I can't help wondering," O'Leary said, "why should you care what happens to me any more than the rest of them? They all seem to want to see me strung up by the ears."

"Just a natural desire to help a stranger in distress," Nicodaeus answered, smiling. "After all, having saved you from a session with the hot irons, I have a sort of proprietary interest in seeing you safely through."

"At one point you just about had Goruble convinced I was a spy."

"A red herring; I wanted to distract him from the sorcery aspect. Like all Artesians, he's prey to superstition."

"Then I was right; you're not native here."

"Actually, I'm not," the magician admitted. "I, ah, come from a country to the south, as a matter of fact. I——"

"They must be way ahead of Artesia, technologically speaking. That lighter, for example. I'll bet you're responsible for the electric lights in the palace."

Nicodaeus nodded, smiling. "That's correct. I do what I can do to add to the amenities of palace life."

"Just what *is* your position here?"

"I'm an adviser to his Majesty." Nicodaeus smiled blandly. "He thinks I'm a master of magic, of course, but among these feather-heads a little common sense is sufficient to earn one a reputation as a wise man." He smiled comfortably. "Look here, my young friend—and I think I have established that I am a friend—isn't there something that you'd care to, ah, confide in me? I could perhaps be of some assistance, in whatever it is you have in mind."

"Thanks, but I don't have anything in mind that I need help with."

"I'm sure we could work out some arrangement, to our mutual benefit," Nicodaeus went on. "I, with my established position here; you Mr. O'Leary, with your, ah, whatever you have . . ." He paused on an interrogative note.

"Call me Lafayette. I appreciate what you did for me, but I really don't need any help. Look, the party must be about to begin. Let's beat it downstairs. I don't want to miss anything."

"You're determined to pursue your course alone, I see," Nicodaeus said sadly. "Ah, well, just as you wish, Lafayette. I don't mind saying I'm disappointed. Frankly, I've gotten just a little bit bored lately. I thought—but never mind." He eyed Lafayette, nibbling his lower lip. "You know, I wonder if it wouldn't be safer for you to just slip away tonight, before the fete. If you wait until later, his Majesty is likely to start having second thoughts and send you along to the rack after all. Now, I can arrange to have a fast horse waiting——"

"I don't want to leave now, before the party," O'Leary said. "Besides," he added grinning, "I promised to kill off a dragon, remember?" Lafayette winked at Nicodaeus. "I think it might be a little difficult to kill a superstition." But I have to at least go through the motions. Meanwhile, I hear this Princess Adoranne is quite a dish."

"Careful, lad. The princess is Goruble's most jealously guarded treasure. Don't make the mistake of thinking——"

"Thinking—that's the one thing I've determined not to do, as long as I'm here," O'Leary said with finality. "Let's go, Nicodaeus. This is the first royal function I've ever been to; I'm looking forward to it."

"Well, then." Nicodaeus clapped O'Leary on the back. "On to the ball! Tonight, revelry, and tomorrow, the fight to the death!"

"Fight to the death?" O'Leary looked startled.

"You and the dragon," Nicodaeus reminded him.

"Oh, that." Lafayette smiled. Nicodaeus laughed.

"Yes, that," he said.

At the high-arched entry to the ballroom, O'Leary paused beside Nicodaeus and looked out over an expanse of mirror-polished white marble the size of a football field, crowded with the royal guests, splendid in laces and satins of every imaginable hue, gleaming in the light from the chandeliers that hung from the gold-ribbed vaults of the ceiling like vast bunches of sparkling grapes. Heads turned as the majordomo boomed out the name of Nicodaeus, then looked inquiringly at O'Leary.

"Better get on your toes, Humphries," the magician advised the beribboned official. "This is Lafayette O'Leary, the young champion who's here to rid the kingdom of Lod's monster."

"Oh, beg pardon, milord. An honor!" He bowed and pounded his staff on the floor.

"Sir Lafayette of Leary!" He trumpted. "The King's champion!"

"I'm not a sir," Lafayette started.

"Never mind." Nicodaeus took his arm and led him along toward the nearest group. "We'll see about an earldom for you at the first opportunity. Now . . ." He nodded casually at the expectant faces that moved in to surround them. "Ladies, sirs, may I present my good friend, Sir Lafayette."

"Are you really going to fight that horrid monster?" a cuddly creature in pale blue flounces breathed, fluttering her fan. A tall, hollow-faced man with thin white hair raised a bony finger. "Ride in fast, smite the brute in the soft underparts and get out. That's my advice, Sir Lafayette! I've always found that boldness pays."

"Will you cut off his head?" a plump blonde squeaked. "Ooooh, how terrible! Will there be much blood?"

"I'd like to be riding with you, lad," a stout gentleman with an imposing nose and a walrus mustache wheezed. "Unfortunately, my gout . . ."

Lafayette nodded, offered breezy comments, accepted a drink from a tray after giving a moment's thought to the contents and feeling the slight jar that signaled successful manipulation. No use drinking cheap booze. He tested the drink: Rémy-Martin. He tossed the first shot down and scooped up another glass. The cognac had a pleasant, warming effect. He took another from a passing tray.

A sudden murmur ran through the assemblage. Horns tootled a fanfare.

"The princess," murmured the crowd. Lafayette looked in the direction toward which necks were craning and saw a cluster of women entering through a wide archway.

"Which is Adoranne?" He nudged Nicodaeus.

"She'll appear next."

A girl strolled into view, leading a tiger cub on a leash. She was tall, slender, moving as gracefully as a swan in a gown of palest blue scattered over with tiny pearls. Her hair—the color of spring sunshine, Lafayette decided instantly—was straight, cut short in a charming style that complemented the coronet perched atop it. She had a short patrician nose—at least it was the kind of nose that suggested that word to O'Leary—large blue eyes, a perfectly modeled cheek and chin line. Her figure was that of a trained athlete: trim, slim, vibrant with health. Lafayette tried to take a deep breath, his lips puckering instinctively for a long low whistle of admiration, but managed only a gasp.

"What's the matter?" Nicodaeus whispered.

"Now I know what they mean by breathtaking," he muttered. "Come one." He started through the crowd.

"Where are you going?" Nicodaeus plucked at his sleeve.

"I want to meet the princess."

"But you can't approach royalty! You have to wait for her to summon you!"

"Oh, don't let's bother with all that protocol. I want to see if she looks as marvelous up close as she does from here."

He pushed through between two bony dowagers just rising from creaky curtsys and smiled at the girl as she turned inquiringly toward him.

"Hi," Lafayette said, looking her over admiringly. "They told me you were beautiful, but that was the understatement of the year. I didn't know

I could imagine anything this nice."

A big young man with curly dark hair and cigarette-ad features stepped forward, flexing Herculean shoulders that threatened to burst his royal blue gold-braid-looped tunic. He inclined his head to the princess, then turned to give O'Leary a warning look.

"Withdraw, bumpkin," he said in a low voice.

O'Leary waved a hand. "Go play with your blocks." He started around the man, who took a quick step to bar his way.

"Are you deaf, oaf?" he rapped.

"No, I'm Lafayette O'Leary, and if you don't mind, I'd like to——"

The young Hercules put a finger against O'Leary's chest. "Begone!" he hissed fiercely.

"Now, now, no rough stuff in front of the princess," O'Leary admonished, brushing the hand aside.

"Count Alain," a cool feminine voice said. Both men turned. Princess Adoranne smiled an intimate little smile at the count and turned to Lafayette.

"This must be the brave man who's come to rid us of the dragon." She tugged at the leash as the tiger cub came snuffling around O'Leary's ankles. "Welcome to Artesia."

"Thanks." Lafayette nudged the count aside. "I didn't exactly come here to kill dragons, but since I'm here, I don't mind helping out."

"Have you slain many dragons, Sir Lafayette?" She smiled at him coolly.

"Nope, never even saw one." He winked. "Did you?"

Adoranne's lips were parted in an expression of

mild surprise. "No," she admitted. "There is but one, of course—the beast of the rebel Lod."

"I'll bring you his left ear—if dragons have ears."

The princess blushed prettily.

"Fellow, you're overbold," Alain snapped.

"If I'm going to go dragon hunting, that's a characteristic I've been advised to cultivate." Lafayette moved closer to the princess. "You know, Adoranne, I really should have demanded half the kingdom and your hand in marriage."

Count Alain's hand spun O'Leary around; his fist hovered under Lafayette's nose.

"I've warned you for the last time."

Lafayette disengaged his arm. "I sincerely hope so. By the way, isn't there a little matter you wanted to attend to?" Lafayette envisioned an urgent physiological need.

Count Alain looked uncomfortable. "Your pardon, Highness," he said in a strained voice. He turned hastily and hurried toward an inconspicuous door.

'O'Leary smiled blandly at the princess. "Nice fellow," he said. "Good friend of yours?"

"One of my dearest companions since we played together as children."

"Amazing," Lafayette said. "You remember your childhood?"

"Very well, Sir Lafayette. Do you not?"

"Well, sure, but let's not get started on that. Would you like to dance?"

The princess' ladies, drawn up in a rank behind her, sniffed loudly and moved as if to close in. Adoranne looked at O'Leary thoughtfully.

"There's no music," she said.

Lafayette glanced toward the potted palms, envisioned a swinging five-man combo behind them. They were in tuxes, and the music was on the stands, and the instruments out. The leader was saying a word to the boys now, raising a hand . . . He felt the small thump.

"May I?" Lafayette held out a hand as the opening blast of the Royal Garden Blues rang across the ballroom. Adoranne smiled, handed the cub's leash to a lady standing by and took Lafayette's hand. He drew her close—a feather-light vision of sky-blue and pearls and a faint scent of night-blooming jasmine.

"Sir Lafayette!" she gasped. "You have a strange manner with a lday."

"I'll show you a quaint native dance we do at home."

She followed without apparent difficulty as he tried out one of the Arthur Murray steps he had so often practiced solo in his room with the instruction book in his left hand.

"You follow beautifully," O'Leary said. "But then, I guess that's to be expected."

"Of course. I've been well instructed in the arts of the ballroom. But tell me, why did you agree to go out against Lod's dragon?"

"Oh, I don't know. To keep from finding out if your pop really meant what he said about hot irons, maybe."

"You jest, sir!"

"Sure."

"Tell me, did you swear some great oath to do a mighty deed?"

"Well . . ."

"And an oath of secrecy as well," she nodded,

brighteyed. "Tell me," she asked in an excited whisper, "who are you—really? The name—Sir Lafayette—does it disguise some noble title in your own land of Leary?"

"Now where did you get that idea?"

"You comport yourself not as one accustomed to bending the knee," she said, looking at him expectantly.

"Well, now that you mention it, where I come from, I don't have to kneel to anybody."

Adoranne gasped. "I knew it! How exciting! Tell me, Lafayette, where is your country? Not to the east, for there's naught but ocean there, and to the west lies only the desert stronghold of Lod."

"No fair to try to worm my secrets out of me," Lafayette said waggishly. "It's more fun if I'm mysterious."

"Very well, but promise me that when you reveal yourself, it will be first to me."

"You can count on that, honey," Lafayette assured her.

"Honey?"

"You know, sweet stuff."

Adoranne giggled. "Lafayette, you have the cutest way of putting things!"

"That's one of the nice things about being here," he said. "Usually I'm pretty dumb when it comes to light conversation."

"Lafayette, you're trying to cozen me! I'll wager there's never a moment when you're at a loss for words."

"Oh, there have been moments. When the musketeers came to arrest me, for example. I'd been having a few quick ones with somebody called the Red Bull——"

Adoranne gasped. "You mean the infamous cutpurse and smuggler?"

"He seemed to have some illegal ideas, all right. A reflection of the anarchist in me, I suppose."

"And they arrested you!" Adoranne giggled. "Lafayette, you might have been lodged in a dungeon!"

"Oh, well, I've been in worse places."

"What thrilling adventures you must have had! A prince, wandering incognito——"

The music stopped with a clatter as though the players had tossed their instruments into a pile. Everybody clapped, calling for more. Count Alain shouldered past O'Leary, ducking his head to the princess.

"Adoranne, dare I crave the honor of the next?"

"Sorry, Al, she's taken," Lafayette took the girl's hand, started past the count, who pivoted to face him.

" 'Twas not *your* leave I spoke for, witling!" he hissed. "I warn you, begone before I lose my temper!"

"Look, Al, I'm getting a little tired of this," Lafayette said. "Every time I'm on the verge of having an interesting chat with Adoranne, you butt in."

"Aye! a greater dullard even than yourself should see when his company's not wanted. Now get ye gone!" People were staring now as the count's voice rose.

"Alain!" Adoranne looked at him with a shocked expression. "You mustn't speak that way to . . . to . . . a guest," she finished.

"A guest? A hired adventurer, by all accounts!

How dare he lay a hand on the person of the Princess Royal!"

"Alain, why can't you two be friends?" Adoranne appealed. "After all, Sir Lafayette is sworn to perform a great service to the crown."

"His kind finds it easy to talk of great deeds," Alain snapped, "but when the hour comes for action——"

"I notice you didn't volunteer, Al," O'Leary pointed out. "You look like a big strong boy——"

"Strong enough to break your head. As for dragon slaying, neither I nor any other man can face a monster bigger than a mountain, armored and fanged——"

"How do you know he's armored and fanged? Have you seen him?"

"No, but 'tis common knowledge——"

"Uh-huh. Well, Alain, you run along now. After I've killed this dragon I'll let you come out with a tape measure and see just how big he is—unless you're too shy, that is."

"Shy, eh!" The count's well chiseled features scowled two inches from Lafayette's nose. "I'm not too shy to play a tattoo on your ill-favored hide, a-horse or afoot!"

"Count Alain!" Adoranne's cool voice was low but it carried a snap of authority. "Mend your manners, sir!"

"*My* manners!" Alain glared at O'Leary. "This fellow has the manners of a swineherd! And the martial skill as well, I'll wager!"

"Oh, I don't know, Al," O'Leary said casually. "I've done a bit of reading on karate, aikido, judo——"

"These are weapons I know not," Alain grated.

"What do you know of the broadsword, the poniard, the mace? Or the quarterstaff, the lance——"

"Crude," Lafayette said. "Very crude. I find the art of fencing a much more gentlemanly sport. I read a dandy book on it just last month. The emphasis on the point rather than the edge, you know. The saber and épée——"

"I'm not unfamiliar with rapier form," Alain said grimly. "In fact, I'd welcome an opportunity to give you lessons."

Lafayette laughed indulgently. "*You* teach *me*? Al, old fellow, if you only knew how foolish that sounds. After all, what could you possibly know that I don't, eh?" He chuckled.

"Then, Sir Nobody, perhaps your worship would condescend to undertake my instruction!"

"Alain!" Adoranne started.

"It's all right, Adoranne," O'Leary said. "Might be fun at that. How about tomorrow afternoon?"

"Tomorrow? Ha! And overnight you'd scuttle for safety, I doubt not, and we'd see no more of you and your pretensions! 'Tis not so easy as that, knave. The inner courtyard is moon-bright! Let's repair to our lessons without further chatter!"

Nicodaeus was at Lafayette's side. "Ah, Count Alain," he said smoothly. "May I suggest——"

"You may not!" Alain's eyes found O'Leary's. "I'll await you in the courtyard." He bobbed his head to the princess, turned on his heel and pushed his way through the gaping circle of onlookers who at once streamed away in his wake.

"All this excitement about a fencing lesson," O'Leary said. "These people are real sports fans."

"Sir Lafayette," Adoranne said breathlessly,

"you need not heed the count's ill-natured outburst. I'll command that he beg your forgiveness."

"Oh, it's all right. The fresh air will do me good. I'm feeling those cognacs a little, I'm afraid."

"Lafayette, how cool you are in the face of danger. Here." She took a lacy handkerchief from somewhere and pressed it in Lafayette's hand. "Wear this and please, deal generously with him." Then she was gone.

"Adoranne——" O'Leary began. A hand took his arm.

"Lafayette," Nicodaeus said at his ear. "Do you know what you're doing? Alain is the top swordsman in the Guards Regiment."

"I'm just giving him a few tips on saber technique. He——"

"Tips? The man's a master fencer! He'll have his point under your ribs before you can say Sam Katzman!"

"Nonsense. It's all just good clean fun."

"Fun? The man is furious!"

Lafayette looked thoughtful. "Do you really think he's mad?"

"Just this side of frothing at the mouth," Nicodaeus assured him. "He's been number one with Adoranne for some time now—until you came along and cut him out of the pattern."

"Jealous, eh? Poor fellow, if he only knew . . ."

"Only knew what?" Nicodaeus asked sharply.

"Nothing." He slapped Nicodaeus heartily on the back. "Now let's go out and see what he can do."

CHAPTER V

The courtyard was a grim rectangle of granite walled in by the looming rear elevations of the servant's residential wings of the palace, gleaming coldly in the light of a crescent moon. The chill in the air had sharpened; it was close to freezing now. Lafayette looked around at the crowd that had gathered to watch the fencing lesson. They formed a ring three or four deep around the circumference of the impromptu arena, bundled in cloaks, stamping their feet and conversing in low, excited mutters. The wagers being made. O'Leary noted, were two to one in favor of the opposition.

"I'll take your coat," Nicodaeus said briskly. O'Leary pulled it off, shivered as a blast of frigid wind flapped his shirt against his back. Twenty feet away, Count Alain, looking bigger than ever in shirt sleeves, chatted casually with two elegant-looking seconds, who glanced his way once, nodded coldly, and thereafter ignored him.

"Ah, I see the surgeon is on hand." Nicodaeus

pointed out a portly man in a long gray cloak. "Not that there'll be much he can do. Count Alain always goes for the heart."

The count had accepted his blade from one of his aides now; he flexed it, tested its point with a finger and made a series of cuts at the air.

"I'd better warm up, too," O'Leary drew his rapier from its scabbard, finding it necessary to use both hands to get the point clear. "It's kind of long, isn't it?" he said. He waved the weapon, took up a stance.

"I hope your practice has been against skilled partners," Nicodaeus said.

"Oh, I just practice by myself." O'Leary tried a lunge, went a little too far, had to hop twice to get his balance.

"This thing's heavy," he commented, lowering the tip to the ground. "I'm used to a lighter weapon."

"Be grateful for its weight; Count Alain has a superb sword arm. He'll beat a light blade aside like a wooden lath."

"Hey," Lafayette said, nudging the magician. "Look over there, in the black cloak. That looks like——"

"It is," Ncodaeus said. "Don't stare. The cloak is accepted by all present as an effective disguise. It wouldn't do for a lady of her rank to witness an affair of this sort."

Lafayette fumbled out Adoranne's hanky, fluttered it at her and tucked it in his shirt pocket. Across the yard, Count Alain, watching the byplay, set his left fist on his hip, proceeded to whip his blade through a dazzling warmup pattern. O'Leary gaped at the whistling steel.

"Say, Nicodaeus," he murmured thoughtfully, "he's good!"

"I told you he was a winner, Lafayette. But if, as you said, you're better——"

"Look, ah, maybe I was hasty." He watched as the count described a lightning series of figure eights, finished with an elaborate *redoublement* and lowered his point with a calculating glance at O'Leary.

"Go ahead," Nicodaeus whispered. "Show him a little swordsmanship. It will give you a psychological advantage if you can slice yours a hair closer to the test pattern than he did."

"Ah, look here, Nicodaeus, I've been thinking; it wouldn't really be fair of me to show him up, in front of his friends."

"He'll have to take that chance. After all, he was the one who insisted on the meeting."

Alain's seconds were nodding now. They turned and started across toward O'Leary.

"Nicodaeus!" O'Leary grabbed his second's arm. "This isn't going just the way I'd figured. I mean, I assumed that since Alain—that is, I don't see how——"

"Later." Nicodaeus disengaged his arm, strode across, engaged in deep conversation with his two opposite numbers. Lafayette hefted the sword, executed a pair of awkward thrusts. The weapon felt as clumsy as a crowbar in his cold-numbed fingers. Now Alain stepped forward a few paces and stood waiting, his slim blade held in his bronzed fist as lightly as a bread stick.

"Come along, Lafayette." Nicodaeus was at his side. "Now, I'll hold a white handkerchief between your crossed blades . . ."

Lafayette hardly heard Nicodaeus, who was talking rapidly as he urged him forward. Perhaps if he fell down, pretended to hurt his knee . . . no, no good. Maybe if he sneezed—a sudden attack of asthma——

It wouldn't do. There was only one course left. Damn! And just when he'd started having a good time. But it couldn't be helped. And this time it had better work. O'Leary shut his eyes, conjured up the image of Mrs. MacGlint's Clean Rooms and Board, the crooked hall, the cramped bedroom, the peeling, stained wallpaper, the alcove, the sardines . . .

He opened his eyes. Nicodaeus was staring at him.

"What's the matter? You're not sick?"

O'Leary snapped his eyes shut, muttering to himself: "*You're asleep, dreaming all this. You're in bed, feeling that broken spring in the mattress–the one that catches you under the left shoulder blade. It's almost morning now, and if you just open your eyes slowly . . .*" He opened one eye, saw Count Alain waiting ten feet away, the rank of expectant faces behind him, the stone wall looming above.

"*It's not real,*" he hissed under his breath. "*It's all a fake, an hallucination! It isn't really here!*" He stamped a boot against the stone paving. "*This isn't real stone, ha ha, just imaginary stone. I'm not really cold; it's a nice night in August! There's no wind blowing . . .*"

His voice trailed off. There was no use in kidding himself: The stone was solid as ever underfoot. The icy wind was still cutting at his face like a skinning knife and Alain waited, light glinting on the naked steel in his hand. Nicodaeus was looking at him concernedly.

". . . instructions," he was saying. "Well, do the best you can, my boy." He took out the white handkerchief and flapped it.

"It's the distractions," O'Leary mumbled to himself. "I can't concentrate, with all these people watching."

"Gentlemen, on guard!" Nicodaeus said sharply. Count Alain raised his sword, held it at the *engagé*. Dumbly, Lafayette stepped forward, lifted his heavy blade, clanged it against the other. It was like hitting a wrought iron fence.

"Say, just a minute!" O'Leary lowered his blade and stepped back. Alain stared at him, his black eyes as cold as outer space. O'Leary turned to Nicodaeus. "Look here, if this is a real duel, and not just a friendly lesson——"

"Ha!" Alain interjected.

". . . then as the challenged party, I have the choice of weapons, right?"

Nicodaeus pulled at his lower lip. "I suppose so, but the meeting has already begun."

"It's never too late to correct an error in form," O'Leary said firmly. "Now, you take these swords—primitive weapons, really. We ought to use something more up to date. Pistols, maybe; or——"

"You demand pistols?" Nicodaeus looked surprised.

"Why not pistols?" At least—O'Leary was thinking of the princess's eyes on him—he wouldn't look as silly missing with a pistol as he would with Alain chasing him around the courtyard slashing at his heels.

"Pistols it is, then," Nicodaeus was saying. "I trust suitable weapons are available?"

"In my room," O'Leary said. "A nice pair of weapons."

"As Sir Lafayette desires," one of Alain's seconds was saying. "Subject to Count Alain's agreement, of course."

"I'm sure the count won't want to chicken out at this point," O'Leary said. "Of course pistols are pretty lethal——" he broke off, suddenly aware of what he was saying. Pistols?

"On second thought, fellows——" he started.

"I've heard of them," Alain was nodding. "Like small muskets, held in the hand." He shot O'Leary a sharp look. "You spoke only of cold steel when you goaded me to this meeting, sirrah; now you raise the stakes."

"That's all right," O'Leary said hastily. "If you'd rather not——"

". . . but I accept the gage," Alain declared flatly. "You're a more bloodthirsty rogue than I judged by the look of you, but I'll not cavil. Bring on these firearms!"

"Couldn't we just cut cards?" But Nicodaeus was already speaking to a mop-haired page, who darted away, looking eager.

Alain turned his back, walked off a few paces, spoke tightlipped to his seconds, who shot back looks at O'Leary. He shrugged apologetically, got scowls in return.

Nicodaeus was chewing his lip. "I like this not, Lafayette," he said. "With a lucky shot, he could blow your head off, even if you nailed him at the same time."

Lafayette nodded absently, his eyes half shut.

He was rmemebering the pistols, picturing them as they lay snug in their jeweled holsters. He envisioned their internal workings, visualized the parts . . . His ability to manipulate the environment seemed to come in spells, but it was worth a try. Tricky business, at this range. He felt a reassuring flicker, faint but unmistakable—or was it? Perhaps it had just been a gust of wind.

The boy was back, breathing hard, holding out the black leather belt with its elegant bright-work and its burden of long-barreled pistols.

"I'll take those." Nicodaeus lifted the guns from the page's hands, crossed to the waiting count and offered both pistol butts. Alain drew one from its holster, hefted it, passed it to his seconds, who turned it over, wagged their heads, muttered together and handed it back. O'Leary took his, noted distractedly that it was a clip-fed automatic with a filed front sight. It looked deadly enough.

"What distance is customary, Lafayette?" Nicodaeus enquired in a whisper.

"Oh, about three paces ought to be enough."

"What?" Nicodaeus stared at him. "At that range, no one could miss!"

"That's the idea," O'Leary pointed out. "Let's get on with it." He licked his lips nervously, hardly hearing as Nicodaeus instructed both combatants to stand back to back, their weapons held at their sides, and at the signal to take three paces, turn and fire.

Alain stepped into position and stood stiffly, waiting. Lafayette backed up to him.

"All right, go!" Nicodaeus said firmly. O'Leary gulped, took a step, another, a third and whirled, raising the gun.

Alain's weapon was already up, pointed straight at O'Leary's heart. He saw the count's finger tighten on the trigger at the same instant that he sighted on the white blob of the other's shirt front and squeezed.

A jet of purple ink squirted in a long arc, scoring a dead center hit as a stream of red fluid from Alain's gun spattered his own shoulder.

"I got you first!" O'Leary called cheerily, snapping another shot that arched across to catch Alain on the ear. It was a good, high-pressure jet, O'Leary noted approvingly. It followed the haughty count as he reeled back, played over his face and down the already empurpled shirt, and piddled out just as Alain, in retreat, collided with his own startled seconds and went down. The crowd, in silent shock until then, burst out with a roar of laughter, above which a distinct titter from the direction of Princess Adoranne was clearly audible.

"Well, I guess I win," O'Leary lowered the gun, smiling and taking the accolade of the crowd. Alain was scrambling to his feet, scrubbing at his face with both hands. He stared at his violet palms, then with a roar leaped at his second, wrested the sword from the startled man's grip and charged.

"Lafayette!" Nicodaeus roared. O'Leary looked around in time to see his rapier flying toward him, hilt first. He grabbed it and brought it up just in time to receive Alain's onslaught.

"Hey!" O'Leary back-pedaled, frantically warding off the count's wild attack. Steel clanged on steel as the bigger man's fury drove O'Leary back, back. His feet stumbled on the uneven pavement and the heavy blows numbed his arm, threatening to knock his weapon from his grip. There was no question of counterattack.

A mighty chop sent Lafayette's blade spinning. He had a momentary glimpse of Alain's face, purple with ink and fury, as he brought back his blade, poised for the thrust.

There was a flash and a resounding clong! as something white shot down from above to strike the count's head, bound aside and smash against the wall. Alain dropped his sword, folded slowly, knees first, and slammed out flat on his face.

A fragment of the missile clattered to O'Leary's feet. He let out his breath in a hoarse gasp, stooped and brought up the shard. It bore a fmiliar pattern of angels and rosebuds: the chamber pot from his room.

He looked up quickly, caught a glimpse of a saucy face, ringed with dark curls, just withdrawing from a darkened window.

"Daphne," he muttered, "nice timing, girl."

Back in the ballroom there was a great deal of hearty laughter and congratulatory slapping of Lafayette's back.

"As pretty a piece of foolery as I've seen this twelve-month," chortled a grizzled old fellow in pale yellow knee pants and a monocle. "Young Alain's had it coming to him, what? Bit of a prig, but a trifle too stout a lad to bait!"

"You handled the situation nicely, my boy," Nicodaeus nodded sagely. "A fatality would have been in rather bad taste, and of course, you've made you point now, statuswise."

Adoranne came up, looking prettier than ever

with her cheeks pink from the cold air. She put a hand on Lafayette's arm.

"I thank you, noble sir, for sparing the count's life. He's learned a lesson he'll not soon forget."

A sudden loud shriek rang out across the crowded ballroom floor, followed by the piercing accents of an angry female voice. At this new diversion, Lafayette's circle of admirers broke up and moved off craning their necks to make out the source of the outbursts.

"Whew!" O'Leary looked around for a waiter and lifted the ninth—or was it the tenth?—brandy of the evening from a passing tray. "Adoranne," he started, "now's our chance to get away from the mob for a minute. I noticed there's a nice garden outside."

"Oh, Lafayette, let's discover what it is that's set the duchess to clamoring like a fishwife spoiled of a copper!" She tugged at his hand playfully. He followed as Nicodaeus moved ahead, calling for way for her Highness.

"It's a chambermaid," someone was passing the word. "The saucy minx was mingling with her betters, wearing a stolen gown, mind you!"

O'Leary had a sudden sinking feeling. He'd forgotten all about his invitation to Daphne. The petite chambermaid, transformed in rose-colored silk set off by white gloves, silver slippers and a string of luminous white pearls, defiantly faced a bony matron buckled into stiff yellowish-white brocade like a suit of armor. The latter shook a finger heavenward, her neck tendons vibrating like cello strings, the coronet atop her mummified coiffure bouncing with the vigor of the verbal assault.

". . . my girl, and I'll see to it that after the flogging, you're sent away to a workhouse where——"

"Ah, pardon me, Duchess," O'Leary stepped forward, winked encouragingly at Daphne and faced the incensed noblewoman. "I think there's been a slight misunderstanding here. This young lady——"

"Lady! I'll have you know this is a common servant girl! The audacity of the baggage appearing here—and in *my* gown! My seamstress completed it only today."

"You must be mistaken," O'Leary said firmly. "The dress was a gift from me and I invited her here."

Behind him there was a sharp gasp. He turned. Adoranne looked at him, wide-eyed, then managed a forced smile.

"Another of our good Sir Lafayette's jests," she said. "Be calm, Veronica dear; the girl will be dealt with."

"No, you don't understand," O'Leary protested. "There's been a mistake. I gave her the dress this evening."

"Please, noble sir," Daphne broke in. "I . . . I'm grateful for your chivalrous attempt to aid a poor servant girl, but it's no use. I . . . I stole the dress, just as her ladyship said."

"She did not!" Lafayette waved his arms. "Are you all out of your mind? I tell you——"

The duchess pointed a skeletal finger at a decorative motif on the bodice of the gown. "Is that, or is that not, the crest of the House of High Jersey?" Her voice was shrill with triumph.

"She's quite right of course," Nicodaeus muttered at O'Leary's side. "What's all this about giving her the dress?"

"I . . . I . . ." O'Leary stared from the duchess to Daphne, who stood now with downcast eyes. A suspicion was beginning to dawn: somehow, his ability to summon up artifacts at will wasn't quite as simple as he'd thought. When he had called for a bathroom, he'd gotten a tub—complete with occupant—transferred, the girl had said, from her garret room. And when he had ordained a dress in the closet, he hadn't created it from nothing; he had merely shifted the nearest available substitute to hand—in this case, from the wardrobe of the duchess.

"I'll pay for the dress," he blurted. "It's not her fault. She didn't know it was stolen—that is, I didn't steal it—not really. You see, I invited her to the party, and she said . . ."

He trailed off. Interested smiles were fading. Adoranne tossed her head, turned and moved grandly away. The duchess was glaring at him like a mother tyrannosaurus surprising an early mammal sucking eggs.

"Adoranne, wait a minute! I can explain——" He caught Daphne's tear-brimmed eye.

"Come along, Lafayette," Nicodaeus tugged at his sleeve. "The joke didn't go over; there people are pretty stuffy about protocol."

"Daphne," O'Leary started. "I'm sorry——" The girl raised her head, looked past him. "I do not know you, sir," she said coldly, and turned away.

"Oh, dammit all!" O'Leary grimaced and let his arms fall at his sides. "I wish I'd never thought of the infernal dress in the first place."

There was a startled yelp from the duchess, a squeak from Daphne, a delighted roar from the males in the audience. Lafayette gasped and caught a fleeting glimpse of a curvaceous white flank as Daphne, clad only in silver slippers, a few bits of lace and blushes, vanished into the crowd, followed by a rising storm of applause.

"Oh, capital, old fellow!" A stout gentleman in deep red velvet slammed O'Leary's shoulder with a meaty hand. "Done with mirrors, I suppose?"

"Ah, Sir Lafayette, you are a sly fox!" boomed another appreciative oldster. The duchess sniffed, glared, stalked away.

"Where's Adoranne gone?" Lafayette rose on his toes, staring across heads.

"This wasn't exactly the kind of prank to impress her Highness with," Nicodaeus said. "You won't see her again this evening, my boy."

Lafayette let out a long sigh. "I guess you're right. Oh, well; the party's breaking up, anyway. Maybe in the morning I can explain."

"Don't even try," the magician advised.

Lafayette eyed him glumly. "I need some time to figure out a few things before I try any more good deeds," he said. "Maybe if I sleep on it—but on the other hand, if I go to sleep——"

"Never mind, my boy. She won't stay angry forever. Go along and get some rest now. There are a few things I want to discuss with you in the morning."

Back in his room, Lafayette waited while a soft-footed servant lit a candle. In the dim light he pulled off his clothes, used the washbasin to slosh water over his head and toweled off. He blew out the taper, then went to the fourposter, pulled back the blankets and clambered in with a grateful sigh.

Something warm and smooth cuddled up against him. With a muffled yelp he bounded from the bed and whirled to stare at the bright-eyed face and bare shoulder of Daphne, looking up tousel-headed from under the covers.

"Count Alain gave you an awful drubbing, didn't he, sir? Come along and I'll rub your back."

"Uh, thanks for dropping that, uh, missile on him," O'Leary started. "But——"

"Never mind that," Daphne said. "It was nothing. But your poor bruises . . ."

"Lucky for me he used the edge." Lafayette moved his arm gingerly. "It is pretty sore, at that. But what in the world are you doing here?"

She gave him an impish smile. "Where else could I go, milord, in my condition?"

"Well . . ." O'Leary froze, listening for a sound. It had been a stealthy sort of creak.

"Hssst!" the voice came from across the dark room. O'Leary tensed, remembering his sword, across the room on the floor in a heap with his clothes.

"Sir Lafayette, come quickly," the voice hissed. "It concerns the welfare of her Highness. Make no outcry! Secrecy is vital!"

"Who are you?" O'Leary demanded. "How did you get in here?"

"No time to talk! Hurry!" The voice was a throaty rasp, unfamiliar. Lafayette squinted, trying to get a glimpse of the intruder. "What's happened?"

"No more talk! Follow me or not, as you choose! There's not a moment to lose."

"All right; wait until I get my pants on. . ." He fumbled his way across to his clothes, pulled on breeches and a shirt, jammed his feet into shoes and caught up a short cloak.

"All right, I'm ready."

"This way!" Lafayette made his way across toward the sound of the voice. As he passed the bed, Daphne's hand reached out, tugged him down.

"Lafayette," she breathed in his ear, "you must not go! Perhaps it is a trick!"

"I've got to," he whispered back, equally quietly. "It's——"

"Who's that?" the voice snapped sharply. "To whom do you speak?"

"Nobody," Lafayette pulled free, went toward the voice. "I always mutter to myself when I don't know what's going on. Look here, is she all right?"

"You'll see."

A line of faint light showed against the wall and widened as a four-foot rectangle of paneling slid aside. A cloaked silhouette showed against it for a moment and then slipped past. O'Leary followed, barely able in the deep gloom to make out a narrow low-ceilinged passage and the stealthy figure of his guide. He cracked his head on a low beam, swore, scraped aside cobwebs that clung to his face. There was an odor of dust and stale air and mice; somewhere wind whined in a cranny in the wall.

The passage led more or less straight, with an occasional jog around a massive masonry column, then turned right, continued another fifty feet and dead-ended at a coarsely mortared brick wall.

"We go up here," the hoarse voice said shortly. Lafayette groped until he found rough wooden slats nailed to a vertical post against the wall. He went up, stepped off into a new passage and hurried after his guide. He tried to estimate his position in the palace. He was on the third floor, about halfway along the east wing.

Just ahead there was a soft creak, a faint rusty squeal. A hand caught his arm, thrust a coarse-textured sack into his hand—a sack heavy with something that clinked.

"Hey, what's——" A hearty shove thrust Lafayette violently forward. He stumbled, struck something with his shoulder, felt a rug underfoot now and caught a scent of delicate perfume. He whirled, heard a panel slam in his face; his hands scraped fruitlessly across a solid-seeming wall. There was a stir behind him in the room, a sharp cry, quickly cut off. 'OLeary flattened himself, trying desperately to see through the darkness. Someone called in the next room. There were hurried footsteps; a door opened across the room, fanning soft light across a wedge of rich-patterned rug, a slice of brocaded wall, an arch of gilded ceiling. O'Leary saw a window with dainty ruffles, a vast canopied four-poster. A short, fat woman in a flounced nightcap puffed through the open door, holding a candle high.

"Your Highness! You cried out!"

Lafayette stood frozen, staring at a vision of bare-shouldered femininity sitting up in the huge bed, staring across at him in astonishment. The fat woman followed Adoranne's gaze, saw Lafayette, screeched, clapped a hand to her broad bosom and screeched again, louder.

"Shhh! It's only me!" Lafayette started forward, shushing the woman frantically; she yelled again and backed against the bed.

"Stay back, villain! Touch not one hair of her Highness's head——!"

"It's all a mistake." O'Leary indicated the wall through which he had entered. "Somebody came into my room and told me——"

There was a pounding of feet, a clash of steel. Two immense guardsmen in flaring helmets, polished breastplates and greaves thundered into the room, took one eye-popping look at Adoranne, who quickly pulled the pink silk sheet up to her chin.

"There!" screamed the fat lady-in-waiting, pointing with a plump finger. "A murderer! A ravisher! A thief in the night!"

"Let me explain how I happened to be here, fellows——" Lafayette broke off as the two men rushed him, pinned him against the wall with six-foot-long doubleheaded pikes at his chest. "It was all a mistake! I was in my room, asleep, and all of a sudden——"

"——you took it into your head to violate the boudoir of her Highness!" the fat woman finished for him. "Look at the great wretch, half-dressed, burning with unholy lust——"

"I was only——"

"Silence, dog," one of the pikemen grated between set teeth. "Who thinks to harm our princess begs for bloody vengeance!"

"Did he—did he——" The other guard was

glaring at O'Leary with eyes like hot coals.

"The monster had no time to achieve his evil purpose," the chubby woman bleated. "I placed my own body between him and that of her Highness, offering it gladly if need be to save her Highness from this fiend!"

"Has he taken anytning?"

"Oh, for heaven's sake," O'Leary protested. "I'm no thief!" He waved his arms. "I——" The bag, still clutched in his hand, slammed the wall. He stared at it dumbly.

"What's he got there?" One of the men seized the sack, opened it, peered inside. Over his shoulder, Lafayette caught a glimpse of Adoranne, an expression of mischievous interest on her perfect features.

"Your Highness!" The man stepped to the bed and upended the contents of the pouch on the rosebud adorned coverlet—a sparkling array of rings, necklaces, bracelets, glinting red, green, diamond-white in the candle light.

The fat woman gasped. "Your Highness' jewels!" Lafayette made a move, felt the pike dig into his chest hard enough to draw blood. "Somebody shoved that into my hands," he called. "I was in the dark, in the passage, and——"

"Enough, thief!" the pike wielder snarled. "Move along now, you! I need little excuse to spit your gizzard!"

"Look, Adoranne, I was trying to help! He told me——"

"Who? Have you an accomplice in your felony?" The guard jabbed again to emphasize the question.

"No! I mean there was a man—a medium-sized

man in a cloak; he came into my room——"

"How came the rogue here?" the fat woman shrilled. "Did you great louts sleep at your posts of duty?"

"I came in through some kind of sliding panel," O'Leary turned to the princess. "It's right over there. It closed up behind me, and——"

Adoranne's chin went up; she gave him a look of haughty contempt and turned away.

"I thank you, Martha," she said coolly to the fat lady-in-waiting. "And you, gentlemen, for your vigilance in my defesnes. Leave me now."

"But, your Highness——" the fat woman started.

"Leave me!"

"Adoranne, if you'd just——" A painful prod in the solar plexus doubled O'Leary over. The pikemen caught his arms and hauled him from the room.

"Wait!" he managed. "Listen!"

"Tomorrow you can tell it to the headsman," the guard growled. "Another word outta you and by the three tails o'Goop I'll spare the crown the expense of an execution!"

In the corridor, Lafayette, still gasping, fixed his eye on the intersection ahead. *Just around the corner,* he improvised. *There's a . . . a policeman. He'll arrest these two.*

The pikemen shoved him roughly past the turn; the corridor was empty of cops. Too bad. Must be a spot he'd already seen and thus couldn't change. *But that door just ahead: it would open, and a python would come slithering out, and in the confusion——*

"Keep moving, you!" the pikeman pushed him

roughly past the door, which failed to disgorge a snake.

A gun, then, in his hip pocket——

He reached, found nothing. He should have known *that* one wouldn't work; he had just put the trousers on a few minutes earlier, and there had been no armaments bagging the pockets then—besides which, how could he concentrate with these two plug-uglies hauling at him? A sharp jerk at his arm directed him down another side way. He stumbled on, assisted by frequent jabs and blows, down stairs and more stairs, into a dim malodorous passage between damp stone walls, past an iron gate into a low chamber lit by smoking flambeaux in black iron brackets. He leaned against a wall, trying to decide which of his bruises hurt worst, while his pike-wielding acquaintance explained his case in a few terse words to an untrimmed lout with thick lips, pale stubble and pimples.

"One o' them guys, huh?" The turnkey nodded knowingly. "I know how to handle them kind."

"Wait . . . till I get my breath," O'Leary said. "I'll . . . visit you . . .with a plague of boils . . ."

A blow slammed him toward a barred gate. Hard hands hustled him through to a mouldy oak-plank door. Keys jangled. The blond jailer cuffed him aside and hauled the door open with a rasp of dry hinges. O'Leary caught a glimpse of a stone floor and a litter of rubbish.

Damn! If he'd just thought to picture something a trifle cosier, before he saw it.

"Kind of crummy quarters fer a dude like youse,

Buster," the turnkey leered. "You got straw, but I'll give ye a clue: Use the bare floor instead. We got a few fleas and stuff, you know?" Then a foot in the seat sent O'Leary spinning inside and the door thudded behind him.

CHAPTER VI

O'Leary sat on the floor, blinking into total blackness. Some day he'd have to read up on Freudian dream symbolism. All this business of stumbling around in the dark being beaten by large men must be some sort of punishment wish, probably arising from guilt feelings due to the Adoranne and Daphne sequences—particularly the former.

O'Leary got to his feet, felt his way to a wall, made a circuit of the cell. There were no windows, unless they were above his reach; and just the one door, massive and unyielding. He heard a furtive scuttling. Rats, no doubt. Not a very nice place to spend the rest of his dream. He sighed, regretting again he had been too rattled to provide a few amenities before it was too late. But perhaps he could still manage something . . .

Light, first. A candle would do. He pictured a two-inch stub lying among the litter in the far corner . . . and a match in his pocket.

There was a thump, as though the universe had gone over a tar strip in the road. O'Leary groped among odds and ends, felt straw, small bones—and a greasy lump of wax with a stub of a wick. Aha! Now for a match. In his pocket, a small item like that could have passed unnoticed. He checked, felt the smooth cover of a match folder, pulled it out and lit up. The candle burned with a feeble yellow flame, its light confirming his first impression of the cramped cell. Well, that part couldn't be helped, but it would be wise to think carefully about his next move.

O'Leary settled himself on the driest spot on the floor. It looked as though he were stuck here unless he could manage to regain the sanctuary of his room back at Mrs. MacGlint's house. The last two tries hadn't worked out, but then that was to be expected. After all, who could focus the Psychic Energies with someone hauling him toward a paddy-wagon or threatening to stick a foot of razor-edged steel into his internal arrangements?

At least it was peaceful here in the cell. But going back was a last resort; he couldn't just vanish without even a chance to explain to Adoranne how he had happened to be in her bedroom with a sackful of loot.

What could he do? If things hadn't happened so fast, he could have dreamed up some way out, some last minute rescue. Maybe it still wasn't too late. Nicodaeus, maybe; *he* could get him out of here. Probably he hadn't heard about his protégé's arrest yet—or, O'Leary amended, he had just heard a few minutes ago. By now he'd be coming along the hall, passing the iron-barred door, ordering guards around, demanding O'Leary's immediate release——

There was a sound from the door. A tiny panel opened; light glared in. O'Leary jumped up as he saw the face at the opening.

"Daphne! What are you doing here?"

"Oh, Sir Lafayette, I knew something terrible would happen!"

"You were right; there's dirty work afoot. Look, Daphne, I have to get out of here! I'm worried about Adoranne; whoever led me to her room——"

"I tried to tell them, sir, but they think I'm your confederate."

"What? Nonsense! But don't worry, Daphne, Nicodaeus will be along soon."

"He tried, sir—but the king was furious! He said it was an open-and-shut case, that you were caught red-handed——"

"But it was a frame-up!"

"At least you won't have a long wait in that awful cell. It's only three hours till dawn; it comes early this time of year."

"They're letting me out at dawn?"

"For the execution," Daphne said sadly.

"Whose execution?"

"Y—yours, sir," Daphne sniffled. "I'm to get off with twenty years."

"But—but they *can't*! King Goruble needs me to kill the dragon, and—and——"

"OK," a guard's rough voice interrupted, "you seen him, kid. Now how about that smooch?" the panel slammed with a bang. O'Leary groaned and resumed his seat. He'd not only reduced his own credit to zero, but dragged an innocent girl down with him. It looked like the end of the line—the second time in the last few hours that imminent death had stared him in the face. Some dream! What if he failed to wake up in time, and the sentence were actually carried out? He'd heard of people dreaming they were falling, and hitting, and dying in their sleep of heart failure. A hard story to check, but that was one experiment he couldn't afford to try. There was no help for it; he'd have to wake up.

Sitting against the wall, he relaxed, closed his eyes. *Mrs. MacGlint's house,* he thought, picturing the front porch in the gray predawn light; *the dark hall, the creaky stairs, the warped, black-varnished door to his room with its chipped brown-enameled steel knob; and the room itself, the odor of stale cookery and ancient woodwork and dust . . .*

He opened an eye. The candle flame across the cell guttered, making shadows bob on the stone wall. Nothing had changed. O'Leary felt uneasiness rising like water in a leaky hold.

He tried again, picturing the cracked sidewalk in front of the boarding house, the dusty leaves of the trees that overhung it, the mailbox at the corner, the down-at-the-heels shops along the main street, the tarnished red brick of the Post Office . . .

That was real, not the ridiculous dream about princesses and dragons. He was Lafayette O'Leary, aged twenty-six, with a steady if not inspiring job at which he was due in a very few hours. Old Man Biteworse would be hopping mad if he showed up late, bleary-eyed from lack of sleep. There was no time to waste, idling in a fantasy world, while his real-life job waited, with its deadlines and eyestrain and competition for the next two-dollar raise.

O'Leary felt a faint jar. A breath of warmth touched his face. His eyes snapped open. He was staring into a bright mist that swirled and eddied. The air was hot, moist. Aburptly, he was aware of dampness soaking into the seat of his trousers. He scrambled up, saw vague pale shapes moving in the fog. Out of the steam, figures appeared—the pink bodies of young girls with wet hair, wearing damp towels, carelessly draped. Lafayette gaped. He had made his escape—not back to Mrs. MacGlint's, it appeared, but to a sort of Arabian paradise, complete with teen-age houris.

There were sudden startled yelps; the nearest girls fled, squealing. Others bobbed into view, saw O'Leary, hastily hitched up towels and dashed away, adding to the outcry.

"Oh, no," Lafayette muttered. "Not again . . ." He moved off quickly to his left, encountered a corner and the sound of running water. He tried the other direction, spotted the darker rectangle of a doorless arch, made for it—and collided with a vast bulk in bundlesome tweeds hurtling through from the room beyond. There was a bleat like the cry of an outraged cow hippo defending her young; a rolled umbrella whistled past O'Leary's ear. He ducked; the shadowy giantess charged again, emitting piercing shrieks against the background of lesser yelps. Lafayette backed away, warding off a rain of blows from the flailing implement.

"Madam, you don't understand!" he shouted over the din. "I just wandered in by mistake, and——" his foot slipped. He had a momentary impression of a square red face like a worn-out typists's cushion closing in, the mouth gaping, tiny eyes glaring. Then a bomb exploded and sent him hurtling into a bottomless darkness.

"The way I see it, chief," a meaty voice was saying, "this character hides out over on the men's side last night, see? Then after the joint's locked up, he goes up a rope, out the skylight, across the roof, in the other skylight, down another rope, and hides out in the shower room until Mrs. Prudlock's early-morning modern dance class gets there——"

"Yeah?" a voice like soft mud came back. "So what'd he do with them ropes? Eat 'em?"

"Huh? How could a guy eat forty feet o' rope, chief?"

"The same way he done all that other stuff you said, lamebrain!"

"Huh?"

"Look, I think I got it, chief," an eager voice announced. "He dresses up like a janitor——"

"Only one janitor at the Y. Ninety years old. Checks out clean. Turned in a complaint last year he seen a nood dame. *Then:* You boys sure you checked that side door?"

"She was locked up tighter'n a card-sharp's money belt, chief."

"Now, my theory is," another voice put in, "he come in dressed as a broad, like. And after he's inside——"

"——he puts on tight britches and a cape, and jumps out at old lady Prudlock. Yah!"

The discussion continued. O'Leary sat up,

winced at a throb from the back of his head and others from various parts of his body representing blows from Alain's sword, jabs from the pikemen and a few assorted kicks, cuffs and falls. He looked around; he was in a small room with walls of white-washed cement, a bare concrete floor, a no-nonsense toilet minus a lid, a tiny washbowl with one water tap and a mirror above. Two bunks were bolted to the wall, on the lower of which he was sitting. Beyond a wide, steel-grilled door he could see a short stretch of two-tone brown-painted hallway, another barred door and beyond it a group of men in baggy dark blue suits with shiny seats and fat leather holsters strapped to wide hips.

O'Leary got to his feet, made it to the small barred window. Outside, early morning sunshine gleamed down on the drowsy view of the courthouse lawn, the park with the Civil War cannon and the second-best shopping street of Colby Corners. He stumbled back and sank down on the bunk. He was home—that much was clear—but how in the name of Goop had he gotten into the county jail? He had been in a dungeon under the palace—the present quarters were a marked improvement over their Artesian equivalent—and then . . .

Oh, yes. The houris and all that steam, and the big woman with the umbrella . . .

"Look, chief," a rubbery-voiced cop was saying, "What's the rap we're hanging on this joker?"

"Whatta ya mean, what's the rap? Peeping Tom, trespasser, breaking and entering, larceny——"

"We didn't find no busted locks, chief. Illegal entry, maybe, but the Y is open to the public."

"Not the *YW*! Not to the *male* public, it ain't! Besides he probably swiped something!"

"Naw, he just come fer the scenery." Guffaws rewarded this sally. The eager one cleared his throat. "What's the penalty for looking at nood dames, chief?"

"Hey, chief, can we hang a peeping Tom on a guy if he's working in broad daylight?"

O'Leary turned out the legal hassle. There was something very strange here. From what the cops were saying, it was clear enough that he'd actually *been* in the YW. That part hadn't been a dream, and the knot on the back of his head where the tile floor had come up and hit it confirmed it. The old battleax had called in the police, hence his presence in a cell. But how—and why—had he gotten into the shower room in the first place? It was a good five blocks from Mrs. MacGlint's; about the same distance, he realized with dawning comprehension, as that from the Ax and Dragon to the palace. Did that mean that he had actually covered the distances that he had dreamed of moving? Had he walked in his sleep? But he never wore pajamas, and—he looked down quickly, confirming that he was wearing pants——

Tight-fitting pants, of a deep blue, with tiny bows at the knee. And low-cut shoes, with thin soles and silver buckles.

He gulped, staring at himself. Excitement started up, like distant drums. There was something strange here, something more than a backfired experiment with self-hypnosis.

Artesia was no dream; the clothes he had gotten there were real. And if the clothes were real—he tugged at the cloth, felt its reassuring toughness—then perhaps all of it . . . .?'

But the whole thing was too idiotic! O'Leary came to his feet, grunted as his wounds throbbed—those were real enough, too—and took a quick turn up and down the cell. You *couldn't* go to bed and dream, and then wake up and find it had all really happened! Maybe he was at home, dreaming that he was in Artesia dreaming that he was in jail?

Hell, if that were so, he was already hopelessly skitzy. He put a hand against the wall; it was rough, cold, solid. If it wasn't real cement, it might as well be.

O'Leary went back to the bunk and sat down. This was all going to be very hard to explain to Mr. Biteworse. When the story got out that he had been arrested in the girl's shower at the Y, wearing funny pants and a shirt with ruffles——

Well, it was goodby job—even if the police released him, which seemed unlikely, in view of the charges being discussed in the outer office. He had to do something—but what? If he were back in Artesia, he could simply conjure up a key to the door, and be on his way. Things weren't quite that simple here in Colby Corners. Solid objects had a way of staying solid. If you wanted a telephone, say, you had to go find one previously installed by the Bell Company. You couldn't just whistle it up . . .

Lafayette sat up, holding a tight rein on a racing imagination. After all, he'd dreamed up all of Artesia; why not just one little old telephone? It could be out in the hall, maybe—mounted on the wall. And if he reached through the bars——

It was worth a try. O'Leary rose, eased over to the barred door and stole a look. The coast was clear. He closed his eyes, pictured a phone bolted to the brick wall, surrounded by scribbled numbers, with a tattered book dangling below . . .

Cautiously, he reached, and found nothing. He drew a deep breath, gathered his resources. *It's there,* he hissed. *Just a little farther to the right . . .*

His groping hand encountered something hard, cool. He grasped it, brought it into view. It was an old-fashioned instrument with a brass mouthpiece. He lifted the dangling ear unit and paused. He hadn't seen a phone in Nicodaeus' lab, but that could be fixed. There had been a lot of locked cabinets with solid wood doors; the phone would be fitted inside one of them—the one just to the left as you entered the lab . . .

"Central," a bright voice said tinnily in his ear. "Number, please."

"Ah, nine five three four . . . nine oh oh . . . two one one," Lafayette said, noticing how the number seemed to spell itself out.

"Thank you. Hold the line, please."

He held the receiver, listening to the hum, punctuated by an occasional crackle, then a loud pop. There was a harsh buzz. Pause. Buzz. Pause. What if Nicodaeus wasn't home? The cops would notice him any minute now, and——

There was a clunk! and the sound of heavy breathing.

"Hello?" a deep voice said cautiously.

"Nicodaeus!" Lafayette gripped the earpiece.

"Lafayette! Is it you my boy? I thought—I feared——"

"Yeah, let's skip that for now. I seem to have made a couple of small errors, and now——"

"Lafayette! Where did you get my number? I didn't think—that is, it's unlisted. And——"

"I have my methods—but I'll go into all that later. I need help! What I want to know is, ah, where—I mean, how—oh, dammit, I don't know what I need! But——"

"Dear me, this is all very confusing, Lafayette. Where did you say you are now?"

"I'd tell you, but I'm afraid you wouldn't understand! You see, you don't actually exist—that is, I just thought of you—but then, when Goruble slapped me in the cell, I decided to wake up—and here I was!"

"Lafayette—you've hurt your head, poor lad. Now, about my telephone number——"

"To heck with your telephone number! Get me out of here! I've got half a dozen stupid cops debating which of six assorted felonies I'm to be held without bail for——"

"Dumb cops, huh?" an ominous voice growled. The phone was yanked from Lafayette's hand and he stared into the bovine countenance of a thick-lipped redhead with old boxing scars on his cheekbones.

"You don't talk to no mouthpiece without the chief says okay, see?" The cop put the phone out of sight. "An' that'll be a dime for the call."

"Put it on my bill," Lafayette said bitterly. The cop snorted and turned away.

With a groan, Lafayette stretched out on the hard bunk and closed his eyes. Maybe it was nutty, but his only chance seemed to be to try to get out of this idiotic situation the same way he'd gotten into it. All he had to do was slide back into some other dream; a nice, restful place this time, he decided; to hell with romantic old streets and cozy taverns and beautiful princesses . . . But Adoranne *had* been gorgeous—and that flimsy nightgown . . .Damn shame he had to go off like that, leaving her thinking he was a liar and a cheat.

The man—the one who had come for him—had there been something familiar about the fellow? Who had sent him—and why? Alain, maybe? No, the count was a stuffed shirt, but not really the devious type; he'd simply have run him through. Nicodaeus? But what motive would he have?

O'Leary's ruminations were cut short by a sudden sensation of sliding, as though the cell had silently skidded a foot in some undefined direction. He sat up, staring across at the window. There were red-checked curtains beside it and a potted geranium on the sill——

Curtains? Geranium? O'Leary jumped to his feet and stared around the room. It was low-ceilinged, crooked-floored, spotlessly clean, with a feather bed in a polished wooden frame, a three-legged stool and a door made of wooden planks. Gone were the iron-grilled door, the concrete walls, the barred window, the cops. He went to the window, looked out at a steep street filled with the ring of a blacksmith's hammer, the shouts of stall-keepers hawking their wares. Half-timbered fronts loomed up across the way, and behind and beyond he saw the pennant turrets of a castle. He was back in Artesia!

O'Leary felt himself smiling foolishly. In spite of himself, he was glad to be here. And now that he was, he might as well take the time to clear up his misunderstanding with Adoranne.

O'Leary washed up quickly at the basin on a stand in the corner, tucked in his shirt tail, smoothed back his hair, dropped on the bed one of the small gold pieces he had found in his pocket and went down to the street. The hammering, he saw, was emanating from a shop with a sign announcing Flats Fixed While U Wait. A wooden steam cart was jacked up with two wheels on the sidewalk while the smith pounded out a new steel-strap tire for a massive oak wheel.

O'Leary turned down the first side street leading toward the palace, threading his way through a bustling throng of plump Artesian housewives doing their morning shopping at the food stalls. He sniffed and caught the aroma of fresh-baked bread. He hadn't realized how hungry he was. But then he hadn't eaten since—when?

The bake shop was just ahead—into a cozy room crowded by two tiny tables. He ordered pastries and a cup of coffee from a red-cheeked girl in starched white. He reached for his money, hesitated. The city guard just might be looking for him. It wouldn't do to leave a trail of gold pieces all over town, but if there were some smaller coins in among the sovereigns . . .

He concentrated, picturing silver pieces, then checked the contents of his pocket. Success! He selected a quarter, handed it to the girl, started for the door——

"Beg pardon, sir," the girl called after him.

"Ye've give me furrin money—by mistake, I don't doubt . . ."

Sure enough, a U.S. two-bit piece. "Sorry," he muttered; he took out a gold piece and handed it over. "Keep the change." He flashed her a quick smile, started out——

"But sir! A whole sovereign! Wait here half a sec and I'll pop across to Master Samuel's stall and——"

"Never mind; I'm . . . ah . . . in a hurry." Lafayette went up the steps, the girl behind him. "Ye must be daft, sir!" she called indignantly. "A sovereign fer tuppence 'orth o' cakes?"

People were staring. A lantern-jawed woman with a basket on her arm jerked as though someone had pulled a wire attached to her neck. She pointed.

"It's him!" she squawked. "Last night, at the grand ball. I seen the rascal, plain as I'm seeing him now, when I come in to trim the wicks!"

Lafayette plunged past her, rounded a corner at a full run. Behind him a shout was rising; feet pounded in pursuit. He glanced back, saw a big-chested man in an open vest round the corner, hair flying, legs pumping.

O'Leary sprinted, bowled over a cart loaded with gimcracks and miniature pink-and-white Artesian flags, skidded into a narrow alley, pounded up a cobbled way toward the looming wall of a church. Someone shot from a side alley ahead, whirled, arms spread; Lafayette straight-armed him, jumped the sprawling body, emerged into an open court. There was an eight-foot wall rimming the yard. He ran for it, leaped, caught the top, pulled himself up and over. He dropped into a tiny back yard where an old man trimming roses with a pair of heavy shears opened a toothless mouth as Lafayette bounded past him through a door, along a short dark hall redolent of wood smoke and burst out onto a quiet side street. He paused a moment, took a deep breath, looked left and right.

The hunt, rounding the corner half a block above, gave a shout as they saw him. He whirled, dashed off down the slope. If he could make the turn ahead in time to duck out of sight before they caught up . . .

The street curved, widened into a plaza with a fountain surrounded by flower stalls and a dense throng of shoppers, vivid in the shafts of morning light pouring down past the cathedral towers. An inviting street turned off to the left just ahead. He ducked into a crouch as he pushed in among the crowd; maybe they wouldn't pick him out in the press if he didn't stick up so high. People gave way before him as he worked his way through, back curved, neck bent. A motherly woman handed him a copper. A legless man seated under the lamp post on the corner with a hat in his lap gave him a resentful look.

"Hey, buddy, you joined the union?"

O'Leary dodged past him, straightened, went up the street at a lope. The geography of the town, it occurred to him, was similar to that of Colby Corners. The main difference was that back home they'd leveled the ground; here the streets wound up and down over the little hills and valleys that in a less romantic clime had been hammered into drab horizontality.

The street he was now in was analogous to the

alley running behind Pott's Drug Store and Hambanger's Hardware. That being the case, if he took a right just ahead, and another right, he'd hit the park—and maybe, among the trees and underbrush, he could lose his pursuers. He could hear them behind him, closing in again. He caught a glimpse as he rounded the corner. A big man with a pitchfork was in the lead now, running hard. Lafayette ran for the next turn, skidded into it, pelted uphill, saw the gap ahead where the buildings ended and the open green began. He leaped for the grass, threw himself flat behind a hedge, twisted to see the pursuit streaming past. Nobody, as far as he could tell, had noticed his dash for the park. Maybe he was safe here for a while.

He cautiously worked his way behind the shelter of the hedge to a clump of arbor vitae. He rested for a moment, then crawled inside the concealment of the ring of trees. It was quiet here, in a green gloom of leaf-filtered sunlight. He settled himself on a carpet of piney mold and prepared to wait until dark. Apparently the story of his having invaded the princess's bedroom was all over town. Until he cleared up that little misunderstanding, there'd be no peace and quiet for him here.

A large, peach-colored crescent moon had risen behind the church towers before O'Leary emerged from his sanctuary. The streets, inadequately illuminated by the yellow gaslights at the corners, were deserted. A few small windows gleamed warm yellow and orange against the dark façades, shedding patches of light on the cobbles below. O'Leary moved along quickly across the park and found the high wall that surrounded the palace grounds. The palace itself, of course, was located in the same relative position as the YMCA back in Plainview. The gate was half a block ahead; he could see the sentry in his bearskin shako standing stiffly at parade rest before the narrow sentry box. No use trying to get through there; he'd be recognized in an instant.

O'Leary turned in a direction opposite to that of the gate. Ten minutes later, in the deep shadow of a clump of tall elms growing just inside the wall, he looked carefully in both directions, then found fingerholds, scrambled up the wall and peered over the top. No guards were in sight. Cautiously, he pulled himself higher, threw a leg over and crouched astride the wall. The tree that provided the shadow was too high, he saw, craning his neck, to be of any help.

Below there was a sudden thump of feet, the unmistakable rasp of a blade sliding from a sheath.

"Hold, varlet!" a hostile voice barked. Lafayette, startled by the sudden interruption, grabbed to retain his balance, missed, went over sideways with a choked yell. He saw the flash of light along a bared blade, had just an instant to picture himself impaled on it as he twisted aside and landed full on the man with an impact that knocked the breath from him. He rolled free and saw the watchman stretched on his back, out cold. Someone shouted—from the left, O'Leary thought. He came to his feet, struggling to breathe, and staggered off in the direction of the deepest shadow. Running feet approached. O'Leary leaned against the three-foot trunk of the largest elm, drawing painful breaths.

"It's Morton," a squeaky voice piped. "Somebody clobbered him!"

"He couldn'a of went far," a deep voice boomed. "You check over that way, Hymie; I'll scout along here."

O'Leary tried to quiet his wheezing; he heard hoarse breathing, the whack of a sword blade beating the bushes against the wall. He eased around the trunk as the searcher passed six feet away. O'Leary then tiptoed toward some shrubbery across the path twenty feet distant.

"Grab him, Hymie!" the deep voice yelled from the other direction. Lafayette sprang into action, dived for cover, hit the dirt, wriggled through, rose to a crouch on the far side, scuttled for the shelter of an ornamental hedge.

Another man, looming tall in a floppy hat and boots, sprang from nowhere into his path, brandished a sword aloft and charged with a yell. O'Leary ducked aside and dashed for the hedge, rounded right end, leaped a marble bench, veered barely in time to miss the lily pool. There was a yell and splash behind him; the pursuer had misjudged the water hazard.

In the clear for the moment, O'Leary sprinted for the tall shadow of the palace, angling to the right to miss a pavilion glowing with strung lanterns. Judging from the yells, he had a dozen men on his trail now, mostly behind him, but some ahead, off to the right. If he could reach the shelter of the wall before they spotted him . . .

Two men dashed into view ahead and skidded to a halt.

"They went that way!" O'Leary shouted. The two newcomers whirled and dashed back out of sight. O'Leary veered sharply, reached a line of trees leading generally palaceward and pounded ahead. A wing of the massive building stretched out toward the trees. O'Leary cleared the end of the row, raced for the refuge of the deep shadows ahead and saw a man back into view fifty yards distant, his attention on the bushes from which he had emerged. Lafayette put on a spurt, dived for the tangle of ivy against the palace wall just as the fellow turned.

"Hey! Here he is, boys!" the man yelled. O'Leary muttered curses and worked his way behind the trailing curtain of vines, forcing his way along against the rough-hewn stone blocks. Feet pelted past and he froze; voices called near at hand. There was the clang of a blade thrust through the vines.

"We got him pinned down, men!" someone exulted. "Spread out and work that ivy!" More clashing of metal against stone, coming closer. O'Leary moved cautiously, gained another foot. Tricky work, trying not to shake the vines. But if he could just get past the corner.

A projecting buttress blocked his way. He felt along its edge; the vine cover ended two feet along it. He was trapped—cornered. Unless . . .

O'Leary closed his eyes, remembering the palace layout. This was the southwest face of the building. He'd never been on this side of the palace, so it ought to be safe.

He pictured a door, just a small one, set a foot or two above ground level. It was made of stout oak planks, weathered but sound, and it was secured by a hasp—a rusty one. Very rusty. It was concealed by the vines, of course, and opened into a forgotten passage which led—somewhere.

At the comforting jolt in the smooth flow of the universe, O'Leary opened his eyes, started feeling over the wall, as steel clashed less than ten feet away. His hands encountered wood, a rough frame, then the door, a squat entry four feet by five, with rust-scaled hinges and a massive padlock dangling from a corroded hasp. O'Leary let out his breath in a preliminary sigh of relief, pushed against the panel. It stirred, came up against the restraint of the hasp. He pushed harder; rusted screws tore out of the wood with a crunching sound.

"Hark, men! What's that?" Hands were tearing at the vines. O'Leary pushed at the resisting door, got it open a foot, slipped inside, forced it shut behind him. A moldering beam lay on the floor; brackets to fit it were mounted on either side of the doorway. He lifted the timber, grunting, settled it into place as a hand slammed the oak from the outside.

"Hey, Sarge! A door! Look!" a muffled voice came through the barrier. More talk, thumps, then a heavy blow.

"He couldn'a got through there, ya dummy, it's locked."

"Hey—if this guy's a like sorcerer . . ."

"Yeah, what's a locked door to a guy like that?"

O'Leary looked both ways along a narrow, low-ceilinged passage, closely resembling the one through which he had been led to Adoranne's room—less than twenty-four hours before, he realized with wonderment; it seemed like days.

As for the passage, it was probably part of a system running all through the building. With a little luck, he'd be able to find his way back to the princess' apartment and explain what had happened without having to venture out into the open.

He moved off, barely able to see by random glints of dim light filtering through chinks in the crudely mortared walls. The passage ran straight for twenty feet, then right-angled. There was a door a few feet beyond the turn. O'Leary tried the latch; it opened, revealing a wide, clean room, smoothly floored, crowded with bulky dark shapes the size of upright pianos. Along the left wall there was a complex pattern of highlights from massed dial faces and polished metal fittings. To the right, more panels, like computer programmer's consoles, were set under wide TV-type screens.

The whole thing, O'Leary thought, looked like a blockhouse where a space shot was being readied. How did all this fit into the simple Artesian scene? True, there were a few electric lights in the palace, and he had seen a number of clumsy mechanical devices in use—but nothing approaching the technology implied here. It didn't make sense—unless Nicodaeus knew something about it. That had to be it. There was definitely something fishy about the court magician. That candid camera he'd used, disguised as a lighter, for example . . .

But that wasn't finding Adoranne. He closed the door, noting the thick metal plate bolted to it. It would take some doing to force your way past that. He went on along the passage, passed a heavy metal-clad door like a butcher's walk-in refrigerator. More modern devices; maybe Nicodaeus had set it up and stocked it with foods in season, which he later miraculously produced. There was nothing like fresh frozen strawberries in the dead of winter to endear a sorcerer to a gourmet king.

Thirty feet past the refrigerator, the passage dead-ended. O'Leary thumped the walls, looking for concealed doors, then started back the way he had come—and stopped dead at a sound from the darkness ahead.

He stood, head cocked, listening, aware of the musty odor of the dead air, the rasp of his own breathing. The sound came again—a soft scraping. He flattened himself against the wall. There was a movement—a stirring of shadows against the darkness. Something was coming toward him—something bulky, crouched, no more than waist-high. O'Leary tried twice, managed to swallow. No wonder the secret passages were deserted; ordinarily, he didn't believe in spectral orges, but——

It was closer now, no more than two yards away, waiting there in the darkness. O'Leary pictured diabolical eyes studying him, goblin fangs gaping . . .

He fumbled in his pockets; he had no weapon—damned careless of him. But he couldn't just stand here and wait to be savaged; he'd rather attack in the blind, come to grips with whatever it was. He took a deep breath, set himself——

"Hiya, Sir Lafayette," a bass voice rumbled. "What you doing down here?"

O'Leary jumped violently, cracking his head, and slumped back against the wall, weak with relief.

"Yokabump," he managed. "Fancy meeting you here."

CHAPTER VII

"You're lucky I run into you," Yokabump was saying. "Duck your head now; low bridge."

Behind him, Lafayette maneuvered around a massive timber that half blocked the cramped way. "You're so right," he agreed. "I never would have found that stairway. I wonder how many people know about all these hidden entrances into their rooms?"

"Not many."

"Well, next time I'm chased at least I'll have somewhere to hide."

"There's some folks around here might say I shouldn't be helping you out," the dwarf said.

"I can explain all that nonsense about me being in her Highness' room," O'Leary began.

"Never mind, Sir Lafayette. I'm just the court jester; I supply the boffs and let the gentry work out their own problems. But I got confidence in you."

"I suppose you mean because of my ring—the ax and dragon."

"Nay, I don't go for that legend jazz. Anyway, that's just a story old Gory cooked up himself, back when he was new on the job. Propaganda, you know; people was restless. They kind of liked the old king, and who ever heard of this Cousin Goruble? There's still lots of folk think her Highness ought to be setting on the throne right now."

"I take it King Goruble isn't too popular?"

"Ah, he's OK—kind of strict, I guess—but you can't blame him, since this bird Lod made the scene. Him and his pet dragon——"

"More folklore, I take it?"

"Well, I never actually *seen* this dragon."

"Hmmm. Funny how nobody I've met has seen it, but they all believe in it."

"Yeah—well, here we are." Yokabump had halted at a blank wall. "This here is the panel that opens into her Highness' bedroom. I guess you know what you're doing—and I ain't going to ask you why you're going in there. When I trust a guy, I trust him all the way."

"Well, that's very decent of you, Yokabump. I have her Highness' best interests at heart."

"Sure. But look, Sir Lafayette, give me about five minutes to do a fade, OK? I don't want to be nowhere around in case anything goes wrong."

"If I'm captured, I won't implicate you, if that's what you mean."

"Good luck, Sir Lafayette," the rumbling voice breathed. There was a soft rustle, and O'Leary was alone. He waited, counting slowly to three hundred, then felt over the panel, found an inconspicuous latch at one side; it clicked as he flipped it up. The panel moved smoothly aside. He peered out into the dark room. Only a few hours ago, a hand had propelled him violently through the same opening; now he was back, voluntarily.

He stepped through onto the deep pile rug. He could see the shape of the big canopied bed.

"Adoranne!" he whispered, moving forward softly. "Don't yell. It's me, Lafayette! I want to explain . . ." his voice trailed off. Even in the dim moonlight filtering through the gauzy curtains at the high windows, he could see that the bed was empty.

A five-minute search confirmed no one was in the apartment. O'Leary stood by the ornately carved gold and white dressing table, feeling unaccountably let down. But after all, why should he have blandly assumed she'd be here? Probably there was a big party going on, and she was there, dancing with Count Alain.

But never mind that train of thought. It was time to go—before the fat lady-in-waiting came in and set up a howl. He went back to the inner doorway leading to the bedroom—and stopped short at the sound of voices. The door on the far side of the bedroom opened, and O'Leary ducked back as the maid came in, accompanied by an old man with a mop. The girl sniffled.

"It . . . it ain't . . . the same . . ."

"Never mind that; tears won't help nothing . . ."

O'Leary ducked across the room and tried the hall door. It opened. He peeked cautiously out; the corridor was dim-lit, deserted. Strange. Usually, ceremonial—or perhaps not ceremonial—

guards were posted every fifty feet along the hall. And it was a little early for Nicodaeus' fifty-volt lighting system to be turned down so far.

He went along the carpeted corridor to the wide, ornate door, white with gold carving, that separated Adoranne's private quarters from the public area. He tried the gleaming golden handle. It opened. He went through and started off toward the next room from which he could re-enter the secret passage system.

Someone was coming; low voices muttered. O'Leary ran for it, ducked down a side hallway, slid to a halt as he saw a guard posted at the next intersection. The man was yawning; he hadn't seen O'Leary.

Just ahead was a narrow door. O'Leary stepped quickly to it, opened it, ducked through. Steps led upward. He could go up or back out into the hall. He paused with a hand on the door, hearing soft footfalls just outside. That narrowed the choice down; he turned and started up the winding stairs.

Five minutes later, winded by the climb, O'Leary reached a heavy door opening from a tiny landing at the top of the stairs. He listened, then tried the latch. The door opened noiselessly. He poked his head in, wrinkling his nose at a heavy stench resembling burnt pork that accompanied a dense cloud of greenish fumes boiling from an open pan placed over a tripod. Through the smoke he saw the tall figure of Nicodaeus, bent over a workbench, absorbed, his back to the door.

O'Leary studied the narrow, granite-walled

chamber, floored with vast stone slabs, lit by giant candles guttering on stands, its ceiling lost in shadows and cobwebs. There were cabinets, shelves, chests, all piled with stuffed owls, alarm clocks, old boots, bottles and jars and cans both full and empty; against the walls wooden crates were stacked, cryptic symbols stenciled on their sides in red and yellow and black. Along one side of the room ran a workbench, littered with tools, bits of wire, odd-shaped bits of metal and glass and plastic. Above it was a black crackle-finish panel, set with dozens of round glass dials against which needles trembled. Double doors at the far end of the room were half-concealed by a heavy hanging. From the ceiling, a gilded human skeleton dangled from a wire.

O'Leary slipped inside, closed the door behind him, silently shot the bolt. The stench was really terrible. Lafayette concentrated, remembering his success with the goaty girl at the tavern. Roasted coffee, say; that would be a marked improvement . . .

He felt the subtle jar that indicated success. The color of the smoke changed to a reddish brown; the greasy smell faded, to be replaced by the savory aroma of fresh-ground coffee beans.

Nicodaeus straightened, went across to the instrument display panel, jabbed at buttons. A small screen glowed pale green. The magician muttered, jotting notes—then paused, ballpoint posed. He sniffed, whirled suddenly——

"Lafayette! Where did—how—what?"

"One question at a time, Nicodaeus! I had a hell of a time getting to you; the whole town's gone crazy. You don't have anything to eat handy, do you? I've been lying under a bush in the park all day."

"Lafayette! My boy, you've repented! You've come to me to make a clean breast of it, to tell me where you've hidden her! I'll go to his Majesty——"

"Hold it!" O'Leary sank down on a wobbly stool. "I haven't repented of anything, Nicodaeus! I told you somebody came to my room, told me Adoranne was in trouble and led me into a secret passage. Then the double-crosser gave me a push and shoved some junk into my hand, and the lights went on."

"Certainly, lad, and now you've decided to throw yourself on his Majesty's mercy."

"You mean apologize for not letting him cut me into slices for something I didn't do? Ha! Look here, Nicodaeus, there's something funny going on around here. I want to see Adoranne and explain what happened. She thinks I stole her crown jewels or . . ." He broke off, seeing the expression on the other's face. "What's the matter?" He came to his feet in sudden alarm. "She hasn't been hurt?"

"You mean—you really don't know?" Nicodaeus blinked through his rimless glasses.

"Don't know what?" O'Leary yelled. "Where's Adoranne?"

Nicodaeus' shoulders slumped. "I had hoped you could tell *me* that, Lafayette. She's been missing since some time before dawn. And everyone thinks you, my boy, are the one who stole her."

"You're all out of your minds," O'Leary said,

finishing off a cracker with sardines—the only rations, it appeared, that Nicodaeus kept handy. "I was locked in a cell. How could I have kidnaped her? And why?"

"But you escaped from the cell. And as to why . . ." Nicodaeus looked wise. "Need one ask?"

"Yes, one need ask! I'm not likely to drag a girl away in the middle of the night just to . . . just to . . . do whatever people do with girls they drag away in the middle of the night."

"But, Lafayette!" Nicodaeus twisted his hands together. "Everyone's assumed you were the kidnaped her? And why?"

"I don't know who! You're supposed to be some kind of a magician; can't you find out things?"

"*Now* who believes in magic?" Nicodaeus inquired sardonically. He shot Lafayette a keen look. "By the way, I noted a severe energy drain recorded in the beta scale at 6:15 this morning. Then about ten minutes later—that would be at 6:25—there was the first of a series of lesser disturbances, that have continued at intervals all day."

"What are you measuring? Is this some sort of seismograph?"

Nicodaeus studied O'Leary's face. "See here, Lafayette, isn't it time you spoke frankly to me? I confess I don't know just what the connection might be between you and the data I've been collecting ever since your arrival—but it's more than coincidence."

"That giant!" O'Leary interrupted suddenly. "Cludd, or whatever his name was! Is there really any such ogre, or is he somebody's pet superstition, like the Phantom Highwayman and Goruble's dragon?"

"Oh, Lod exists. I can vouch for that, my boy. He visited the city, not a month ago. Thousands of people saw him; three meters tall, as broad as I can reach with both arms wide, and ugly as a wart hog!"

"Then he must be the one! Didn't they say he came here courting Adoranne? Then, when he was turned down, he planned this kidnapping——"

"And how, dear lad, would Lod—enormous, ungainly, with a price on his head and known to every subject in the country—slip into town, remove the princess from the midst of her guards and get away clean?"

"Somebody did, and it wasn't me! There are secret passages in the palace—I wouldn't be surprised if one of them led to a tunnel that would take you right outside the city walls. I want a good horse——"

"But Lafayette, where would I get a horse?"

"You've got one waiting at the postern gate, remember? Don't stall, Nicodaeus! This is serious!"

"Oh, *that* horse . . . Mmmmm. Yes, perhaps. But——"

"Stop saying 'but'! Get me the horse and stock the saddlebags with food and a change of socks and . . . and whatever I might need. And don't forget a road map."

"Umm. Yes. Look here, Lafayette, you may be right. Lod *could* be the kidnapper. A difficult trip, though. Do you really intend to try, single-handed?"

"Yes, and I need help! You've double-crossed me a few times, but maybe that was just misguided loyalty. You *are* fond of Adoranne, aren't you?"

"Double-crossed? Why, Lafayette——"

There was a thunderous hammering at the door. Lafayette jumped. Nicodaeus whirled to him, pointing to the heavy hangings at the narrow end of the room.

"Quickly!" he whispered. "Behind the drapes!"

Lafayette sprang to the hiding place Nicodaeus had indicated and slipped behind the heavy hangings. There was a cold draft on his back. He turned, saw double glass doors standing ajar. A tiny balcony was dimly visible in the darkness beyond them. He stepped out into cold night air and a light drizzle of icy rain.

"Swell," he muttered, huddling against the ivy-covered wall beside the door. Through a narrow gap in the draperies he could see the magician hurrying across the room, drawing the bolt. The door burst open and armed men pushed through—two, three, more. Word must have spread that he had gotten into the palace. Probably they were searching every room.

Two men were coming across toward the hangings behind which O'Leary had been hidden a minute before. He threw a leg over the iron railing, slid down, found a toehold in the tangled vines beneath the balcony, his eyes at floor level. Through the glass door, he saw a sword blade stabbing through the drapes. The point struck the door and glass broke with a light tinkle. O'Leary ducked down and clambered in close under the shelter of the overhang of the balcony, gripping the wet vines. Above, the doors crashed wide open. Boots crunched glass above his head.

"Not out here," a gruff voice said.

"I told you——" the rest of Nicodaeus' speech was cut off by the clump of boots, the slamming of doors. Lafayette held on, shivering in the cold wind; water dripped from the end of his nose. He looked down. Below, there was nothing but darkness and the drumming of rain, heavier now. Not a very enticing climb, but he couldn't stay here.

He started down, groping for footholds on the wet stone, clinging to the stiff vines with hands that were rapidly growing numb. Wet leaves jabbed at his face, dribbling water down inside his sodden jacket.

Twenty feet below the level of the balcony, he found a horizontal stone coping and followed it along to the corner. The wind was stronger here, buffeting him, driving stinging rain into his eyes. He retreated to the opposite side of the tower. He was about fifteen feet above the slanting, copper-green plates of the roof over the main residential wing now. He'd have to descend, get past the eaves and then make it to the ground without being seen. Far below, torches moved about the gardens; faint shouts rang out. The palace guard was out in force tonight.

It was a tricky climb down from the ledge to the roof below; only the thick-growing vines made it possible. O'Leary reached the roof, braced himself with one foot in the heavy copper gutter, now gurgling with runoff from the gable above, and rested five minutes. Then he gripped the vines firmly and lowered himself out and over the wide overhang of the roof. He swung his legs, groping for support, but found nothing. The vines here were sparser than above; probably they had been thinned to clear the downspout.

He let himself down another foot; the edge of the roof was at chin level now. He tried again and again failed to find a foothold. The strain on his icy hands was getting a bit tiresome. He slipped farther down, hanging at arm's length now, and ducked his head under the overhang. The face of the building was a good three feet distant—and as bare of ivy as a billboard. There was a window there, six feet to the left—but it was dark, shuttered and out of reach even if it had been wide open.

O'Leary grunted, hitching himself along to the left. Quite suddenly, he was aware of the hundred feet of empty night air yawning below him. Was that where he was going to end, after all? His hands were stiffening; he couldn't tell if he was gripping the vines hard, or if his hold was weakening, slipping . . .

With a desperate surge, O'Leary swung his legs and managed to slam one toe against the boarded window. Out of reach; he couldn't make it. Could he go back? He struggled to pull himself up, felt the edge of the roof cutting into his wrists; he kicked his legs vainly, then hung slackly. *Maybe five minutes,* he thought. *Then my grip will loosen and down I'll go . . .*

Abruptly, the shutters on the window clanked open. A pale, frightened face looked out, framed by dark hair.

"Daphne!" O'Leary croaked. "Help!"

"Sir Lafayette!" Her voice was a gasp. She thrust the shutter back and the wind caught it, thumping it against the stone. Daphne stretched out her arms. "Can you—can you reach me?"

O'Leary summoned his strength, swung his foot; Daphne grabbed and the buckled shoe came off in her hand. She tossed it behind her, brushed back a strand of hair with the back of her hand and leaned farther out.

"Again!" she said. O'Leary sucked in air, swung himself back, kicked out; the chambermaid's strong fingers gripped his ankle. She leaned back, pulled his lower leg across the sill, then grabbed the other foot as it swung forward. O'Leary felt his grip going as the girl tugged. He gave himself a last thrust; his hands came free, and he was swinging down.

His back slammed the wall with a thud that knocked the wind from his lungs. Dizzily, he groped upward, caught the sill with one hand. Daphne seized his arm and tumbled him inside.

"You're . . . strong for a . . . girl . . ." O'Leary managed. "Thanks."

"Comes of swinging a broom all day, sir," she said breathlessly. "Are you all right?"

"Fine. How'd you happen to be there at just the right moment?"

"I heard the outcry above; I ran up to Nicodaeus' tower to see what was afoot. The guardsmen were in a pet, dashing about and cursing. Nicodaeus whispered to me it was you—that you'd gone over the balcony rail. I thought maybe I could catch a glimpse of you from the window—if you hadn't fallen, that is . . . and——"

"Look, Daphne, you saved my life. But——" he frowned, remembering his last conversation with the girl. "Why aren't you in jail?"

"King Goruble pardoned me. He was quite sweet about it; said a child like me couldn't be guilty. He wouldn't even let them hold a hearing."

"Well, the old grouch has a few redeeming traits, after all." O'Leary got to his feet, rubbing his lacerated wrists. "Listen, I have to get out of here. It's a bit too hot for me right now. I've just heard about Adoranne's kidnapping, and I——" he broke off. "*You* didn't think I was mixed up in that, did you?"

"I . . . I didn't know sir. I'm glad if you're not. Her Highness is so lovely, though, and a gentleman like you . . . ." She looked at her feet.

"A gentleman like me doesn't resort to kidnapping to get a girl. But I think I may have a lead. If you'll get me to one of the entries to the hidden passage system, I'll try to follow it up."

"Hidden passages, sir?"

"Sure, they run all through the palace. There are entries from just about every room in the building. Where are we now?"

"This is an unused storeroom, just down the hall from the suite of the Earl of Nussex."

"Is he in?"

"No, sir; he's off with one of the troops searching for her Highness."

"That'll do, then."

He found his shoe, put it on and followed as Daphne checked the corridor. She led him along to a locked door which she opened with one of the keys on the ring at her waist. He took her hand.

"By the way, you don't happen to know where Lod's headquarters is, do you?"

"In the desert to the west."

"Um. That's all anyone seems to know. Thanks for everything, Daphne." He leaned and kissed her smooth cheek.

"Where will you go?" she asked, wide-eyed.

"To find Lod."

"Sir—will you be safe?"

"Sure. Wish me luck."

"G-good luck, sir."

He slid inside the room, crossed to the panel. Yokabump had pointed out to him earlier and stepped through into close, musty darkness.

Two hours later, O'Leary was in a twisting alleyway under the shadow of the city wall three-quarters of a mile from the palace grounds. Sheltered in the lee of a tumble-down shack, he breathed hard from the climb, the dash from one covering shrub to another across the wide palace lawns, the sprint through the gate while the sentry investigated a sound made by a thrown pine cone, the rapid walk through the streets to this noisome corner of the city slum. He was soaked to the skin, shivering. His hands were cut and scratched, yesterday's bruises still ached. The scant meal Nicodaeus had given him hardly assuaged the pangs of a day's fast.

It was raining harder now. O'Leary felt his teeth clatter; his bones felt like something rudely chipped from ice. At this rate he'd have pneumonia before morning—particularly if he spent the night standing out in the chill, raw wind.

He couldn't knock at a door and ask for shelter; every citizen in town seemed to know him. The clever thing to do would be to abandon this foolishness, shift back to Colby Corners and his room, and get what sleep he could. Tomorrow he could call Mr. Biteworse and explain his absence as being due to a sudden attack of flu . . .

But what about Adoranne? He pictured her waking up to find someone's hand over her mouth. The villain must have gotten in via the secret passage, of course. He probably gagged her, bound her hand and foot, slung her over a hard shoulder and carted her off to some robber hideout.

O'Leary couldn't abandon her. He might fail, but he couldn't leave without trying. But what could he do? At the moment he was a hunted fugitive with no one to turn to. His only friend, Nicodaeus, had been suspiciously quick about letting the soldiers in—and they'd rushed directly to his hiding place. If he hadn't climbed outside, prompted by some obscure instinct, he'd have been run through. Had the magician deliberately betrayed him? What reason would he have? True, he'd been eager to see the last of O'Leary; all that talk about fast horses at the postern gate—but then Nicodaeus *had* helped him at the trial . . .

He'd been lucky to get clear of the palace. The outcry inside had drawn off most of the guard force, fortunately, so he hadn't had to lie low in the mud more than half a dozen times before reaching the gate. He wiped his muddy palms on sodden trousers and shivered again. Briefly, he thought of conjuring up the image of the princess locked in the nearest hut, say. He could break in the door, and there she'd be . . .

It was no use. He didn't believe it. He was too tired to conjure up the impossible. She was miles from here, and he knew it. He needed food, warmth, sleep; then perhaps he could make his mind work again. He looked at the sagging structure against which he huddled. It was a shed no more than six feet by eight, with a roof of sodden thatch. The door was a battered agglomeration of mismatched boards, held together by a pair of rusting iron straps and hanging crookedly from one rotten leather hinge. He prodded it and it slumped even farther; O'Leary caught a glimpse of a dark interior.

He looked away quickly; no point in making *that* mistake again. There was no telling what that rude exterior might house—or be made to house. Perhaps it was a secret hideaway, fitted out by some adventurer with a need for private quarters away from the hubbub of busy streets—well camouflaged, of course . . .

No use carrying the rationalization too far, O'Leary reminded himself. Firmly, he pictured sound walls under the moldering slabs, a snug, waterproof roof concealed by the defunct thatch, a weatherproof door, an adequate heating system—a gas fire with artificial logs, perhaps, fed by bottled propane. Add a rug—cold floors were rough on bare feet, a shower stall with plenty of hot water—there'd been a shortage of that, even in the palace, a tiny refrigerator, well-stocked, a bunk—a wide one, with a good quality mattress . . .

O'Leary completed his mental picture, filling in the details with loving attention. Of course, it was there, he told himself; he needed a hideout.

Time seemed to hesitate for an instant; then O'Leary smiled grimly and reached for the door . . .

Half an hour later, with the door locked firmly against intruders, clean and warm after a hot shower, O'Leary finished off his second Bavarian ham on Swiss rye, quaffed the last of the sixteen-ounce bottle of lager, pulled the feather comforter up snug about his ears and settled down to catch up on some much needed rest.

The alarm clock he had thoughtfully provided woke him with chimes at dawn. He stretched, yawned, blinked at the glass door to the shower stall, the pale green walls, the olive-carpeted floor, the dark green wall-mounted refrigerator, the cherry fire on the hearth. Now, just where was he? There was Mrs. MacGlint's or had that been an evil dream? And his room at the palace, and the bunk in the cell at the police station, and a room with a flowerpot . . . and oh, yes, the converted hut here. Quite cozy. He nodded approvingly. He was always waking up in different places these days, it seemed.

O'Leary threw back the coverlet, checked the refrigerator, nibbled a cold chicken leg, then showered while sorting out kaleidoscopic impressions of the day before. It was getting harder and harder to recall just what had been a dream and what hadn't—or whether there was any distinction. The visit to the palace, now. Had that been real? He looked at his hands. They were badly scraped. Uh-huh, that had been real all right. Nicodaeus had nearly gotten him killed, the skunk—unless it was S.O.P. to run swords through curtains first thing when searching a room.

And Adoranne was gone, kidnapped. That was the important fact. He'd have to do something about that, right away. Funny how different everything seemed in the morning, with a meal and a night's sleep behind him. He wasn't worried. Somehow he'd recover Adoranne, explain the business of the midnight visit and the bag of loot, and then . . . Well, then he could play it by ear. And now to business.

He tried the door to the clothespress, discovered a handsome outfit consisting of modern-style whipcord riding breeches, a heavy gray flannel shirt, cordovan boots, a short lined windbreaker, a pair of pigskin driving gloves, and—incongruously—a rapier in a businesslike sheath attached to a Western-style leather belt. He dressed, quickly fried three eggs and half a dozen strips of bacon and washed up after breakfast.

The rain had stopped when O'Leary closed the door carefully behind him. The shack, he noted with approval, looked as derelict as ever. Now to action. The first step . . .

He paused, standing in the garbage-strewn, dawn-lit alley. What *was* the first step? Where did Lod stay when he wasn't off on a raid? What was it they had said? In the desert to the west? Not much in the way of travel directions. He had to have more information—and he couldn't just collar a passer-by. The first question put to a local citizen would have the pack howling on his heels again before he could say "post-hypnotic suggestion."

Heavy boots clumped along the alley, coming closer. O'Leary made a move to duck into concealment . . .

Too late; a heavily built man in a greasy sheepskin jacket hove into view and halted at sight of him. Under the damp brim of a wide, shapeless hat, a battered face stared truculently. Then it broke into a crafty, gap-toothed smile.

"Duh Phantom Highwayman!" the newcomer squeaked. "Thay, am I glad to thee *you*! I wanted to thay thanks fer handing the copperth a bum thteer the other night. I don't know how youse thwung it, but they didn't theem to know me from Adam'th off okth."

"Oh, it's the Red Bull," O'Leary said cautiously. "Ah, glad to help out. Well, I have to run along now."

"I hear you're duh one dat thnached duh princeth. Ith dat duh thtraight goodth?"

"What, you, too? I had nothing to do with it! I've got an idea this fellow Lod is the guilty party. Maybe you can tell me: exactly where are his headquarters?"

"Youse can level wit' me, bo. I got contacth; we'll work togedduh and thplit duh take."

"Forget it. Now about Lod's hideout——"

"I get it. Youse figger to thell her Highneth to duh Big Boy. What youse figger theyee'll bring?"

"Listen to me you, you numbskull!" O'Leary shook a fist under the flattened nose. "I'm not involved in the kidnapping! I'm not selling her to anybody! And I'm not interested in any shady deals."

The Red Bull's thick finger prodded O'Leary's chest. "Oh, thtingy, huh? Well, lithen to me, bo—what'th duh idea of working my thection of town, anyway? You thtick to yer highwatyh, and leave duh thity to me, thee? And I'm cutting mythelf in on duh thnatch caper, thee? And——"

"There ithn't any thnatch caper—oh, for heaven's sake stop lisping! You've got me doing it!"

"Huh? Look, bo . . ." the Red Bull's voice dropped abruptly to its accustomed bass. "Yuh split wit' me or I cave in yer mush—and den call cooper fer duh reward an' a free pardon."

O'Leary slapped the prodding finger aside. "Tell me where Lod's hideout is, you dimwit, and stop babbling about——"

A large hand gathered in the front of O'Leary's new jacket, lifted him to his toes.

"Who yuh calling a dimwit, bo? I got as good a mind as duh next gazebo."

"I happen to be the next gazebo," O'Leary said in a voice somewhat choked by the pressure at his throat. "And I'm an idiot for standing here chinning with you while there's work to be done." He brought up a hand and chopped down in a side-of-the-palm blow at the base of the Red Bull's thick neck. The grasp on his shirt relaxed as O'Leary delivered a second hearty stroke across the big man's throat that sent him stumbling back. The Red Bull shook his head, roared, started for O'Leary with apelike arms outstretched, and met a kick in the pit of the stomach that doubled him over with a grunt in time to intercept a hard knee coming up to meet his already blunted features. He stumbled aside, one hand on his stomach and the other grasping his bleeding nose.

"Hey, dat's no fair!" he stated. "I never seen duh udder two guys!"

"Sorry. That was in Lesson Three, Unarmed Counterattack. Worked quite well. Now, tell me where I can find Lod. And hurry up—this is important!"

"Lod, huh?" The Red Bull looked disapprovingly at the blood on his hand and moved his head gingerly, testing his neck. "What kind of a split yuh got in mind?"

"No split! I just want to rescue her Highness!"

"How about forty-sixty, and I t'row in a couple o' reliable boys to side yer play wit' Lod?"

"Forget it! I'll ask somebody else." O'Leary straightened his jacket, rubbed the bruised side of his hand, gave the Red Bull a disgusted look and started off up the alley.

"Hey!" The Red Bull trotted to his side. "I got a idea! We split thoidy-seventy; what could be more gennulmanly dan dat?"

"You amaze me; I didn't know you knew that much arithmetic."

"I taken a night course in business math. How about it?"

"No! Get lost! I have things to do! I'm conspicuous enough without Gargantua padding along at my heels!"

"I'll settle for a lousy ten percent, on account of you got such a neat left hand, and duh knee work was nice, too."

"Go away! Depart! Dangle! Be missing! Get

hence! Avaunt thee, varlet! No deal!" A small man probing hopefully in a sodden garbage bin gave O'Leary a look as the two passed.

"You're attracting attention!" O'Leary halted. "Listen, I give in. You're just too smart for me. Now here's the plan: Meet me an hour before moonrise at, uh——"

"How about duh One-Eyed Man on duh West Post Road?"

"Sure—just the place I had in mind. Wear a red carnation and pretend you don't know me until I sneeze nine times and then blow my nose on a purple bandanna. Got it?"

"Dat's duh way to talk, bo! Nuttin' I like better'n a slick plan, all worked out wit' snazzy details an' all. Uh . . . by duh way, where do I get duh carnation, at dis time o' year?"

O'Leary closed his eyes, concentrated briefly. "Just around the next turn," he said. "On top of the first garbage bin on the left."

The Red Bull nodded, eyeing Lafayette a trifle warily.

"Sometimes when youse ain't in such a hurry, pal, I want youse should clue me how yuh work some of dese angles."

"Sure," O'Leary said. "Hurry along now, before someone steals your flower." The Red Bull hustled away along the street; O'Leary turned into a side alley to put distance between himself and his volunteer partner. He'd like to know himself how he worked the angles, he reflected. He was beginning to take all this as seriously as though it were really happening. It was becoming increasingly difficult to remember which was the illusion, Artesia or Colby Corners.

In a small cafe consisting of a faded striped awning over a patch of cracked sidewalk, Lafayette sipped a thick mug of strong coffee. He had to have the location of the rebel HQ—but any question on the subject would immediately point the finger at him. As a matter of fact, the girl behind the charcoal stove where the water boiled was giving him sidelong glances right now. Maybe it was just sex appeal, but he couldn't afford to take the chance. He rose abruptly and moved on. His best bet was to keep moving and hope to overhear something.

It was a long day. O'Leary spent it wandering idly through open-air markets, browsing in tiny crack-in-the-wall bookshops, watching the skillful gnarled hands of silversmiths and goldsmiths and leather and wood workers as they plied their crafts in stalls no bigger than the average hot-dog stand back home in Colby Corners. He ate a modest lunch of salami and ale at an inn where low-sagging foot-square beams black with soot crossed above an uneven packed-earth floor. An hour before sunset he was near the East Gate, pretending to eye the display in a tattoo artist's window, while keeping an eye on a lounging sentry who gave him no more than a casual glance. It would be no trick at all to slip through, if he just knew where to go from there . . .

A large man standing a few yards away was looking at him carefully from the corner of a red-rimmed eye. O'Leary whistled a few bars of *Mairzey Doats* with suddenly dry lips. He eased around the corner into a dark alleylike passage. He stepped along briskly and when he looked back he saw only looming shadows. He went on, following twists and turns. The last of the light was rapidly fading from the sky.

The alley abruptly ended in a garbage-strewn court. He cast about, found another narrow way leading off into blackness, ducked into it and turned to see a dark figure, then another, step into dim view. He whirled silently and started off at a trot. He had gone twenty feet when he tripped over a tub of refuse and sent it clattering. At once, there was a rasp of feet breaking into a run. By instinct, O'Leary ducked, threw himself aside as a dark cloaked figure slammed past, tripped and fell with a clangor of steel and a choked-off curse. Lafayette crouched, squinting into the dark and saw the man rise to hands and knees, groping for a dropped weapon.

It was no time for niceties. He took a quick step and planted a solid kick in the side of the jaw. The man skidded to his face and lay still. O'Leary moved off up the alley, scanning the way for other members of the reception committee. There had been at least two of them—maybe more. This would be an excellent place to get away from—fast. But there was no point in running into the waiting arms of an assassin.

A shadow moved against deeper shadow ahead. One of the party, it seemed, had circled to cut him off. O'Leary stooped, picked up a hand-filling cobblestone and stood flat against the wall. The shadow came closer; he could hear hoarse breathing now. He waited; the man came on, staring into the shadows, not noticing O'Leary.

"Hold it right there," O'Leary hissed. "I've got a musket aimed at your left kidney. Put down your weapon and stand where you are."

The man stood like a wax figure illustrating Guilt Caught in the Act. He stooped slowly, put down something that glittered in the moonlight and took a hesitant step.

"That's close enough," O'Leary breathed. "How many of you are there?"

"Just me and Moe and, and Charlie, and Sam and Porkeye and Clarence——"

"Clarence?"

"Yeah; he's a new boy, just learning the trade."

"Where are they?"

"Spotted around front. Hey, how'd you get past 'em, bud?"

"Easy. I went over them. How did you happen to be staked out here?"

"Well, after all, you had to try one of the gates if you planned to get clear of the city."

"How did you know I was still in the city?"

"Look here, fellow—you expect me to rat on my own chief? I'm not saying any more."

"All right, there's just one more thing I want from you: Where's Lod's headquarters lo cated?"

"Lod? Out west someplace. How do I know?"

"You'd better know, or I'll be annoyed. When I get annoyed, my finger gets twitchy, very twitchy."

"What the heck, everybody knows where Lod hangs out, anyway. I guess if I don't tell you, somebody else will, so what's the percentage in me being a hero, know what I mean?"

"Last chance—the finger is getting nervous."

"Ride west—you'll hit the desert after a half a day's travel. Keep going; there'll be a line of mountains to your left. Follow the foothills till you come to the pass. That's all." O'Leary thought he heard a snicker.

"How far is Lod's stronghold from the pass?"

"Maybe five miles, maybe ten, due west. You can't miss it—if you get that far."

"Why shouldn't I get that far?"

"Let's face it, pal; we got you outnumbered five to one."

O'Leary took a quick step and slammed the five-pound stone in his hand against his informant's skull just above the ear. He folded silently and lay on his face, snoring gently. O'Leary stepped past him, moving off up the alley. He emerged five minutes later half a block from the East Gate. Ready to duck and run if necessary, he strolled past the guard just as the fellow yawned, showing cheap silver filling. Once past him, O'Leary let out a long breath and set out to circle the town. His feet were already getting sore; the new boots had a tendency to pinch. Too bad he hadn't taken the time to steal a horse. He had a long trek ahead; maybe three miles around the town walls, then ten to the desert, then another ten . . .

Well, there was no help for it—and thinking about blisters didn't help. He settled down for the hike ahead, watching the moon rise above the castellated city wall.

There was a light ahead, glowing in the window of one of the buildings huddled against the wall near the West Gate. Lafayette made his way to it, clambered over a heap of rubbish and came around to the front that faced the twenty-foot wide dirt road that led off to the west. He was ready for a good meal and a bottle of stout ale before he tackled the long night's walk ahead. The shack with the light seemed to be an inn; a sign nailed to a post bore a horrendous portrait of a bush-bearded pirate with a patch over one eye. Not a prepossessing establishment, but it would have to do.

Lafayette pushed through the door and found himself in a surprisingly cozy interior. There were tables to the left, a bar straight ahead, a gaming area to the right where half a dozen grizzled gaffers were arguing querulously over a checkerboard. Oil lanterns on the bar lent a warm light to the scene. O'Leary rubbed his chilled hands together and took a seat. A vastly fat woman wobbled from a shadowy corner and plucked a heavy pewter mug down in front of him.

"What'll it be, love?" she demanded cheerfully. O'Leary ordered roast beef and baked potato and then sampled the beer. Not bad at all. He'd stumbled into a pretty fair eating place, it seemed.

"Hey, youse is late, bo," a familiar voice rasped in O'Leary's ear. He jerked around. A red face with flattened features looked at him reproachfully. "I been waiting around dis dump for an hour."

"Listen here, Red Bull," O'Leary said quickly. "I told you not to speak to me until I blew my nose six times and, uh, waved a red handkerchief."

"Naw, youse said you'd sneeze nine times and blow yer schnozz on a poiple hanky. An' look, I got my red carnation; kind uh wilted, but——"

"It's the coolest, Red. I can see our partnership is going to be a fruitful one. Now, I have further instructions for you. Just go along to the palace;

most of the guard force is away, looking for the princess. You can sneak inside without much trouble, and gather in all kinds of loot before they get back."

"But duh city gates is locked."

"Climb over the wall."

"Yeah—dat's a nifty idear—but what about my horse? He ain't so good at climbing."

"Hmmm. Tell you what I'll do, Red. I'll take care of him for you."

"Say, dat's white of yuh, bub. He's hitched out back. Now, where'll we meet?"

"Well, just stick around the palace gardens; there's good cover there. We'll rendezvous under a white oleander at the second dawn."

"Duh scheme sounds slick, chum. By duh way, what'll youse be doing in duh meantime?"

"Ill be scouting some new jobs."

The Red Bull rose, gathered his cloak about his broad frame. "OK, I'll see youse in duh hoosegow." He turned and strode off. The waitress stared after him as she clanked O'Leary's platter down before him.

"Hey, ain't that the well known cutpurse and footpad——"

"Shhh. He's a secret agent of his Majesty," O'Leary confided. The woman looked startled and withdrew. Half an hour later, well fed and with three large beers inside him, O'Leary mounted the Red Bull's horse—a solidly built bay with a new-looking saddle—and, keeping in mind all he'd read about the equestrian art, spurred out of the inn yard and off along the West Post Road.

CHAPTER VIII

By dawn, O'Leary had crossed the fertile miles of plain west of the capital, passing tiny villages and lonely farmhouses sleeping in the night. Far ahead, he could see a smoky-blue line of rocky peaks catching the first light of morning. The verdant green of tilled fields had given way to dry-looking pasture spotted with scrubby trees, under which a few lean cattle stood listlessly. He rode up a final slope, the dust of the road rising like stirred talcum powder now, leaned aside from the taking branches of thorn trees beside the trail, and looked out across an arid expanse of pale terra cotta colored clay. He halted, frowning.

Somehow he had expected to encounter some sort of warning before reaching the desert—a saloon with a sign reading "Last Chance Charlie's," or something of the sort, where he could buy some supplies for the long ride still ahead. Instead, here he was, already worn out from an unaccustomed night in the saddle—the book hadn't mentioned blisters on the thighs—facing the desert.

And he was getting hungry again. He jogged on, thinking of food. Taffy, now; that was nourishing, compact, durable. O'Leary felt the glands at the side of his jaws ache at the thought. Beautiful, tawny, delicious taffy. Funny how he'd never really gotten enough taffy. Back in Colby Corners you could buy it in any desired amount at Schrumph's Confectionary, but somehow he'd always felt a little foolish walking in and asking for it. That was one thing he'd correct as soon as he got back—he'd lay in a larger stock of taffy and eat it whenever he felt like it.

He squinted across the hazy flat ahead, concentrating on the idea of saddlebags well stocked with good, mouth-watering, nourishing food. All he had to do was dismount, open them up, and there it would be. Concentrated rations that wouldn't suffer from the desert heat, enough to last him for—oh, say, a week.

There was a tiny jar—the familiar sense of a slipped gear in the cosmic machinery. O'Leary smiled. OK, he was set now. He'd ride on a mile or so into the desert, just to give himself a clear view of the trail behind so that no one could sneak up on him, and then he'd enjoy a long-delayed meal.

It was hot out here. O'Leary twisted, riding in a semi-sidesaddle position to ease the pain in his seat. The early sun was beating on his back, reflecting into his eyes from every projecting rock and desert plant. Too bad he hadn't thought to equip himself with a pair of Ray-Bans—and a hat would have helped, too; a wide-brimmed cowboy model. He reined in, turned in the saddle and looked back, squinting into the sun. Aside from his own trail of hoofprints and the settling dust of his passage, no sign of human life marred the expanse of dusty sand. It was as though the world ended a mile or two behind, where the low plateau met the dazzle of the morning sky. Not a very choice spot for a picnic, but the pangs were getting bothersome.

He swung stiffly down from the saddle, unbuckled the strap securing the flap on the left-hand saddlebag, groped inside and brought out a cardboard box. A bright wrapper showed a plate of golden-brown goodies. *Aunt Hooty's Best Salt Water Taffy,* O'Leary read delightedly. Well, that would make a fine dessert but, first, the more staple portions of the feast. He dropped it back in, came out with a familiar-shaped tin. *Sailor Sam's Salt Water Sardines,* the purple print announced, and beneath in small red letters: Finest Pure Taffy Confections. The next container was a square box containing *Old-Fashioned Taffy, a Treat for Young and Old.* O'Leary swallowed hard, dropped the box, probed for another; came up with a dozen eggs—chocolate-covered, taffy inside.

The other saddle bag produced a five-pound tin of taffy—a large gob of taffy artfully shaped to resemble a small ham, three square cans of *Old Style Taffy Like Mother Used to Make,* a flat plug of *Country Taffy—Pulled by Contented Clods,* and a handful of loose taffies wrapped in cellophane lettered *Taffy Kisses: Sweet as a Lover's Lips.*

O'Leary looked over the loot ruefully. Not what

you'd call a balanced diet; still, it could have been worse. After all, he *did* like taffy. He sat down in the shade of the horse and started in.

It was worse after that, riding on in the later morning sun. His soreness stiffened into pain that made him wince at every jolt of the animal's hoofs. His mouth puckered with the cloying taste of candy, his stomach feeling as though a dollop of warm mud had been dropped into it. His fingers were sticky with taffy, and the corners of his mouth were gummed with it. Ye Gods! Why hadn't he dwelt on the idea of ham sandwiches or fried chicken, or even good old Tend-R Nood-L! And it would have been clever of him to have supplied himself with a canteen while he had the chance.

Well, he was committed to the venture, ill-prepared though he was. There was no turning back now; the cops would be out in force after the fiasco in the alley. Nicodaeus had shown his colors; he could reduce the tally of his friends here in Artesia from one to zero. Still, when he came riding back with Adoranne before him, all would be forgiven. That part of the trip would be a little more fun than this. She'd have to sit snuggled up close, of course, and naturally he'd have to have at least one arm around her—to steady her. Her golden hair would nestle just under his chin, and he'd ride slowly, so as not to fatigue her Highness. It would take all day, and maybe they'd have to spend a night, rolled up in a blanket—if he had a blanket—by a little campfire, miles from anywhere . . .

But right now it was hot, dusty, itchy and exceedingly uncomfortable. Ahead, the line of peaks showed as a sawtoothed ridge, angling in from the left, marching on without a break to the horizon. Keep going until he reached the pass, the fellow had said back in the alley—not that he could depend on his directions. But there was nothing to do now but keep going and hope for the best.

The sun was low over the mountains to the west, a ball of dusty red in a sky of gaudy purple and pink, against which a clump of skinny palm trees stood out in stark silhouette. O'Leary rode the last few yards to the oasis and reined in under the parched trees. The horse moved impatiently under him, stepped on past a low, half-fallen wall, dropped his head to a dark pool, and drank thirstily. O'Leary eased an aching leg over the saddle and lowered himself to the ground. He felt, he decided, like an Egyptian mummy buried astride his favorite charger, and just now unearthed by nosy archaeologists. He hobbled to a spot on the bank of the pond, got awkwardly to his knees and plunged his head under the surface. The water was warm, a little brackish and not without a liberal sprinkling of foreign particles, but these trifles detracted hardly at all from the exquisite pleasure of the moment. He scrubbed his face, soaked his hair, swallowed a few gulps, then rose and tugged the horse away from the water.

"Can't have you foundering, old boy, whatever that is," he told the patient beast. "Too bad you can't enjoy taffy—or can you?" He rooted in the bag and unwrapped a Taffy Kiss; the horse nuzzled it from his palm.

"Bad for your teeth," O'Leary warned. "Still, since it's all there is, old fellow, it'll have to do."

He turned to the rolled bundle behind the saddle, unstrapped it, found that it consisted of a thin blanket with holes and a weather-beaten tent with four battered pegs and a jointed pole; the Red Bull's equipage left much to be desired. Fifteen minutes later, with the patched canvas erected and a final taffy eaten, O'Leary crawled inside, shaped a hollow in the sand for his hip, curled up on his side and was instantly asleep.

He awoke with a sudden sense of the ground sinking under him, a blip! as though a giant bubble had burst, followed by an abrupt silence broken only by a distant carrump! and the lonely *skriii* of a bird. O'Leary's eyes snapped open.

He was sitting alone on a tiny island with one palm tree in the center of a vast ocean.

CHAPTER IX

From the top of the tree—a stunted specimen with half a dozen listless fronds bunched at the top of a skinny trunk—O'Leary gazed out to sea. Beyond the white breakers that ploughed across the bright green of the shoal to hiss on the flat beach, deep blue water stretched unbroken to the far horizon. A few small petrellike birds wheeled and called, dropping to scoop up tidbits as the waves slid back from the shelf of sugar-white sand. Three or four small white clouds cruised high up in the sunny sky. It was a perfect spot for a quiet vacation, O'Leary conceded—wherever it was—though rather barren. His stomach gave a painful spasm as he thought of real food.

He slid to the ground, slumped against the trunk of the tree. This was a new form of disaster. Just when he'd thought he had a few of the rules figured out—*zip!* Everything had gone to pieces. How had he gotten to *this* ridiculous place? He certainly hadn't wished himself here—he'd never even given a thought to inhabiting a desert isle as a population of one.

And, of course, his efforts to shift the scene back to the oasis and his horse failed. Somehow, he couldn't seem to keep his mind on the subject while his stomach was shooting out distress signals. Just when he needed his dreaming abilities most, they deserted him. He thought of Adoranne, her cool blue eyes, the curl of her golden hair, the entrancing swell of her girlish figure. He got to his feet, paced ten feet, reached the water's edge, paced back. Adoranne had given him a hanky and was doubtless expecting him to come charging to her rescue—and here he sat, marooned on this loony island. Damn!

Never mind. Pacing and chewing the inside of his lip wasn't going to help. This was a time to think constructively. He put his hands to his hollow stomach; the pangs interfered with his mental processes. He couldn't even think about escape until he'd had some food! The palm tree wouldn't help: it was devoid of coconuts. He eyed the water's edge. There might be fish there . . .

O'Leary took a deep breath, concentrated, pictured a box of matches, a package of fish hooks, and a salt shaker. Surely, that wouldn't overtax his power, a modest little hope like that . . . There was a silent thump. Quickly, O'Leary checked his capacious pockets, brought out from one a book of matches labeled *The Alcazar Roof Garden: Dancing Nitely*, and a miniature container of Morton's salt with a perforated plastic top; the other produced a paper containing half a dozen straight pins.

"The Huck Finn bit, yet," he muttered, bending one of the pins into a rude hook. He remembered then that he had neglected to evoke a length of line to go with the hooks. That, however, could be easily remedied. He picked a thread loose from the inside of the beaded vest, unraveled four yards of tough nylon line. For bait . . . hmmmm . . . a cluster of the tiny pearls from his vest ought to attract some attention.

He looped the thread to the hook, pulled off his boots, waded out a few yards into the warm surf. A school of tiny fish darted past in the transparent crest of a breaking wave; a large blue crab waved ready claws at him and scuttled away sideways leaving a trail of cloudy sand. He cast his line out, picturing a two-pound trout cruising just below the surface . . .

Nearly two hours later O'Leary licked his fingers and lay back with a sigh of content to plan his next move. It had taken three tries to land his fish—the pins, he discovered, tended to straighten out at the first good tug. The sharp-edged rock had been a clumsy instrument for cleaning his catch but as a skillet, it had served well enough, laid in the driftwood fire that still glowed in the hollow he had scooped in the sand. All things considered, it hadn't been a bad meal, for something improvised in a hurry.

And now the time had come to think constructively about getting off the island. It would help if he knew where he was; it didn't seem to be any part of Artesia—and it certainly didn't look like Colby Corners. Suppose he tried to transfer back home now, and wound up in the humdrum world of foundries and boarding houses? Suppose Artesia, once lost, could never be regained?

But time was precious. Already the sun was

sinking toward the orange horizon; another day nearly gone.

He closed his eyes, gritted his teeth and focused his thoughts on Artesia: the narrow, crooked streets, the tall, half-timbered houses, the spires of the palace, the cobbles and steam cars and forty-watt electric lights—and Adoranne, her patrician face, her smile . . .

He was aware of a sudden stress in the air, a sense of thunder impending, then a subtle jar, as though the universe had rolled over a crack in the sidewalk.

He felt himself drop two feet, and a gush of cold salt water engulfed him.

O'Leary sputtered, swallowed a mouthful, fought his way to the surface. He was immersed in a choppy, blue-black sea, riffled by a chilly breeze. The island was nowhere in sight, but off to the left—a mile or more, he estimated as a wave slapped him in the face—was a shoreline, with lights.

He was sinking, dragged down by the heavy sword and the sodden clothes. The belt buckle was stubborn; O'Leary wrenched at it, freed it, felt the weight fall away. His boots next . . . He got one off, surfaced, caught a quick breath; the clothes were dragging him down like a suit of armor. He tried to shrug out of the vest, snarled it around his left arm, nearly drowned before he got his head free of the surface for another gulp of air.

It was all he could do to hold his own; he was out of breath, tiring fast. The cold water seemed to paralyze his arms. His hands felt like frozen cod. He managed a glance shoreward, made out a familiar projection of land: the blunt tower of the Kamoosa Point Light. He knew where he was now: swimming in the Bay, twenty miles west of Colby Corners!

He went under again, shipping more water. His arms . . . so tired. His lungs ached. He'd have to breathe soon. What a fool he'd been . . . shifted himself back to the Colby Corners . . . and since he'd traveled twenty miles to the west, naturally he'd wound up in the Bay . . . too tired now . . . can't swim any longer . . . cold . . . going down . . . too bad . . . if he could have just seen her turned-up nose once more . . .

——and something slammed against his back. The cold and pressure were gone, as though they had never been. O'Leary gasped, coughed, spat salt water, rolled over and coughed some more. After a while his breathing was easier. He sat up, looked around at an expanse of twilit sand—lots of it, stretching away to a line of jagged peaks black against the blaze of sunset.

Apparently he was back in Artesia. He looked up at the stars coming into view now in the darkening sky. The best bet would be to get a few hours of sleep and then start on. But he was too chilled to sleep. Perhaps if he walked a bit first, he'd warm up and his clothes would dry.

Wearily O'Leary put one foot in front of another—hay foot, straw foot, hay foot—— He stumbled over a bundle half buried in the sand. Clothes, dry clothes—pants, shirt, boots, a jacket; probably left behind by some picnicker. He knew he'd been too tired to think of them, and besides he hadn't had that universe-slipping feeling.

Hastily, O'Leary put on the dry clothes. There that was better. He felt in the pockets. Miraculously, if that was the word, they were filled with Taffy kisses. He was too bushed to figure this one out now. He scraped a hollow in the sand, building the sand up on one side as a windbreak, and went to sleep.

By midmorning, O'Leary estimated, he had covered no more than five miles of loose sand, in which his feet floundered and slipped with the maddening sense of frustrated progress so familiar in dreams. At each step his boots sank in to the ankle, and when he thrust forward, they slid back. Every time he lifted his blistered feet, it was like hauling a cast-iron anchor out of soft mud. At this rate, he'd never reach the mountains.

He sat down heavily. He pulled loose the bandanna he had tied over his head as an ineffective shield against the increasingly hot sun and mopped his forehead. He wouldn't sweat much more today; there was no moisture left in his body. No hope of a drink in sight, either. He shaded his eyes, scanning the stretch of rippled sand ahead. There was a slight rise to a wind-sculptured crest three hundred yards distant. What if there should happen to be water on the far side of the hill . . . And why shouldn't there be? He envisioned the scene, marshaling what was left of his Psychic Energies. There—had he felt the slight jar that signaled success?

With a sudden sense of urgency, he scrambled up, made for the ridge, stumbling and falling. He was getting weak, he realized, as he rested on all fours before getting up and plowing on. But just over the rise would be an oasis, green palms, a pool of clear, cool water, blessed shade.

Only a few yards now; he lay flat, catching his breath. He was a little reluctant to top the rise; suppose the oasis wasn't there after all? But that was negative thinking, not the sort of thing Professor Schimmerkopf would approve of at all. He got up, tottered on, reached the hilltop and looked down across a gentle slope of sun-glared sand at the square bulk of a big red Coke machine.

It stood fifty feet away, slightly tilted, a small drift of sand against one side, all alone in the vast wasteland. O'Leary broke into an unsteady run, stumbled to a halt beside the monster and noted approvingly the soft hum of the compressor. But where did the power come from? The heavy-duty electric cable trailed off a few yards and disappeared into the sand. But never mind the nit-picking details!

O'Leary tried his left pants pocket, brought out a dime and dropped it with trembling fingers into the slot. There was a heart-stopping pause after the coin clattered down; then a deep interior rumble, a clank and the frosted end of a bottle banged into view in the delivery chute. O'Leary snatched it up, levered the cap off in the socket provided, and took a long, thirsty drag. It was real Coke, all right, just like uptown. Funny; it was a long way to the nearest bottling plant. Lafayette lifted the bottle, peered at its underside. *Dade City, Florida,* said the raised letters in the glass. Amazing! Civilization was penetrating even into the most primitive areas, it appeared.

But what about Artesia? Surely it wasn't included on the rounds of the soft-drink distributors. Ergo, it could only have come from the "real" world—transported here by the concentrated O'Leary will.

He had already established that, when he evoked conveniences like bathtubs and dresses, his subconscious merely reached out and grabbed the nearest to hand. The idea that he could reach them all the way from Dade City was a bit frightening. Still, it was a comfort in a way; it lent a note of some sort of rationality to what had heretofore seemed pure magic.

What it boiled down to was that he had somehow stumbled onto the trick of moving objects around from one spot to another—not dreaming them up out of whole cloth. But that seemed to imply that Artesia was a real place! If that were so, where was it?

O'Leary put the question aside.

Ten minutes later, refreshed and with two spare bottles tucked in his hip pockets. O'Leary resumed the march toward his distant objective.

It was late afternoon when he reached the foothills—bare angles and edges of broken, reddish rock, thrusting up from the sea of sand. Cool air moved here in the shadow of the peaks above, soothing his sunburned face. He rested on a flat ledge, finished his last Coke, emptied the sand from his boots for the twentieth time since dawn, then resumed his trek, bearing northwest now, following the line of the escarpment. Still a long way to go, but the footing was better here. The sand was firmer, and there were patches of pebbly ground and even a few stretches of flat rock—a real luxury. With luck he should make the pass by dark; then tomorrow the final leg to Lod's HQ. As for water, that was no problem; he'd just provide a nice spring up ahead somewhere—and while he was at it, why not a steed, too?

O'Leary stopped dead. Why hadn't he thought of that sooner? Of course, it would have been a little difficult to convince himself that there was a horse standing by, all by himself, out in the desert. An animal wasn't like a Coke machine; he had to have food and water. A long extension cord wouldn't do the job.

But here, with plenty of opportunities for nice deep caves, and hidden fastnesses up in the hills, sure, a mount could be wandering around here. In fact, he'd find him, just around one of those outcroppings ahead. A fine, sturdy beast, adapted to the desert, strong, high-spirited, bright-eyed, and not too nervous to get close to . . .

Four outcroppings and two hours later, O'Leary's pace had flagged noticeably. No horse yet—but that didn't mean, he reminded himself, that he wouldn't find him soon. He hadn't said which outcropping he'd be behind. Probably this next one, just another half a mile ahead.

He plodded on. Getting thirsty again. He'd have to produce that spring pretty soon—but first, the mount. His boots had been designed for riding, not hiking. The sand inside his collar and under his belt was wearing the hide away, too. Not much fun, walking across a desert—but then, Adoranne probably hadn't enjoyed her crossing, either.

He reached the point of rock, thrusting out like the prow of a ship, a vertical escarpment looming up forty, fifty feet above the sands. He angled out to skirt the far end, rounded the point, and found himself looking along a canyonlike ravine, cut through the towering mass of rock. The pass! He had reached it!

He hurried out into the lane of late sunlight streaming down through the gap, his long shadow bobbing behind him. The sun was an orange disc above the flat horizon, reflecting bloodily from the walls of the defile. The sand here was disturbed, as though by the passing of many feet; the low sun etched the prints of boots and hoofs in sharp relief. A horse had passed this way not too long ago—several horses: Lod and his party, with Adoranne, no doubt. There were other prints, too, O'Leary noted—the trail of a small lizard, a row of catlike paw marks—and over there—what was that?O'Leary followed the tracks with his eye. They were large—impossibly large, great three-toed impressions like something made by a giant bird. But who ever heard of a bird with feet a yard across? He smiled at the whimsy. Probably just a trick of light on shifting sand. But where was his horse? He had definitely ordered it for delivery before clearing the pass . . .

There was a sound from ahead, startling in the stillness. Ah, there he was now! O'Leary stopped and cocked his head, listening. The sound came again, a scrape of hoof on rock. He smiled broadly and tried out the whistle Roy Rogers used for calling Trigger. With his parched lips, it came out a weak *tweet*. Far up the pass, a shadow moved.

Something grotesquely tall detached itself from the deep shadow of a buttress of stone at the side of the ravine—a shape that stood fifteen feet high, slender necked, great bodied, stalking on two massive legs like a monstrous parody of a

Thanksgiving turkey, except that the knees bent forward. A head like a turtle's turned his way, eyed him with bright green eyes. The lipless mouth opened and emitted a whistling cry.

"Th-that wasn't exactly wh-what I had in mind," O'Leary announced to the landscape. It occurred to him to run, but somehow his feet seemed frozen to the spot. Through them he could feel a distinct tremor in the rock at each step of the titan. It came on, moving with ponderous grace, its relatively small forearms folded against a narrow chest, the great curve of the belly gleaming pink in the failing light. Fifty feet from O'Leary, it halted, staring over his head and out across the desert as though pondering some weighty problem unrelated to small, knee-high creatures who invaded its domain. O'Leary stared, rooted to the spot. The seconds were ticking past with agonizing slowness. In a moment, O'Leary knew, the iguanodon—he recognized the type from an admirable illustration he had seen in a recent book on dinosaurs—would notice him again, remember what had started it lumbering in his direction. He pictured it wandering on, an odd leg hanging carelessly from the corner of the horny mouth, half swallowed, already forgotten.

He caught himself. No point in helping disaster along with vivid imaginings. He wasn't dead yet. And maybe he wouldn't be, if he could just think of something—anything!

A second lizard, to engage the first in mortal combat while he scuttled away to safety? Too risky; he'd be squashed in the sparring. How about a tank—one of those German Tiger models, with the big 88mm. gun! No, too fantastic. A diversion, perhaps—a herd of nice fat goats wandering by. But there weren't any goats out here. Just himself and the dinosaur—Lod's dragon, the thought dawned suddenly! And he'd dismissed the whole thing as a superstitious fancy. He'd been wrong about that—and about a lot of other things. And now he'd never have a chance to correct his errors. But he couldn't give up yet. There had to be something.

The great reptile stirred, swung his head about; O'Leary clearly heard the creak of scaled hide as it moved. Now it was turning back, dropping its gaze, fixing on the small figure of the man before it. A low rumble sounded from its stomach; it raised a foot, came striding forward.

O'Leary reached to his back pocket yanked out a handful of taffy kisses. With a roundhouse swing, he hurled them straight at the oncoming monster's snout. The mouth opened with the speed of a winking eye and engulfed the tidbits. O'Leary turned to run, twisted an ankle, fell full length. The shadow of the giant fell across him. He tried to evoke the image of Colby Corners, willing himself there. Even drowning in the bay was preferable to serving as hors d'oeuvre to an oversized Gila monster—but his mind was a shocked blank.

There was a peculiar, sucking sound from above, like a boot being withdrawn from particularly viscous mud. He turned his head, looked up; the monster was poised above him, chewing thoughtfully, strings of sticky taffy linking the working jaws. O'Leary hesitated. Should he lie still and hope the monster would forget him or try a retreat while it was occupied?

A pointed tongue flicked out, snagged a loop of taffy dangling by one horny cheek. The behemoth cocked its head and eyed O'Leary. It was a peculiarly unnerving scrutiny.

O'Leary edged away, scrabbling backward on hands and knees. The dinosaur watched; then it took a step, closing the gap. With a final snap, it downed the last of the candy. O'Leary scuttled faster; the titan followed. O'Leary reached the wall of the canyon and started along its base. The monster came after him, watching with the same sort of interest that a cat evinces in a wounded mouse.

Ten minutes of this race, O'Leary decided, flopping down to breathe, were enough. If the thing was going to eat him, it could go ahead. Unless he could banish it, somehow.

Go away, he thought frantically. *You've just remembered your–your mate, that's it–and you have to hurry off now.*

It wasn't going to work. The dinosaur was too close, too real, with its warty, crevassed hide, its cucumber smell, its glittering eye. He couldn't begin to concentrate. And now the big head was dropping lower, the jaws parting. This was it! O'Leary squeezed his eyes shut . . .

Nothing happened. He opened them. The vast reptilian face was hanging before him, not two yards away—and the look in the eyes was . . . hopeful?

O'Leary sat up. Maybe the thing wasn't a man-eater. Maybe it was tame. Maybe——

But of course! He had ordered a steed! This was it! Back in the palace, when he'd ordered a bath, he had gotten the next best thing. This time it seemed he had somehow summoned the neighborhood dragon—and it like taffy!

O'Leary tossed another sample of Aunt Hooty's best to the monstrous beast. It caught it like a dog snapping at a fly, except that the clash as the jaws met was louder.

O'Leary tossed half a dozen together, then the rest of the handful. The dinosaur leaned back on its tremendous tail with a sigh like a contented submarine and munched the goodies. O'Leary sighed too, slumped back against the rock. That had been a harrowing quarter hour—and it wasn't over yet. If he could just sneak away now.

He started off, moving as unobtrusively as possible. The iguanodon watched him go. Twenty feet, thirty feet; just around that next turn now, and he'd bolt.

The reptile came to its feet and padded after him, dainty as an earthquake. O'Leary halted; the huge creature squatted, holding its head low, as though waiting.

"Go 'way," O'Leary squeaked. He made shooing motions. The dinosaur regarded him gravely—almost expectantly.

"Scram!" he shouted. "Who do you think I am, Alley Oop?"

Then an idea struck him. He'd already deduced that the monster had appeared in response to his yearnings for a steed. Could it be? What an impression he'd make on Adoranne if he came cantering up to Lod's hideout on *that!* And since it didn't appear that he'd ever shake the brute, he might as well give it a try. He wouldn't be any more vulnerable seated on its back than he was jumping around under its nose, and anyway—hadn't that book said the iguanodon was a vegetarian?

O'Leary straightened his shoulders, set his jaw and crept cautiously around to the side. The giant head swung, following him. He paused at a leg like the warty trunk of a tree. Not much chance of climbing that. He went on, reached the tail, thick as a fifty-gallon molasses drum, tapering away across the sand. He ought to be able to make it up that route. O'Leary followed the tail out to a point where he could swing aboard, then walked up its length. As he passed the juncture with the hind legs, he found it necessary to lean forward and use his hands, but it was easy going; the fissured hide offered excellent footholds. The saurian waited patiently while he scaled the stretch from haunch to shoulder; then it lowered its head. O'Leary straddled the neck behind the head and the monster straightened, lifting him up to ride fifteen feet clear of the floor of the pass. There was a magnificent view from up here, he noted; far away across the sands to the west he fancied he saw a smudge of vegetation, a tiny glint of light on windows. That would be Lod's hangout. He clacked his heels against the horny hide.

"Let's go, boy," he commanded. At once, the dinosaur set off at an easy canter—in the wrong direction. O'Leary yelled, kicked with one heel; the mighty mount veered, came about on the port tack and headed back up the pass. In five minutes, they were clear of the ravine, striding out across the parched plain at a mile-eating pace. The sun was gone now; deep twilight was settling across the desert. "Steady as she goes, boy," O'Leary commented aloud. "In about an hour we'll be giving this Lod character the surprise of his life."

CHAPTER X

It was dark night with no moon as O'Leary sat his mighty steed behind a dimly seen screen of tall eucalyptus that marked the edge of the grounds surrounding the great building that towered up against the stars—fifteen stories at least, O'Leary estimated. Faint starlight glinted on hundreds of windows; there was dim illumination behind three of them. Blazoned across a strip of what looked like dark plastic twelve-foot-high lavender neon letters spelled out *LAS VEGAS HILTON*. Between him and the nearest corner of a projecting flank of the structure, a ten-foot iron fence ornamented with spearheads thrust up.

"This isn't quite what I expected, fellow," O'Leary muttered. "I pictured a collection of tin shacks, or maybe some wooden huts we could walk right through. Wouldn't do to slam into that; it might fall on us. And Adoranne might get hurt."

The dinosaur stretched its neck across the fence. O'Leary looked down at the sharp points below.

"Wouldn't do to fall on those, Dinny," he said nervously. The iguanodon leaned against the bars; they creaked, bent like soda straws, went down.

"Nice going, boy. Hope nobody heard the clatter . . ."

The monster lowered its head to ground level. O'Leary jumped off onto a carpet of knee-deep grass which the reptile sniffed and began peacefully cropping.

"All right, boy," he whispered. "The place is big, all right, but it seems sparsely manned. Wait here while I reconnoiter—and keep out of sight."

There was a soft snort from the great head, now lifted far above him, investigating the lower branches of a big oak. O'Leary moved off silently, skirted a waterless fountain in the shape of an abstract female, crossed a stretch of pavement marked with faint white lines at ten-foot intervals, hopped a strung chain and entered the rustling, leaf-strewn shadow of a stand of poplars.

From here he had an excellent view of the building. Nothing stirred. He emerged from the trees, made his way around to the front. There was a broad, paved drive—concrete, by the feel of it—which swept past a flight of wide steps leading up to a rank of glass doors, above which a cantilevered marquee thrust out fifty feet. Great, unpruned gardenia bushes bunched up from planters set along the terrace; the warm night air wafted the heavy fragrance of their blossoms to O'Leary.

Inside, beyond the doors, he could see a plushly carpeted foyer, dimly lit, its pale fawn walls decorated by framed pictures and gilt and white lamp brackets. Large soft-looking divans and easy chairs were placed in conversational groups around low coffee tables.

The peaceful order of the scene was marred only by a scattering of papers, bones, empty tin cans and the charred ring of a small camp fire beside a potted yucca. Someone, it appeared, had desired more informal cooking arrangements than the hotel kitchens afforded.

O'Leary went up the steps, approached the doors and jumped as the one before him swung in with a whoosh of compressed air. Magic, after all? He felt the untrimmed hair at the nape of his neck rising. But then, maybe it was just electronics—magic rationalized. He edged through the door and looked around the two-acre lobby.

Adoranne was here—somewhere. It was going to be a long search through fifteen floors of rooms to find her, but he had to make a start somewhere. He picked a corridor at random, went along it in the eerie light to the first door, tried the knob . . .

An hour and a half later O'Leary was working his way through the southwest wing of the ninth floor. So far he had encountered nothing but empty rooms, most of them immaculately made up, with dusty dresser tops and vases of withered flowers the only signs of neglect, but a few with rumpled beds and muddy bootprints on the pastel carpets—like the one he was in. Some careless occupant had plucked a chicken in the bathroom, leaving a clot of feathers in the toilet bowl. A chair had been disassembled for some reason not clear; its component parts lay about the room. A smashed wastebasket was on its side half under the bed. Something bright showed among the rubbish—a key, attached to a turquoise plastic disc with the number 1281 impressed on it in gilt. O'Leary picked it up. Maybe this was a clue. It was worth checking out, anyway. So far he'd seen nothing to indicate that Adoranne was here. Perhaps Lod and his merry men were off on a raid; maybe they'd be back at any moment. He'd better hurry.

As he emerged from the stairwell at the twelfth floor, the sounds of voices came to his ears. He felt his heart thump in unpleasant excitement. He was getting warm, it seemed. He went along the hall in the direction indicated by a glowing arrow. When he rounded a corner the sounds were louder. Room 1281 would be at the end of the hall—beyond the room from which the loud conversation was coming. O'Leary approached the door standing half ajar with a stripe of light falling across the carpet from inside the room.

". . . seen him in the palace, two days ago," a rusty voice was complaining. "An' I says to him, look, I says, if you got some kind of idear we're doing all the dirty work while you grab the loot, your aggies is scrambled."

"But he give the boss a promise he'd get the broad——"a second voice started, cut off with a sound like a croquet mallet striking a side of beef. "It ain't perlite to call a dame a broad," the rusty voice cawed. "And I know what he promised. But it's up to us to collect. Don't worry. The boss's got his plans all doped out. He's got a couple surprises up his sleeve fer his high-and-mightiness."

"Chee, you can't buck *him*!" a third voice said, "Wit' his power——"

O'Leary, straining to catch every word, was suddenly aware of footsteps approaching along the corridor. He looked, dived for a door across the hall, slid inside and flattened himself against the wall.

"Hey!" a voice yelled. "Who ast you in?" A large man with lather on his face stood in the open door to the bathroom, glowering. "Go find yer own flop." His tone changed. "Who're you? I ain't seen you before."

"Ah—I'm a new man, just signed up," O'Leary improvised. "The lure of adventure, you know, the companionship of kindred spirits. Now, about the, ah, girl. What room's she in?"

"Huh?"

"I just wanted to nip up and make sure the door's locked. Our boss, Lod, wouldn't appreciate it if she flew the coop, eh?"

"What are ya, nuts or sumpthin'?" The big man was frowning darkly, working with a forefinger in a cauliflowered ear. "She——"

The door banged open. "Hey, Iron-bender," a peglegged John Silver type in a torn undershirt growled out. "Could I borry yer second-best brass knucks?" The newcomer's gaze fell on O'Leary. "Who's this?" he demanded.

"A new guy; some kind of a ladies' maid. How's come yer always on the scrounge, Bones? You ain't give back my thumbscrew yet, the one Ma give me."

"A *what* kind of a maid?" Bones was eyeing O'Leary.

"I dunno; he was asting about where the dame was. The dummy don't even know——"

"Never mind what he don't know. He's prob'ly

one o' the new reinforcements. That right, bub?"

"Absolutely," O'Leary nodded. "But about the, er, prisoner. Just tell me her room number, and I'll be off. I don't want to trouble you gentlemen further."

"This dope thinks—" Iron-bender started.

"The room, huh?" Bones gave Iron-bender a look. "It's kind of hard to find. Me and him better show ya the way. Right, Iron-bender?"

The thug wrinkled his broad, flat face. "Look, I got things to do."

"You can spare a few minutes to take care o' the demands o' hospitality. Let's go."

"Oh, you needn't bother, fellows," O'Leary protested. "Just give me the room number."

"Not a chanct, matey; we got to do this right. Come on. It ain't far."

"Well . . ." O'Leary followed the two out into the hall. It might help, at that, to have an escort. It would save some embarrassing questions if he encountered anyone else. He followed the two slope-shouldered heavyweights along the passage to a stairway and up two flights. They emerged in a corridor identical to all the others.

"Right this way, bud," Bones said with a smile like a benign crocodile.

They went along past silent doors and halted before one numbered 1407. Bones thumped with his knuckles.

A deep grunt sounded from inside.

"That doesn't sound like Adoranne," O'Leary said. "That sounds like——"

Bones jumped for him, missed as O'Leary spun aside and dropped a side-hand chop across the bass of the thick neck. Iron-bender, slow on the uptake, watched his companion stagger past with a muffled yell before he turned on O'Leary, in time to take the latter's stiff fingers in a hard jab to the sternum. He doubled over and caught a smashing uppercut with his massive chin. He shook his head.

"Hey, what goes on?" he inquired in a pained voice, reaching for O'Leary, who caught his arm, whirled, levered it across his hip—and felt himself being lifted, tossed aside. He rolled away and saw Iron-bender rubbing his arm, a pained expression on his face.

"Ow," the heavyweight said. Bones was coming back now, a little hunched to the left, but an expression on his face which prompted O'Leary to leap to his feet, dash past Iron-bender and make for the stairwell at flank speed. He reached it, slammed through, hammered down one flight, plunged out into the corridor—and into the waiting arms of a grizzly bear.

It was impossible, O'Leary had discovered, to concentrate on escape schemes while in a position of extreme stress—such as now, for example. The man who had gathered him in—a seven-footer with hands like machinst's vises, shoulders like football armor, and a variety of muscles to match—held him in an awkward grip, his arms crossed behind him and raised until he danced along on tiptoe in an effort to relieve the pressure.

"I'll go quietly," he assured his captor. "How about just leaving my arms in the same old sockets they've been in all along; I like them that way."

The thick arm jerked him sideways, heading down along a new passage. O'Leary scrambled to keep the weight off his arms. Through open doors he glimpsed unmade beds, soiled garments on unswept floors, empty cracker boxes, sardine tins, bean cans. His captor came to a halt, struck a closed door two blows with his fist. The door slid back, revealing the interior of an elevator. O'Leary's jailor pushed him inside, worked a handle; the car rose one floor. They stepped out into the corridor where Iron-bender and Bones stood in heated debate.

". . . we tell him the guy pulls a knife, see, and——"

"Naw, we don't tell him nothing. I'll say you was drunk——" the conversation broke off as the two spotted O'Leary.

"Hey!" Bones said. "Crusher got him!"

"Gee, thanks, Crusher," Iron-bender said. "We'll take him off yer hands now."

Crusher make a low rumbling sound in his throat. The two lesser thugs withdrew hastily. Crusher marched O'Leary along to the door Bones had knocked on earlier. This time the knock shook the panel in its frame.

A deep voice called, "It's open, curse you!" Crusher twisted the knob, flung the door wide, and propelled O'Leary into the room.

A man sat in an immense chair placed under the window across the room. He was taller sitting down than Crusher was standing: that was O'Leary's first startled impression. The second was that the man was wider, thicker, heavier, more massive, than any human being he had ever seen before—by far. The third was a shocked wondering whether this *was* a man.

The massive head—carried at an angle as though the neck had been broken once and badly set—was adorned by a dark leathery face, like some heroic carving of a demon. The nose was sharply chiseled, with great flaring nostrils. The mouth was wide, thin-lipped, with a long sparsely bristled upper lip, over a massive jaw with a receding chin. Small, bright eyes stared from the oversized face; deep brown eyes, with no white showing. Coarse hair, short-cropped, covered the wide, knobby skull; the leg-thick neck was muffled in a great scarf, and the ponderous body was draped in shimmering folds of a dark wine-colored stuff. The hands that rested on the arms of the chair were big enough to hold two footballs each, O'Leary estimated. Great jewels glistened on the thick, hairy fingers. The giant twitched one of the latter members, and Crusher released his grip and backed from the room.

"So you reach my citadel," a thickly accented voice near the lower level of the audible range rumbled. "I thought you might—though sage Nicodaeus think otherwise."

"You're—you're darn right," O'Leary said, trying hard to control a quaver in his voice. "And if you know what's good for you, you'll turn Adoranne over to me right now and mayby I'll put in a good word for you with King Goruble."

"If I know what is good for me? Alas, little man, none ever know what is good for him. And if one knew, would he follow that path?"

"I'm warning you, Lod—you *are* Lod, aren't you? If you've hurt her Highness——"

"Yes, Lod is my name." The giant's voice rang with a harder note. "Undertake to offer me no warnings, small creature. Instead, speak to me of the errand that brought you hither."

"I came for Princess Adoranne . . ." O'Leary stopped to swallow. "I know you've got her, because who else——"

"At first lie, I give you pain," Lod said. "Like this." He leaned forward with a swift motion, gripped O'Leary's shoulder with one huge hand and squeezed. O'Leary yelped in agony.

Lod rolled back, eyeing him with a touch of amusement. "At second lie, I give disfigurement; the loss of an eye, perhaps, or a crushed limb. And at third, I condemn you to hang in the cage of tears, where you will die with a sloth that will surprise you."

"Who—who's lying?" O'Leary managed, blinking away pain tears. "I heard Adoranne was missing; everybody thought I did it, but that's nonsense. You're the one with the motive and the organization——"

"What? Must I inflict lesson two already?"

"He's telling the truth, you great ugly imbecile," a sharp, though muffled voice piped up from somewhere. Lod halted in mid-reach, looking disconcerted.

"Of course I'm telling the truth," O'Leary moved his shoulder. Nothing seemed to be broken. What a pity he hadn't equipped himself with a .45 automatic while he was at it; it would be a pleasure to plug this leering man-mountain.

"Who sent you here?" Lod barked. "Nicodaeus, I think, that sly traitor!"

"Nicodaeus tipped off the palace guard when I paid him a visit in his room," O'Leary said. "I'm no messenger of his."

"Ask him who *he* is, not the name of his master," the snappish voice came again. It seemed to

O'Leary that it emanated from behind Lod. He craned to see who might be crouched behind the chair.

"Name yourself then, little man," Lod commanded.

"I'm Lafayette O'Leary. What's that got to do with it? I demand——"

"Where do you come from?"

"I left Artesia yesterday, if that's what you mean. Before that—well, it's kind of complicated——"

"I sense a strangeness in this man," the shrill voice piped. "Let him go, let him go!"

Lod's eyes narrowed. "You came alone and unarmed against mighty Lod. How did you pass dragon who guards my eastern gate? How——"

"As well ask the west wind why it blows," the shrewish voice shrilled. "You face power here, vile usurper! Have the wit to turn from it in humility!"

"Speak up!" Lod's voice was a snarl. "I think you fairly beg for torment!"

"Look, all I want is the girl and my freedom," O'Leary said desperately. "Tell your gorillas to release us, unharmed, and——"

Lod's immense hands jumped, caught O'Leary between them and lifted him off his feet, bruising his ribs.

"Must I tear you in two, stubborn mite?"

"Aye, kill him now—ere he tells you that which you fear to hear," the shrill voice snarled. "Shut off the voice of doom impending!"

Lod snarled, tossed O'Leary from him. He came to his feet, stood over O'Leary, ten feet tall, a mountainous, crook-backed orge. "Must I boil you in pitch?" he boomed. "Impale you on bed of thousand needles? Drop you in the dark well of serpents? Bury you neck deep in broken bottles?"

O'Leary picked himself up, half-dazed by the blow his head had struck the floor. "No, thanks," he faced the giant towering over him. "Just . . . give me Princess Adoranne and a good dinner and . . . I'll let you off easy this time."

Lod roared; the other voice squealed in wild laughter. The giant whirled, stalked back to his chair, threw himself in it, his face working through a series of Hallowe'en expressions before setting in a grim stare.

"Kindness avail nothing with you, I see," Lod grated in a tone of forced calm. "That being case, stern measures are called for." He twitched a wrist. The door opened. Crusher stood in it, looking like a dwarf in the shadow of Lod.

"Take him to interrogation room," the giant rumbled. "Prepare him. Then await my coming."

It seemed as though hours had passed. O'Leary felt himself swaying again, tried to catch himself; then the stabbing pain as the sharp spikes set in the cage stabbed at his right shoulder. He jerked away, struck his left elbow an agonizing crack on the neatly placed projection on that side. Then again he was huddled in the only position possible in the cage; half-bent, half-crouched, his head cocked sideways. His knees and back ached; the throb of a dozen shallow puncture wounds competed for attention. He shifted minutely to relieve the cramp developing in his thigh, felt the prod of the waiting needle points.

"This won't get you anything, Lod," he croaked. "I can't tell you who sent me, because nobody sent me. I'm operating on my own." The giant was lounging at ease in a vast chaise lounge, dressed in pale pink robes now, a voluminous scarf of purple silk wound around his grotesque neck. He waved a ringed hand as big as a brief-case.

"Be stubborn as you like, little man. It gives me pleasure to watch you fret there, surrounded by pain, weighing one punishment against another. An artful device, the cage of tears, for as it torments body with its spiked caresses, so does it agonize the mind with the need to make frequent, painful decisions." Lod chuckled contentedly, lifted a gallon-sized leathern jack, quaffed deeply, then plucked a leg from a roast turkey-sized creature and sucked the meat from the bone in one gulp.

Moving only his eyes, O'Leary looked around the room for the fifteenth time, scanning the high, beamed ceiling, the damp earth floor, the rich rug on which Lod's chaise rested, the trophies hung carelessly on the rough, stone walls. There were heads of great reptiles—not cured and stuffed, merely rotting empty-eyed skulls—broken weapons twice normal size, a great ax with a leather-wrapped haft and a rusted, double-bitted head. There was nothing here he could work with—not that he could concentrate, with pain stabbing at him from every side. There was just one door, and he knew where that led. It was fruitless to try to imagine the U.S. cavalry charging in to the rescue. King Goruble's subjects, fond though they were of the princess, were too much in dread of Lod and his dragon to attempt to storm his citadel.

"I see you admire my little souvenirs," Lod rumbled cheerily. He was growing more talkative as he downed mug after mug of brown ale. "Mementos of early years, before my elevation to present eminence."

"Eminence?" O'Leary put all the scorn he could manage into the word. "You're just an ordinary crook, Lod. A little uglier than most, maybe, but there's nothing special about kidnapping and torture. The dregs of humanity have been at that sort of thing for thousands of years."

"Still you pipe merry tune," Lod boomed, smiling genially as he chewed, showing immense, square teeth. "But pain and thirst and hunger are faithful servants; they do their work, aided by their ally, fear."

"Only the fool knows no fear!" the strange, shrill voice screeched suddenly. "You toy now with forces you know not of, foul tyrant!"

"Where's that voice coming from?" O'Leary croaked.

"Voice of my conscience," Lod growled, then guffawed and drank.

"Some conscience; I can hear it all the way over here. Why don't you pay some attention to it? It's smarter than you are."

Lod lifted his lip in a snarl. "One day I kill conscience," he muttered as though to himself. "And day grows close." A shriek of insane laughter answered him. He drank again, spilling the ale down his chin, slammed the jack to the table and eyed O'Leary balefully.

"You babble of her Highness, Princess

Adoranne, my bride-to-be," he growled. "He swore to me: wench would be my prize! And now my agents bring word that he spirit her away. Time grows close; his plots ripen—and now he needs me not, thinks he! He do away with girl, threat to his grip on throne, and cast me aside—me, to whom he swore his oath!"

"You mean . . . Adoranne really isn't here?" O'Leary stared with pain-blurred eyes at the horrendous face.

"Aye, he is sly one," the giant went on, slurring his words now. "With his promises and his gifts and his treachery. But the fool fail to remember that in my own land, I was king!" Lod banged the mug again, sloshing ale. "By force of my arm and guile of my nature, I *made* myself king! My father was mighty one, but I slew him! I!"

"He trusted you, unnatural son and brother!" the voice piped. "You cut him down while he slept."

"To victor belong spoils!" Lod boomed. He refilled his mug, drank, tore a great chunk off the roast bird while the thin voice screamed curses.

"But——" Lod pointed a finger at O'Leary, as the latter twitched away from the stab of a spike digging into his thigh. "Does traitor who plots in palace deal fairly with me? Does he fear powers that made me king? No! He thrust me aside, think to confine me here in this parched land while richness of cities and fields goes to him!"

"Why not?" O'Leary heard himself taunting. His mind was fogging now; only the recurrent prick of the dagger points kept him from fainting. "Nicodaeus knows it's safe to cheat you, because you're stupid."

"Stupid?" Lod laughed, a sound like a stone tower falling. "Yet he sent you, a weakling, here."

"How did this weakling pass the guardian?" the voice piped. "Ask him that, mighty imbecile!"

"Yes, now you will talk!" Lod leaned forward unsteadily. "Why did the gray magician send you? Why *you*? Who are you? *What* are you? How——"

O'Leary managed a creditable Bronx cheer.

Lod started to his feet, then sank back heavily. "I exercise myself needlessly," he muttered. "But a little time, and the cage will do its work."

"But a little time, and you die," the disembodied voice screeched. "Then will the foul ghosts of the ancestors rend your stinking corpse, and that of my father will be foremost."

"Silence!" Lod bellowed. He poured and drank, slopping the ale. "If I die, who then feed you, evil leech?" The giant slumped back in his chair, watching O'Leary with red-rimmed eyes. "I tire of this sport," he rumbled. "Speak now, little man! What are secret schemes of Nicodaeus? What double-dealing lies behind his promises? Why did he send you? Why? Why? Why?"

"Don't you . . . wish you knew . . ." O'Leary managed. If the cage were made of something soft, like taffy . . . or if he had thought to provide a small gun . . . or if someone—anyone—would burst in now, open the cage . . .

It was no use. He was stuck here. His powers didn't work under stress like this. True, when he'd been drowning, he had managed to jump back to Artesia at the last instant. But at least he had been drowning in comfort, and perhaps he hadn't yet reached the last minute. If he ever got out of this, he'd have to set up some controlled experiments, determine the extent and nature of his abilities.

But this time he wouldn't escape. He'd die here; and Adoranne would never know he'd tried.

". . . now, before it's too late," the tiny voice was chanting. "Let him go, foul parricide, turn back from disasters you know not of."

"Almost," Lod rumbled blurrily, "I think stubborn runtling has suborned you, so merrily you cry his cause! But I am Lod, king and master, and I fear neither man nor devil nor caster of spells."

"Fool! Let him go! I see death, and rivers of blood, and all your vile plans fallen to ruin! I see the shadow of the Great Ax that hovers over your head!"

"Great Ax hangs there amid my trophies," Lod laughed wildly. "Who's to wield it against me here?" He finished off another gallon of ale and refilled the jack with unsteady hands.

"How say you, starveling?" he called to O'Leary. "Do you tire of game? Do red-hot knives of pain loosen your tongue?"

"I'm fine," O'Leary said blurrily. "I like it here. It's restful."

"Let him go!" the voice snarled. "Let him go, cretinous monster!"

Lod shook his head in drunken stubbornness. "You see, little man, what a burden even greatness must bear. Day and night, waking and sleeping, that foul voice ever shrilling at my ear! Is enough to drive lesser man mad, eh?" He peered owlishly at O'Leary.

"I . . . don't hear . . . anything," O'Leary got out. "You've already . . . gone nuts, I guess . . ."

Lod laughed again, hiccupped. "No ghostly voice, this," he rumbled. "It issues from hideous lips as ever body nourished."

"That's . . . the first sign," O'Leary gasped. "Hearing voices . . ."

Lod grinned. "And you, little man—you draw comfort from the impertinence you hear pass unpunished. You guess you gain an ally, eh?" Lod's chuckle was not an encouraging sound. "Small help you'll have from that quarter," he cried. "But I've been discourteous! I've not made introductions! An oversight, believe me! But I'll soon set that aright." Lod reached to his throat, fumbled at the scarf, tore it free.

From the base of his bull-neck, a second head grew—a shrunken, wizened, hollow-cheeked copy of the first, with eyes like live coals.

"Behold my brother!" Lod mumbled; then he fell back in his chair, mouth open, eyes shut, and snored.

CHAPTER XI

For a long minute, there was silence. Lod's snores grew louder, deeper. He stirred, flung out an arm that knocked over the ale mug. Dark fluid gushed, splashed on the floor, then settled down to a steady drip. O'Leary watched, wide-eyed, as Lod's second head stirred, staring across at him. The lips worked.

"The . . . great brute . . . sleeps," it whispered shrilly. "The strong ale tugs at my mind also . . . but I will not heed it."

O'Leary stared. The spilled ale dropped. Lod snuffled, snorted in his sleep.

"Hearken, small one," the head hissed. "Will you do my bidding, if I help you now?"

O'Leary tried to speak; his tongue seemed paralyzed. It was too much effort. He felt himself slumping against the spikes. He knew they were cutting in, but the blessed relief of a moment's rest . . .

"Don't die now, fool!" the head whispered harshly. "I can free you—but first your word that you will do the task I set you!"

"What—what is it?" O'Leary tried to keep his mind on what the head was saying. He knew it was important, but a great pit of soft blackness was waiting, and if he just let go, he would sink down, down . . .

"Listen to me! Freedom! If you swear to serve me!"

The voice penetrated the fog. His chest hurt—how it hurt! Spikes were digging in as he slumped against them. Something sharp was cutting into his cheek, and another against his jaw.

He gasped and pulled himself off the daggers. The eyes in the shrunken head caught him, glaring.

". . . now, fool! Catch at the chance Fortune throws in your path! Give me your word and I'll set you free!"

"What—what do you . . . want me to . . . do?" O'Leary managed.

"See the great ax on the wall yonder? It was written—ah, long and long ago—that by its keen edge the betrayer would meet his doom! Take it! Raise it high! Strike off his head!"

"His . . . head?"

"The murderer of his king and father has sworn to do the like by me," the head hissed. "He swore that none should witness his nuptial revels when he makes the Princess Adoranne his bride! The finest surgeons in the land will he summon, and under their knives I'll suffer living decapitation. He hates me, and he fears me. Me, who has suffered with him through thick and thin, ever ready with a word of advice. And now he says I will shame him before her quaking loveliness! Ah, the vile creature! He'd remove me like a wart, cut me down in my prime! His brother!"

"How . . . can you . . . release me?"

"When he sleeps in drunken sottishness, as now, I can, a little, control the body; *our* body, soon to be mine alone. How say you, little man? Is it a bargain?"

"I . . .I'll try."

"Done!" The glittering eyes narrowed. O'Leary saw perspiration pop out on the brown and furrowed brow under a lock of giant's hair. One hairy hand stirred, groped clumsily in the folds of the gown, crept inside. There was a jingle of metal. The hand emerged, holding a ring of keys. Lod snored on, his tongue lolling from his gaping mouth.

"The pain—the mortal pain of it," the second head whimpered. "But soon, soon victory is mine!"

O'Leary watched, goggle-eyed as the hand lifted the keys—then, with an awkward motion, tossed them. They struck the cage, caught on a spike, dangled inches from his hand.

"I can't reach them," he whispered.

"Try! Only a little pain stands between you and freedom! Try!"

O'Leary moved his hand an inch; spikes caught at his arm. He twisted his body sideways, feeling the thrust of other stiletto points against his ribs and hip. He inched the arm forward and up, gritting his teeth as the skin scraped, the blood started, joining the dried blood from earlier cuts. Another inch . . . almost there . . . His finger caught the key ring, teased it . . .

It dropped into his palm, and he clutched it, his heart thudding. Lod snorted, stirred. O'Leary watched him, holding his breath. The giant's breathing steadied once more. Painfully, O'Leary worked his arm back to his side, then forward, enduring the stab of the knives. His clothes were a bloody mess, he realized dimly. He was bleeding from dozens of separate small wounds; none deep, but all painful. He was losing a lot of blood.

"The key of black iron," the head keened softly. "Quickly, now! He sleeps but lightly!"

One more effort. O'Leary took a deep breath, gripping the key in slippery fingers. He reached, forgetting the damage he was doing to his hide, concentrating on the objective. The key touched the dangling lock; it swung away, clattering. The head cursed softly. O'Leary dropped the keys, pushed up on the lock with a finger. In the chair, Lod moved his feet, reached up to rub a thick finger under his nose. The second head watched, cracked lips parted . . .

The lock rose, teetered, fell with a clatter. Lod half-opened his eyes, smacked his lips noisily, relaxed again. O'Leary pushed against the hinged front of the cage. It swung wide. He stumbled out, stood swaying before the sleeping giant.

"Adoranne," he said thickly. "Was he lying? Is she here?"

"He spoke the truth, foolish man. Doubtless He-Who-Plots-in-the-Palace can tell you of her. There is no time to waste! Quickly, to your duty!"

O'Leary straightened his aching back, wiped his bloodied hands on his thighs, tottered to the wall. The ax hung high, out of reach. He turned, dragged a three-legged stool over to the wall, stood on it, nearly fell, clutched at the wall for support. The dizziness passed. The haft of the ax was as big around as his wrist, diagonally wrapped with tough animal hide, dry and hard. He gripped it, lifted it free from the rusted spike it dangled from.

The heavy weapon slipped from his grasp, came clanging down against the hard earth floor. Lod grunted; O'Leary scrambled down, reached, brought up the ax. It was heavy, awkward, too long by a yard. The broad steel head was red with fine rust, twelve inches wide at each blade, two feet from edge to edge, set in a notch in the wood and wrapped with leather strips.

"Haste, small man!" the thin voice screeched. Lod's eyes flew open. He stared blankly, then shook his head, muttering. His gaze fell on O'Leary as the latter gripped the ax at midpoint, brought it up across his shoulder. Lod roared, tried to rise, slipped, fell back, bellowing.

With a heave, O'Leary swung the ax from his shoulder, took two steps, brought it over and down with all the force of his arms behind it, square on the juncture of Lod's neck and chest. The great head leaped up six inches, like a grotesque beach ball balanced on a spurting column of crimson; then it fell aside, bounced once on the massive shoulder, struck the floor with a meaty thud, spun, came to a stop staring up at O'Leary with a hideous leer.

In the chair, the great body, still fountaining blood, rose unsteadily to its feet.

"Now I am master," the tiny head croaked.

Then the body toppled—dead.

O'Leary groped to the table, feeling blackness

closing in; he found the ale jug with his hands, tilted it, drank, then leaned on the table and waited while the cool liquid burned away the fog. There was food here—a feast fit for a giant. He sank down on a stool, picked up a roast pigeon, fell to, oblivious of the immense body lying at his feet in a spreading pool of tar-black blood.

After eating, O'Leary pulled off his shirt and examined his wounds. He was cut, slashed, scraped in fifty places. None of the cuts were deep, but he'd look like a schoolgirls's embroidery project when the doctors finished stitching him up. Using a little of the ale, he cleaned the slashes, wincing at the sting. He wiped away the drying blood, then tore strips from Lod's voluminous scarf to bind up the worst cuts.

He went to the door—there was no sound from outside. Was Crusher or another of Lod's bulky bodyguard standing by, awaiting a summons? He needed a weapon. There were plenty of them on the wall, but all were broken—war trophies, taken from fallen enemies, Lod had boasted. The ax was too big to be handy, but it would have to do—and maybe its bloody condition would impress the locals. He hefted it, got it across his shoulder, flung the door open. There was no one in sight in the dark tunnel.

The rough-hewn passage led upward at a slant, angled around a massive reinforced concrete footing, ended at a crude doorway hacked in the ceramic tile cellar wall, covered over by an untanned hide of some scaly animal. O'Leary thrust it aside, emerged into a gloomy basement crowded with vast air-conditioner and furnace units, festooned with aluminum-wrapped duct work, piping, and heavy electrical cables. At one side, a 50 kw diesel generator chugged patiently—the source of the remaining electric power in the hotel, O'Leary deduced.

He crossed the wide room, went up stairs and came out into the kitchens, foul with a faint odor of rotted food. Windows at the far side showed the gray light of early dawn. They were sealed shut, he saw. Still, there was no point in venturing out into the frequented area of the building. His mission now was merely escape, and return to the capital as quickly as his pet dragon could canter. Nicodaeus had been clever, tricking him into setting off on a wild goose chase while he completed his plans for seizure of the kingdom undisturbed. Lod had said that the plotter planned to dispose of Adoranne. If he had hurt her——

Time to think about that later. O'Leary swung the ax at the window. Glass burst outward. He knocked free the jagged shards remaining in the frame, stepped up on a table, ducked through to a wide stone sill and jumped down to the untrimmed turf six feet below. So far, so good. Now, where was his mount? He gave a low whistle. There was an answering hiss from beyond the nearest clump of trees, only dimly visible through the early-morning fog. O'Leary set off in that direction and saw the stir of a tall body among the trunks. A mighty figure stalked forth to meet him, looking bigger than ever through the mist.

"That's the boy, right on the job," O'Leary called in a low voice. He trotted forward to meet the tremendous beast as it advanced, emitting a rumble like a dormant volcano stirring to life. O'Leary admired the play of the massive thigh muscles under the greenish hide, the great column of the neck, the jaws——

Jaws? He didn't remember a head the size of a Volkswagen, opening like a vast power shovel to reveal multiple rows of gleaming ivory daggers, nor did he recall red eyes, pinning him down like spears, or talons like curved bone scimitars.

He turned, dropped the cumbersome ax and dashed for shelter. A huge foot struck the earth just beside him; something immense swooped down and O'Leary caught a glimpse of a steaming red-lined cavern big enough to stable a pony. He dived; there was a tremendous boom! as the jaws met inches behind him; a blow sent him spinning.

He rolled over, came to hands and knees, his shirt in shreds. He saw the strange dinosaur whirl, a tatter of cloth dangling from its teeth, and come prancing back, jaws ready for a second try. O'Leary backed, met the solid resistance of thick-growing shrubbery——

With a crash of rending branches, a second, smaller reptile stepped into view. Dinny!

The herbivore took two steps into the clear. The meat-eater bellowed. Dinny gave a leap when he apparently saw the tyrannosaur for the first time. He bleated, took three hasty steps backward, turned and made for cover.

"Smart dinosaur," O'Leary muttered. He readied himself for a desperate sprint as the carnivore veered to plunge after the tame saurian, jaws gaping even wider. A few yards in the lead, the iguanodon skidded to a halt, rocked forward, swept his heavy fleshy tail to one side, and brought it around in a swipe that caught the meat-eater solidly across the knees. The tyrannosaur stumbled, crashed through a screen of trees in a tangle of broken boughs and trailing vines, and went down out of sight with an impact like a falling skyscraper. There was one terrific blast of sound, like a calliope gone mad; the unbelievable legs kicked out, subsided to a regular twitching, shuddered, were still. O'Leary tottered across the patch of lawn, peered through the fallen foliage; the spearheads of the steel fence across which the monster had fallen protruded through the massive neck. O'Leary stooped, recovered his ax.

"Nice placement, boy," O'Leary said. "Now let's saddle up and ride—and hope we're not too late."

It was a two hours' ride into the desert. O'Leary shaded his eyes, watching a moving caterpillar of dust approaching, miles away across the parched sands. The column had halted. Men on horseback were milling, fanning out. One or two deserters or couriers had turned and were cutting trails back toward the distant faint line of green that marked the dessert's edge, fifteen miles away. Now a single horseman spurred forward, riding out alone in advance of the deployed troop. O'Leary slowed his mount to a walk. The lone rider was a tall man, buckled into black armor, a long sword slapping at his side, a long lance in its rest. He reined in his handsome black charger a hundred yards distant, and O'Leary saw the black hair and clean-cut features of Count Alain. The count raised a gauntleted hand to wipe the sweat from his forehead.

"As I expected, the traitor, Sir Lafayette!" he

shouted. "I warned the king you were in Lod's pay, but he seemed to find the suggestion amusing."

"I don't blame him, it's a very funny idea," O'Leary called back. "What are you doing out here in the desert?"

"I've come with a hundred loyal men to demand the return of her Highness, unharmed. Will you yield now, villain, or must we attack?"

"Well, that's very nobly spoken, Al," O'Leary said. "And I admire your nerve in facing up to Dinny here. But I'm afraid you're barking up the wrong dinosaur. I don't have Adoranne."

"Then your master, the unspeakable Lod——"

"He's not my master. In fact, he's not anybody's master now. I killed him."

"You? Ha! I'm laughing!"

O'Leary held up the bloodied ax. "Then laugh this off. But let's cut the chatter. Adoranne isn't back there; she never was. Nicodaeus is the man we want. He's plotting to take over the kingdom. He had a deal with Lod, but it seems he's decided he doesn't need him any more, so he double-crossed him and instead of delivering her Highness to him as a consolation prize, he intends to do away with her."

"Lies!" Alain shouted, rising in his stirrups and shaking a mailed fist. "You're trying to drag red herrings across the trail. But if you think I'm fool enough to swallow that tale——"

"Go ahead—see for yourself. You'll find Lod in his private interrogation room, at the end of a tunnel from the cellar under the kitchens. He had fifty or more thugs hanging around the place, so be careful. Don't worry about his dragon, though; Dinny here killed it."

"You take me for an idiot? You're perched on the Lod's dragon at this moment, in living testimony to your false alliance!"

"OK. I can't wait around. I've got to get to the capital before it's too late. Too bad you can't see your way clear to join me." O'Leary kicked his heels against the saurian's skull: it obediently started forward. Alain spurred aside, watched as O'Leary rode past.

"First I ride to rescue her Highness," he shouted. "Then I settle accounts with you, Sir Lafayette!"

"I'll be waiting for you. Ta-ta!" O'Leary waved and then settled down for the long ride ahead.

The sun was high when he crossed the cactus-grown borderland and rode down the last slope into the green countryside of Artesia. News of his approach had spread ahead of him: his fifteen-foot-tall mount must have been visible for the last quarter hour as it tramped across the sandy waste. The road was deserted now; shops stood empty; the windows of the houses along the way were tight-shuttered. O'Leary's cuts and bruises were aching abominably and his reflections were gloomy.

By agreeing with his theory that Lod was the abductor, Nicodaeus had neatly set one nuisance against another, with a chance that O'Leary and the giant might manage to destroy each other. The magician had been a plausible scoundrel; poor king Goruble had given the schemer quarters right in the palace, where he could carry out his plot with the greatest convenience. The plan had been well worked out, O'Leary conceded; and only luck had given him this chance to thwart the would-be usurper—if he wasn't already too late.

He entered the suburbs—the collection of squatters' huts and merchants' stalls clustered outside the city wall proper. All was silent, the narrow alleys empty. A damned shame he couldn't find someone to spread the word that he was on their side, that he needed their help now in his attack on Nicodaeus. No telling what the magician might have rigged in the way of defenses. There might be a battery of artillery waiting inside the palace walls. Well, if so, that was just a risk he'd have to run.

The city gates just ahead were closed tight. From his perch, O'Leary could see over the wall into empty streets beyond. Well, if they wouldn't let him in, he'd have to make his own way. He urged Dinny ahead; the saurian balked, sidled, then turned, lashed out with its tail. A twenty-foot section of the ancient wall went over with a crash and rumble of falling masonry. The dinosaur picked its way delicately through the rubble into the street of shuttered shops. Far away, O'Leary heard the sound of a church bell tolling out a warning. Except for that, and the scrape and clack of the iguanodon's horny bird-feet on the cobbles, the city was silent as death.

The palace gates were shut, O'Leary saw, as he rode up the avenue leading through the park toward the high iron grilles. Two frightened sentries stood their ground inside the wall, nervously fingering blunderbusses. One raised his weapon as O'Leary halted fifty yards from the gates.

"Don't shoot," he called, "I'm——"

There was a loud boom! and a jet of black smoke spurted from the flared muzzle of the gun. O'Leary heard a sharp whack! against the dinosaur's hide. The latter turned his head casually and cropped a bale of leaves from an arching branch.

"Listen to me!" Lafayette tried again. "I've just escaped from Lod's fortress, and——"

The second guard fired; O'Leary heard the ball shriek past his head.

"Hey!" he yelled. "That could be dangerous! Why don't you listen to what I've got to say before you make a serious error?"

Both men threw their guns aside and bolted.

"Oh, well, I guess it's what you'd expect," O'Leary muttered. "All right, boy, here we go again." He urged the dinosaur forward; it stalked up to the gates, leaned on them, trampled them down without slowing, continued along the wide, graveled drive. Ahead the palace loomed, windows aglitter in the afternoon sun, silent. A movement caught O'Leary's eye at the top of one of the towers. He turned toward it across the lawn and waved an arm.

"Hello in there!" he shouted. "It's me, Lafayette O'Leary——"

All along the parapets, from the castellated tops of towers, from the archer's slits set in the stone walls, arrows sprang, arching up in sibilant flight, converging, dropping.

O'Leary ducked, closed his eyes and gritted his teeth. An arrow clacked off Dinny's snout, inches from his boot tip. Something plucked at his torn left sleeve. Other darts clattered down, glancing from the dino's tough hide, bounding off to fall in the grass. Then silence. He opened an eye; ranks of men were in view at the ramparts now, fitting new bolts to strings, bending bows.

"Let's get out of here, Dinny!" O'Leary dug in his heels; the big reptile started forward as a second flight of arrows swept past to thud into the turf and rattle off the iguanodon's tail. The balustraded grand entry was just ahead. The dinosaur took the graceful flight of wide steps at a stride and halted at O'Leary's command.

"No use knocking the wall down," he panted, sliding down to the smooth tiles of the terrace as Dinny lowered his head to investigate the geranium boxes along its edge. "You wait here."

Still carrying Lod's ax, O'Leary ran to the wide glass doors—less substantial than the oak panels opening from the courtyard side, he noted gratefully—kicked them in. The great hall echoed his steps. Somewhere in the distance he could hear a hoarse voice yelling commands. Those archers at the battlements would be arriving on the scene at any moment—and at close range, they could hardly miss.

The entrance from the great hall to the secret passage system was on the far side, he remembered; right about there, where the tall mirrors reflected gilt ceilings and a vast crystal chandelier. Feet were clattering above. O'Leary ran, reached the wall, felt quickly over it. To the left? No, more to the right.

There was a loud yell from above: O'Leary looked up, saw a beefy-faced household guardsman with three wide yellow stripes on his sleeve leaning over a gallery rail, pointing. More men crowded up behind him. Bows appeared, and muskets. O'Leary searched frantically. He had seen the chandelier when Yokabump had opened the panel for him to peek out—he remembered that. And the fountain there——

A section of wall slid aside, just as the roar of a shot boomed through the hall. A bullet smacked the wall above his head. Bowstrings twanged and an arrow struck the wall beside him as he ducked, stepped inside and hauled the ax in behind him. A second arrow shot between his knees and thumped into the wall inside the passage. O'Leary slammed the panel, heard half a dozen hammer blows as more bolts struck, just an instant late. He leaned against the rough brickwork and let out a long sigh.

Now for Nicodaeus.

The heavy door was closed and the tower room silent, as O'Leary stood before it listening. From below, he could hear shouts ringing back and forth as the agitated guardsmen scurried about, looking for the lost trail. They might start up the stairs at any moment and if they cornered him here, it was all over. An ax wasn't much good against guns and bows. He hammered on the door.

"Let me in, Nicodaeus," he called in a low voice, then put his ear to the panel. There might have been a faint rustle from within.

"Open up or I'll knock the door down!" This time he was sure; there was a soft thump from beyond the door. Perhaps there was another passage, one Yokabump hadn't known about; maybe the magician was making a backdoor escape while he stood here like a Fuller Brush man.

O'Leary raised the ax, swung it high.

The door creaked open six inches. There was a hoarse yell as the ax came down against the panel with a crash that slammed the door wide. O'Leary looked past it at Nicodaeus, backed against a table, making gulping motions.

"Dear boy," the magician managed to gasp out, "you startled me."

O'Leary wrenched the ax from the oak door. "You can skip all that 'dear boy' schmaltz," he said coldly. "I'm a little slow to think unkind thoughts about anybody I've shared a drink with, but in your case I managed. Where is she?"

"Where—where is who?"

"Adoranne. And don't bother with the innocence routine either. I know all about you. Your friend Lod spilled the beans just before I killed him."

"You *killed* Lod?" Nicodaeus' eyebrows shot up toward his receding hairline.

"With this." O'Leary hefted the ax. "And I'm prepared to use it again, if I have to. Now start talking. Where have you got her stashed? Right here in the palace, I suppose. It would be easy enough, with all these passages in the walls."

"You must believe me, Lafayette!" The magician straightened himself. "I know nothing of her Highness' disappearance, no more than any other——"

O'Leary advanced. "Don't stall; I have no time to waste. Talk fast, or I'll hack you into stew-sized chunks and find her myself. I know the back routes pretty well."

"Lafayette, you're making a mistake! I don't know what the rebel, Lod, said of me, but——"

"Never mind what he said. What about the way the cops pounced, five minutes after I came into your inner sanctum here, looking for help, a couple of evenings ago?"

"But—but—I had nothing to do with it! It was a routine search. I didn't have time to summon the guard, even if I'd wanted to. And they couldn't have responded that quickly if I had."

"I guess you had nothing to do with framing me with that silly episode in Adoranne's boudoir, either—to get me out of the way, so you could carry on with your schemes unmolested!"

"Of course not! I was as amazed as you were."

"And I should just disregard what Lod said about your plans."

"Lafayette, I did, I admit, approach Lod on one occasion, but only in an effort to learn certain facts. I offered to, ah, grant him certain compensations if he would tell me all he knew of, well, certain matters . . ." Nicodaeus's face was damp, his eyes bugging slightly as they followed the glint of light on the brown-crusted edge of the ax in O'Leary's hands.

"Uh-huh. Certain compensations—like Adoranne."

"No!" the magician yelped. "Did he say that? In his own crude way, Lod was a man of directness, not guile. Surely he didn't accuse me of such an act!"

"Well . . ." O'Leary went back over the conversation with Lod. "He called you a traitor—and he accused me of being your agent."

"But the other—did he say that *I* had promised him the person of her Highness?"

"He kept babbling about the plotter in the palace—how you were out to seize the throne, and do away with Adoranne."

"The plotter in the palace?" Nicodaeus frowned. "It wasn't *I* he was talking about, dear lad. I promise you that. What else did he say?"

"He said you didn't need him any more, so you were welching on your promises."

"Lafayette, I made the giant a promise—this I admit. But it was only that if he would tell me all he knows of—of the matters I spoke of—that I would confirm him in his local power, and see to it that he received a reward in cash—an offer which he promised to consider. But as for thrones, and murder——"

"Get specific, Nicodaeus! What were these certain matters?"

"I'm . . . not at liberty to say."

"All right, play it mysterious then. But if you think I'm going to let you talk your way out of this . . ." O'Leary advanced, bringing the ax up.

"Stop!" Nicodaeus raised both hands. "I'll tell you, Lafayette! But I'm warning you, it's a gross violation of security!"

"Make it good!" O'Leary waited, ax ready.

"I'm a . . . a representative of an organization of vast importance; a secret operative, you might say. I was assigned here to investigate certain irregularities."

"Don't give me that 'certain' routine!"

"Very well; I was sent here by Central. There

was the matter of a highly localized Probability Stress. I was sent to clear it up."

"Not very good," O'Leary said, shaking his head. "Not very convincing. Try again."

"Look . . ." Nicodaeus groped inside his flowing robe, brought out a shiny shield-shaped object. "My badge. And if you'll let me get my lock box, I'll show you my full credentials . . ."

O'Leary leaned forward to look at the badge. There was a large 7-8-6 engraved in its center on a stylized representation of what appeared to be an onion. Around the edge O'Leary spelled out:

SUBINSPECTOR OF CONTINUA

He frowned at the older man and lowered the ax reluctantly. "What does that mean?"

"One of the jobs of Central is seeking out and neutralizing unauthorized stresses in the Probability Fabric. They can cause untold damage to the orderly progress of entropic evolution."

O'Leary hefted the ax. "That's over my head. Tell me in simple language what this is all about."

"I'll try, Lafayette—not that I'm at all sure I know myself. It seems that this coordinate level, this, ah, um, universe? Dimension? Aspect of multi-ordinate reality?"

"You mean world?" O'Leary waved a hand to encompass all of Artesia.

"Precisely! Very well put. This world was the scene, some decades ago, of a Probability Fault, resulting in a permanent stress in continuum. Naturally, this required clearing up, since all sorts of untoward events can occur along the stress line, particularly where matter displacement has occurred."

"OK, let's skip over that. I'd say you were nutty as a pecan roll except for a few things that have happened to me lately. Too bad we don't have more time to discuss it. But what's that got to do with Adoranne?"

"I was merely attempting to establish my bona fides, dear boy. Some sort of skulduggery took place here twenty or thirty years ago; the situation still remains unresolved. It's my job to find the center of the stress pattern, restore all anachronisms and extra-continual phenomena to their normal space-time-serial niches, and thus eliminate the anomaly. But I confess I've made no progress. The center is here, nearby. At one time, I even suspected you, Lafayette—after all, you appeared under rather mysterious circumstances—but, of course, you checked out as clean as a scrublady's knees." He smiled glassily.

"What do you mean, checked out?"

"I took readings on you when I visited you in your room, before the ball. The lighter, you know. You gave a neutral indication, of course. You see, only an outsider—a person native to another continuum—would elicit a positive indication. Since you're a native, you gave no such reading."

"Mmmmmm. You'd better have your dials checked. But look—this isn't finding Adoranne. I was sure you had her. If not . . ." O'Leary looked at Nicodaeus, feeling suddenly helpless. "Who does?"

Nicodaeus stroked his chin. "The plotter in the palace you say Lod spoke of?"

"I wasn't paying much attention; I thought he

meant you. He was pretty drunk, but still cagy enough not to mention the name."

"Who would gain by the disappearance of her Highness? Someone with ambitions of usurpation, someone close to the throne, someone unsuspected," Nicodaeus mused. "Could it be one of Goruble's painted dandies?"

"Lod is the one who had his eye on the throne—and a yen for Adoranne, too. Maybe Alain—but somehow he strikes me as honest, in his blundering way. Then there's you—but for some reason I believe your story. But I'd still like to know who spread the word that I'd been here. They were staked out at the city gates, waiting for me. Are you sure you didn't spill the beans?"

"I assure you, I was discretion itself. Even King Goruble . . ." Nicodaeus paused, looking thoughtful.

"What about Goruble?" O'Leary said sharply.

"I had a few words with his Majesty, just after you were here. He questioned me closely. I wondered at the time what he was hinting at; he appeared to suspect I'd been shielding you."

"Did you tell him I'd been here?"

"No . . . and yet, now that you mention it, he seemed to know . . ." Nicodaeus' eyes were round. "Great heavens, Lafayette! Do you suppose? But how could it be? I've been looking for someone, an outsider—but the king——"

"Lod said someone who *wanted* to take over the throne; Goruble already has it."

Nicodaeus frowned. "In these cases there's usually some individual—often a renegade agent of Central, I confess—who sees his chance to establish himself comfortably in a subtechnical environment and make himself dictator. To which Central would have no particular objection, if it weren't for the resultant chain of anomalies. But it never occurred to me——"

". . . that he'd already taken over," O'Leary finished for him. "I don't know much about the history of Artesia, but from a few hints dropped here and there, I've gotten the impression King Goruble is far from beloved, and that he came to power some twenty-odd years ago under rather vague circumstances."

"I've been blind!" Nicodaeus exclaimed. "I've never tested him, of course. Who would have suspected the king? But it fits, Lafayette! It fits! He had the opportunity. He could walk into the princess's apartment without an alarm, lure her away, then presto—pop her into a locked room, and raise the outcry!"

"But what for? She's his niece."

"Not if our theory is correct, lad! He's an outsider, an interloper, a usurper, with no more claim to the throne than you! And Adoranne, as the niece of the previous king, represents a very real threat to his security—particularly since he is himself unpopular, while the masses adore the princess!"

"Then *he* was the one who was doing business with Lod—the plotter in the palace!" O'Leary nibbled his lip. "But hold it, Nicodaeus. There's one big flaw in the picture: Lod—from what I could guess—was brought in from . . . somewhere else. One of these other continua of yours, I'd say. The same goes for that dinosaur he kept in his front yard. And his HQ itself—it looked like something that had been plucked up by the roots and dumped in the desert for Lod's use. The plotter we're looking for was using Lod as a diversion, to keep the people's minds off his own power grab, and the fancy quarters and the personal dragon were part of the bargain. But the only one around here with outside resources—is *you!*"

"Me? But Lafayette! I'm an inspector! I can't go moving buildings and tyrannosauri about at will! My workshop here suffices for a few modest surveillance instruments, nothing more! You're forgetting that our culprit was himself an outsider. If he transported himself here, why couldn't he have manipulated the rest?"

"You're still holding out on me, Nicodaeus. What about your *real* workshop? I saw some pretty big machines down there; they aren't just for checking suspects' vibrations."

"Real workshop? I'm afraid I don't know what you mean, Lafayette."

"In the cellar—the big room with the iron door, and the smaller room that looks like a walk-in refrigerator."

"Like . . . like . . .?" Nicodaeus' eyes bugged. "Lafayette—did you say—walk-in refrigerator?"

"Yes, and——"

"With a large door—with a big latch mechanism, like this?" He sketched in the air.

"Right. What's it for?"

Nicodaeus groaned. "I fear, Lafayette, we'll not see Adoranne again. The device you describe is a Traveler—used to transport small cargoes from one coordinate level to another. I was dropped here in one, and expect, in due course, to be picked up by another. If Goruble had one here—a stolen vehicle belonging to Central, no doubt—

then I fear Adoranne is already beyond our reach."

"You really think Goruble's our man?"

"None other. Alas, Lafayette, she was such a charming girl."

"Maybe it's not too late," O'Leary snapped. "Come on, we'll pay a call on His Majesty—and this time I won't be bluffing!"

The red-faced sergeant of the guard spotted them as they stepped off the main stairway at the third floor. He gave a yell and dashed up, gun in hand.

"Hold, my man!" Nicodaeus called. "I'm taking Sir Lafayette to interview his Majesty on a matter concerning the security of the realm! Kindly call your men in as an honor guard!"

"Honor guard?" The noncom raised his musket threateningly, "I'll honor-guard the louse, kidnapping our princess."

"I didn't," O'Leary cut in, "but I think I know who did. If you want to shoot me before I can tell, go ahead."

The sergeant hesitated. "Better lay down that ax, buster. Drop it right there."

"I'm keeping it." O'Leary said shortly. "Come with us or stay here, I don't care which, but don't get in my way." He turned, strode off toward the royal quarters. Behind him, after a moment of hesitation, there was a curse and a snapped order to fall in. A moment later the ten-man detail closed in around Lafayette and Nicodaeus, guns ready, eyes rolling ominously at the pair.

"Better not try nothing," the nearest man muttered. "I got a yen to clear my barrel."

O'Leary halted at the door to the king's chambers, ignoring the two gaping sentries. He tried the elaborate gold knob, pushed the door wide.

"Hey, you can't——" someone gasped.

"All right, Goruble, come on out!" O'Leary called. He looked around at cloth-of-gold hangings, high windows, rich rugs, spindle-legged furniture with the gleam of rare wood. The room was empty. He walked across to an inner door, threw it wide; it was an ornate bath, with a sunken tub and gold fittings.

The next door let into a vast bedroom with a canopied bed looking like a galleon under full sail. O'Leary checked two more rooms, Nicodaeus at his side, the troop of soldiers following, silent, awed by this rude invasion of the royal privacy.

"He's not here," Nicodaeus said as O'Leary prodded the hanging clothes in the closet of the last room.

"But—he's got to be here," a guardsman said. "He couldn'a left without we knew about it; after all, we're the royal bodyguard."

"I think I might know where he went," O'Leary said. "I'll go check."

"You ain't going no place, bud." The sergeant stepped forward to assert his damaged authority. "I'm taking you down to the dungeons, and when his Majesty shows up——"

"Sorry, no time." O'Leary brought the butt of the ax up in a swipe from the floor, caught the sergeant under the third button; he oofed and doubled over. O'Leary tossed the ax, handle-first, at the man behind him, straight-armed the next, ran for the door, whirled and slammed it behind him. There were shouts and loud thuds as he turned the key in the lock. In three jumps he was across the room, pulling aside the drapes that framed a portrait of the king as a frowning youth. He slapped panels; a section of wall tilted outward. He slipped through, clicked it shut behind him, turned—and froze at a scraping sound from the darkness.

"Nice footwork, O'Leary," the cavernous voice of Yokabump said. "I kind of figured you'd be taking to the woodwork soon. Where you headed?"

"I'm glad you're here," O'Leary said tensely. "You remember the rooms in the cellar? The ones with all the big machines?"

"Oh, you mean old Goruble's thinking rooms. Sure . What about 'em?"

"I need to get down there—fast!"

"Maybe you better stay clear o' that section for a while. The old boy himself walked right past me in the dark, not an hour ago, headed in the same direction—and I'd say he was in a lousy mood."

"An hour ago? Then maybe there's a chance! Come on, Yokabump! Lead the way as fast as you can, and hope it's fast enough!"

The polished slab door was closed tight as O'Leary came softly up to it, his tread muffled by the carpet of dust in the narrow passage.

"He's still in there," Yokabump whispered. There was a sound like a dynamo growling to a halt. "His footprints go in, and don't come out."

"You must have eyes like a cat," O'Leary said. "It's all I can do to see where I'm going." He put his ear to the door. Silence.

O'Leary narrowed his eyes. There was a keyhole, just there, near the edge, he told himself;

a small inconspicuous aperture. And the key—it would be hanging from a nail on the beam . . .

There was the faintest of bumps in the smooth flow of the timestream. O'Leary smiled grimly, groped over the rough-hewn member, found the tiny key.

"Hey, O'Leary!" Yokabump rumbled. "How'd you know that was there?"

"Shhhh." O'Leary quietly fitted the key into the door; there was a tiny click. He leaned against the door; it swung silently inward, revealing the dim-lit interior of the room, the massed dials and indicator lights, the tall shapes of the massive equipment housings, the festooned conduits and, in the center of the room, King Goruble, seated in a chair, holding a compactly built machine gun across his knees.

"Come right in, Sir Lafayette," Goruble said grimly. "I've been awaiting you."

CHAPTER XII

O'Leary gauged the distance to the rotund monarch. If he jumped to one side, then hit him low——

"I wouldn't recommend it," Goruble said. "I'm quite adept at the use of firearms. Come away from the door. I don't want you to be tempted. Just take a chair there." The king nodded to a seat beside the panel. O'Leary moved across, sat down gingerly, his legs under him, ready to move fast when the moment came.

"You look a trifle uncomfortable," Goruble said. His voice was hard. "Just lean back, if you please, and stretch your legs out. That way I think you'll be less likely to attempt anything foolish."

O'Leary followed orders. This was a new Goruble; the theories that had seemed farfetched minutes before were taking on a new plausibility. The small eyes that stared at him now were those of a man capable of anything.

"Where's Adoranne?" O'Leary demanded abruptly.

"Speak when spoken to," Goruble said harshly. "There are a few facts I want from you—before I make disposition of you."

"With that?" O'Leary glanced at the gun.

"Nothing so gory—unless you force me to, of course, in which case I can put up with the inconvenience. No, I'll merely remove you to a place where you can cause me no trouble."

"And what place would that be?"

"Don't bother your head about that," Goruble retorted coldly. "Now, tell me how much you know. If I find you holding back, I'll consign you to a certain small island I know of—capable of sustaining life, but not offering much in the way of amusements. But for each fact you confide in me, I'll add another amenity to your exile."

"I think I know the place you mean, but I didn't like it there, so I left—if you'll recall." O'Leary watched the stout ruler for a reaction to the shot in the dark. Goruble's mouth twitched in a frown.

"This time you'll have no confederate to snatch you back. Now, kindly start your recital. How much is known at Central?"

O'Leary considered and rejected a number of snappy answers. "Enough," he said after the momentary pause.

"You, I take it, are fully in the confidence of Nicodaeus. How did he discover your identity?"

"I told him," O'Leary hazarded.

"Ah." Goruble looked crafty. "And how did *you* discover your identity?"

"Someone told me," O'Leary replied promptly.

Goruble's brow furrowed. "I suggest you speak plainly!" he rapped. "Tell me all you know!"

O'Leary said nothing.

"You'd best discover your tongue at once," Goruble snapped. "Remember, I have it in my power to make it highly uncomfortable for you—or, on the other hand, to leave you in a situation of comparative ease."

O'Leary was studying the half-open door of a cabinet on the wall behind the king. If there should be a small glass container lying just inside—and if it should be on its side, ready to roll out—and if there should be just the slightest jar, such as a sneeze . . .

"Surely you're not childish enough to imagine that you can distract me by eyeing some imaginary intruder behind me," Goruble smiled sourly. "I'm . . ." his nose twitched. "I'm far too . . . tooo . . ." He drew a sharp breath, blasted out a titanic sneeze, then grabbed for the gun, brought it back on target.

"It requires bore thad a bere sdeeze to distragd be." He fumbled for a handkerchief in his breast pocket. "I'm quite accustomed to the dust in these unused ways."

There was a soft creak as the cabinet door stirred in the faint gust of air raised by Goruble's explosion. Light glinted for an instant on something on the dark shelf; an eight-ounce beaker rolled into view, dropped——

At the impact of glass against concrete, Goruble leaped from the chair. The gun went off with a shattering roar, stitched a row of craters across the floor, blasted tufts of cotton from the chair seat as O'Leary dived from it, slamming Goruble aside with a shoulder. He snatched the gun as it flew from the king's hands and whirled, centered the sights on the monarch's paunch.

"Nice weapon," he said. "I'll bet a few of these made a lot of difference, back when you were stealing the throne."

Goruble made an unpleasant, snarling noise.

"Sit down over there," O'Leary ordered. "Now, let's cut the chatter. Where's Adoranne?" He was fingering the unfamiliar stock of the weapon, wondering which projecting button was the trigger. If Goruble had another gun stashed, and went for it now . . .

"Look here, you utter fool," Goruble snapped. "You don't know what you're doing."

"You wanted facts," Lafayette said. "Here are a few: You're sitting on somebody else's throne. You've kidnapped her Highness—who isn't your niece, by the way—because she's a potential threat to you. You brought Lod in from Outside, and his pet lizard, too. Unfortunately, I had to kill both of them."

"You——" Goruble dropped flat as O'Leary's questing finger touched a concave button on the breech of the gun and sent a round screeching past the king's ear to blast a pocket in the stone wall.

"Just a warning shot," O'Leary said hastily. "Now, open up, Goruble. Where is she?"

The king crouched on all fours, looking badly shaken; his jowls had lost their usual high color.

"Now, now, don't get excited," he babbled, coming shakily to his feet. "I'll tell you what you want to know. As a matter of fact, I'd intended all along to propose an arrangement with you." He slapped at the dust on his velvet doublet. "You didn't think I intended to hog it all, did you, my dear fellow? I merely wished to, ah, consolidate the improvements I've made, before summoning you—that is, inviting you—or——"

"Get to the point. Where is she?"

"Safe!" Goruble said hastily.

"If she's not, I'll blow your head off!"

"I assure you she's well! After all, *you* suffered no harm, eh? I'm not bloodthirsty, you know. The, ah, earlier incident was just an unfortunate accident."

O'Leary raised his eyebrows. "Tell me about the accident."

Goruble spread his hands. "It was the purest misfortune. I had come to his chambers late one evening, with a proposal, a perfectly reasonable proposal——"

"By 'he', I suppose you mean your predecessor?"

"My, ah, yes, my predecessor. Hot-tempered man, you know. He had no reason to fly into a pet. After all, with my, ah, special resources, the contribution I would make would be well worth the consideration I sought. But he chose instead to pretend that I had insulted him—as though an offer of honorable marriage to his sister could be anything but an honor to the primitive—that is, underdeveloped—or——"

"Get on with it."

"I was a bit put out, of course; I spoke up frankly. He attempted to strike me. There was a struggle; in those days, I was a rather powerful man. He fell . . ."

"Hit his head, I suppose?"

"No, there was a sword—his own, of course—and somehow, in the excitement, he became, er, impaled. Through the heart. Dead, you know. Nothing I could do."

Goruble was sweating. He sank down in the bullet-pocked chair, dabbing at his temples with a lace hanky. "I was in an awkward spot. I could hardly be expected to summon the guard and tell them what had happened. The only course open to me was . . . to dispose of the body. I brought it down through the inner passage, and, ah, sent it away. Then what? I racked my brain, but I could evolve only one scheme: to assume supreme authority—temporarily, of course—until such time as more, ah, regular arrangements could be made. I made certain preparations, called in the members of the council, explained the situation and enlisted their support. There were one or two soreheads, of course, but they came around when the realities of their position were explained to them."

"I get the general idea." O'Leary moved up and pressed the muzzle of the machine gun against Goruble's chin. "Take me to Adoranne—right now. I'll get the rest of your confession later."

Goruble's eyes crossed as he stared down at the cold steel jabbing his throat. "Certainly. The dear child is perfectly well."

"Don't talk; just show me."

Goruble rose carefully and led the way onto the passage. O'Leary glanced both ways, but saw no sign of Yokabump. The clown must have fled at the first inkling of the strange doings here in the palace catacombs. Goruble was picking his way in the near-darkness, moving along toward the chamber O'Leary had likened to a walk-in refrigerator. The king fumbled out keys under O'Leary's watchful eye, manipulated locks; the heavy panel swung silently open. Goruble stepped back as bright light gleamed through the widening opening. He indicated the interior of the eight-by-ten cubby-hole.

O'Leary moved clear of the opening door, took in the dial-covered walls, the console installation like an all-electric kitchen—and at one side, Adoranne, bound hand and foot, gagged with a silken scarf and tied to a gold-brocaded easy chair. She tugged frantically at her bonds as she saw O'Leary, her blue eyes wide. She was wearing a pale blue nightgown, he saw, an imaginative garment as substantial as a spiderweb. O'Leary smiled encouragingly at the girl and motioned with the gun at Goruble.

"After you, your borrowed Majesty," he said. Goruble quickly stepped through the door, went to Adoranne's chair, skipped behind it and faced O'Leary.

"There are a few other matters I must mention to you," he said, looking unaccountably smug. "First——"

"Never mind that. Untie her."

Goruble held up a plump hand. "Patience, if you please. I hardly think you dare fire the shatter-gun in such intimate juxtaposition to the object of your anxieties . . . He put a palm familiarly on the bare, rounded shoulder of the princess. "And if you should feel impelled to some more animalistic assault, let me point out that the controls are within my easy reach." He nodded to a variety of levers set in the wall to his left. "True, you might manage to halt me—but the danger of ricochets . . ." he smirked. "I'd suggest you exercise caution."

O'Leary looked from Adoranne to the monarch, noting the close-set walls, the nearness to hand of the levers . . .

"All right," he said between his teeth, "spit it out."

"The Traveler here—as perhaps you're aware—is a standard utility model. It can place its cargo at predetermined triordinates and return to base setting, requiring a controller at the console, of course. But what you *don't* know is that I have made certain special arrangements, to fit my, ah, specialized needs here."

The king nodded to a point between himself and O'Leary just outside the half-open door. "If you'd take a step forward so that I can point out the modifications—ah, that's close enough," he said sharply as O'Leary reached the threshold. "I found it convenient to so arrange matters that I could despatch useful loads to random locations without the necessity for my accompanying them."

He pointed to a number of heavy braided copper cables dangling across the panel. "My modifications were crude, perhaps, but effective. I was able to bring the entire area of the corridor there, to a distance of some fifteen feet, well within effective range." He smiled contentedly, reached for a lever. O'Leary jerked the gun up, had a quick mental image of the explosive pellets smacking into Adoranne's soft flesh; he tossed the gun aside, leaped——

——and landed on his face. He was lying in a

drift of powdery snow packed against a rocky wall that rose from a gale-swept ledge of glittering ice. He gasped as a blast of arctic wind ripped at him; through a blur of tears he saw a small purple sun low in the black sky, a ragged line of ice peaks. His lungs caught at the thin air—like breathing razor blades.

He tried to scramble to his feet; the wind knocked him down. He stayed low then, rolled, reached the inadequate shelter of a drifted cranny. He wouldn't last long here. There had to be some place to get in out of the cold . . . He picked a spot ten feet distant, where the rock wall angled sharply. *Just out of sight around that outcropping,* he thought desperately, *there's a door set in the stone. All I have to do is reach it.* He pictured it, built the image, then . . . There!

Had he felt the familiar faint thump in the orderly flow of entropy? It was hard to tell, with this typhoon blasting at him. But it had to be! It must be a hundred below zero here. The stone at his back and the ice under his hands had burned like hot coals at first. Now everything was getting remote, as though he were encased in thick plastic.

He forced himself to move, crawled forward, almost went down on his face as the full force of the wind struck him. His hands were like wooden mallets now. He made another yard, skidded back as a particularly vicious gust slammed against him, tried again—and saw the soft glow of yellow light across the snow ahead, a cheery reflection in the ice. He rounded the shoulder of rock; there it was, a glass door in an aluminum frame, a tall rectangle of warmth against the cold and dark.

No point in dwelling on the incongruity of it—just reach it. The latch was a foot from his hand. He lunged, caught it, felt the door yield and swing in. He fell half-through the door into a sea of warmth.

He rested a moment, then pulled himself farther inside. The door whooshed shut behind him. Soft music was playing. He lay with his cheek against a rug, breathing in short, painful gasps. Then he sat up, looked around at oil-rubbed, wood-paneled walls, a built-in bar with gleaming glasses and a silver tray, a framed painting showing colors aswirl on a silvery field. He got to his feet, lurched across to the bar, found a bottle, poured a stiff drink, took it at a gulp.

OK, no time to waste; no time to wonder what sort of place this was he'd found, or where it was in the universe. It certainly wasn't anywhere on the familiar old planet Earth.

He had to get back. Goruble had obviously been all ready to travel, just waiting to finish off his enemy before he left. O'Leary closed his eyes. Ignoring the throb of returning sensation in his hands and feet and ears, he pictured the dark, musty passage under Goruble's palace. Adoranne was there; she needed him . . .

There was a thump as though the world had grounded on a sand bar. O'Leary's eyes flew open. He was standing in pitch darkness, in an odor of dust and mildewed wood. Had he made a mistake?

"Over this way, Sir Lafayette," a rumbling voice whispered. "Boy, you sure get around."

"Yokabump!" O'Leary groped toward the voice, felt a massive shoulder under his hand at belt height. "Where is he? I've got to get there before——"

"Wow! Your mitts are like a couple of ice bags!" Yokabump tugged O'Leary forward. "Just around the corner here, there's a door. I was staying out of sight and I couldn't see what was happening, but I heard you yell. Then old Goruble was snickering and talking to himself, and I sneaked a peek. I pretty near jumped him myself when I seen her Highness, tied to a chair. But then I figured——"

"Then they're still here?"

"Sure. His Majesty's working away like a one-man band, switching wires around. I'm glad you didn't stay away long."

"How did you know where I was?"

"I heard the air sort of whoosh. I noticed that before, when you did the fade from the dungeon——"

"Oh, you were hanging around then, were you?"

"Sure, I like to keep in touch."

"Shhh." O'Leary pushed through the rough wooden door into the passage he had vacated so precipitously five minutes earlier. He was fifteen feet from the open door to the Traveler—roughly the distance he had crawled on the ice ledge. Goruble was peering anxiously at dial faces; in the chair, Adoranne tugged futilely at the bell cord binding her arms. O'Leary eased out into the passage, started softly forward. He would reach the door, then in one jump, grab Goruble and hustle him away from the controls.

O'Leary's head cracked a low beam in the dark. Goruble looked up sharply at the sound, stood gaping for an instant as O'Leary, half-stunned, staggered toward him; then the usurper whirled and reached as O'Leary jumped——

——Light glared abruptly; something caught at O'Leary's foot, pitching him headlong into a mass of thorny shrubbery. Steamy air redolent of crushed foliage, rotted vegetation, humid soil and growing things closed around him like a Turkish bath. He floundered, fought his way clear of clinging tendrils of rubbery green, ducked as an inch-long insect buzzed his face. Sharp-edged red and green leaves scraped at him. Small flying midges swarmed about him, humming. There was a rasp of scales on bark; a wrist-thick snake of a vivid green hue slid into view on a leafy bough just ahead, raised a wedge-shaped head to stare. Somewhere above, birds were screeching back and forth from the tops of the towering trees.

O'Leary struggled upright, groped for footing in the tangle of fallen greenery. This time he'd fool Goruble: about ten feet in *that* direction, he estimated. The snake was still there, looking him over. He ducked aside from it, crawled over a fallen tree limb and fanned at the swarming insects. About here, he decided . . .

A movement caught by at the corner of his eye made him whirl. A great striped feline with a bushy yellowish mane was poised in the crotch of a yard-thick tree six feet above O'Leary's head, the green eyes fixed on him like stabbing spears. The jaws parted in a roar that fluttered leaves all around. The cat drew in its hind legs, gathering itself for a leap, roared again and sprang.

O'Leary squeezed his eyes shut, muttered a quick specification, threw himself to one side as the heavy body hurtled past. He slammed into an unyielding wall as a tremendous impact sounded behind him, followed by an ear-splitting yell, a ripping of cloth.

He staggered upright. He was back inside the Traveler, just behind Adoranne's chair. The big cat recovered from its first thwarted spring, whirled toward the fleeing figure of Goruble, whose velvet doublet had been split from top to bottom in the first near-miss, revealing a monogrammed silk undershirt.

O'Leary caught an instant's glimpse of Yokabump's bignosed face in the dark passage beyond the king. Then Goruble was going down face-first as the attacking predator sailed over him, skidded to a halt, rounded to renew the assault. O'Leary grabbed for the lever Goruble had used and pulled it down as the half-lion, half-tiger bounded across Goruble, sprang for the threshold—and disappeared with a sharp whack! of displaced air.

O'Leary sagged and let out a long sigh. Yokabump waddled to the door and bent to rub his shin.

"The old boy moves pretty good," he said. "I nearly missed. He's down for the count, though."

O'Leary went to Adoranne, "I'll have you loose in a minute." He started in on the knots. Yokabump produced a large clasp knife and sawed at the heavy cord on her wrists. A moment later she rose out of the chair and threw herself into O'Leary's arms.

"Oh, Sir Lafayette . . ." He felt hot tears on the side of his neck and discovered that he was beaming broadly. He patted her silken hip in a comforting way.

"Now, now, your Highness," he soothed, "it's all over but the singing and dancing."

"Oh-oh, he's coming around." Yokabump indicated the fallen monarch, stirring and groaning on the floor.

"Better tie him up," O'Leary suggested. "He's too tricky to let wander around loose."

"By your leave, Sir Lafayette." The dwarf stepped to Goruble's side and squatted down on bowed legs.

"Ah, there, your Majesty," he said in a lugubrious tone. "Have you got any last words to say before . . . before . . ."

"What . . ." The king gasped. "Where——"

"Just lie quiet, your Majesty; it's easier that way, they say."

"Easier? Ow, my head . . ." Goruble tried to sit up. Yokabump pressed him back. "It was the best, your Majesty; he got you. Tore your insides out. Don't look. It's too horrible."

"My insides? But—but I don't feel a thing, just my head."

"A merciful provision of nature. But about those last words—better hurry."

"Then—it's all over for me?" Goruble slumped back. "Ah, the pity of it, Yokabump. And all because I was too tender hearted. If I'd done away with the infant——"

"Tender hearted?" O'Leary cut in. "You killed the king, stole his throne, lived it up for twenty-odd years, then brought in a goon to terrorize your own would-be subjects, gave him a dinosaur to assist in the job, and finally tried to do away with her Highness. That's tender hearted?"

"One thing leads to another," Goruble gasped, "as you'll find for yourself. I needed a distraction; the people were grumbling about taxes and even after all these years, still asking too many questions about the former king's death. They weren't too happy with the story that I was his wandering cousin come home. So I made a number of trips in the Traveler, found Lod living in a cave and brought him here. Then I fetched along that great ugly reptile; it fitted in with the old legend of a dragon. Eventually, of course, I intended to do away with it and reap the plaudits of the yokels. But the scheme backfired. Lod grew stronger, while I heard the muttering daily grow louder. The people wanted Adoranne, and always there were rumors of the lost prince." He sighed. "And to think that I could have saved all this, if I could merely have brought myself to murder a tot."

"What's a tot got to do with it?"

"Eh? Why, I refer to the infant prince, of course. Exile was the most I could manage. And now see what it's brought me to."

"You . . . exiled the little prince?" Adoranne gasped. "You horrid, wicked man! And to think I thought you were my uncle! And all these years, you've known where the lost crown prince was."

"No, my dear, I didn't. He was crying in his crib, poor motherless tot—orphaned by my hand, though accidentally. I sent him—I didn't know where. But he thrived—ah, all too well. Cosmic justice, I suppose. And now——"

"How do you know he thrived?" Adoranne exclaimed.

"Just look at him for yourself," Goruble said.

"There he is, standing over me, looking down at me with that accusing expression."

Adoranne gasped. O'Leary looked to left and right, puzzled. Yokabump nodded his heavy head wisely.

"Now you're seeing visions, eh?" O'Leary commented. "But it's a little late for regrets."

Goruble was staring up at O'Leary. "You mean—you didn't know?"

"Know what?"

"The prince—the child that I sent away, twenty-three years ago—is *you*!"

Beside O'Leary, Adoranne gasped aloud. "Then . . . then you, Sir Lafayette . . . are the rightful king of Artesia."

"Now, hold on," O'Leary protested. "Are you all crazy? I'm an American. I never saw this place until a week or so ago."

"I knew you by the ring," Goruble said weakly.

"What ring?" Adoranne asked quickly.

O'Leary held out his right hand. "You mean this?"

Adoranne seized his hand, turned the ring to show the device.

"The ax and dragon—the royal signet!" She looked at O'Leary wide-eyed. "Why didn't you show it sooner, Sir Lafayette—your Majesty?"

"He told me to reverse it," Lafayette said. "But——"

"I should have known then that my plans would come to naught," Goruble went on. "But I thought that by casting suspicion on you, I could dispose of you painlessly."

"Your jail's a long way from painless," O'Leary put in.

"Then you escaped somehow. Sterner measures were called for. I employed my specialized remote control equipment to send you away. How you returned, I still don't know. I followed your progress and waited here for the showdown, only to have it—alas—end in my defeat, disemboweled by a ravening monster unleashed by my own hand."

"Oh, that," Yokabump called from inside the Traveler, where he was gazing at dials and levers, "that was just a gag, your ex-Majesty. You're not hurt. On your feet now, and we'll toss you into your own dungeon until your trial comes up."

"Not hurt?" Goruble sat up, felt gingerly over his corpulent frame. "You mean . . ." His eyes went to the open door to his stolen machine. In an instant, he was on his feet, plunging between O'Leary and Adoranne, dashing for the entry.

Yokabump reached for a lever, waited, threw it just as the fat monarch sprang for the entry. There was a clap of air and Goruble was gone.

"I hope he lands in the same spot as the cat," the jester said, dusting his hands. "The skunk. Leaves me out of a job, I guess—unless your new Majesty wants to take me on?" He looked hopefully at O'Leary.

"Wait a minute," Lafayette protested. "Adoranne's the heir to the throne! I'm just a guy who wandered into the scene."

The princess took his arm and looked up at him warmly. "I know a way to solve the dilemma," she said softly. "The whole question will become merely academic if we . . . if I . . . if you . . ."

"Oh, boy," Yokabump chortled. "Wait'll I spread the word. There's nothing like a royal wedding to cheer everybody up!"

CHAPTER XIII

A glittering assemblage filled the ballroom, hanging back shyly from O'Leary in his new eminence.

"As I see it, Lafayette—that is, your Majesty," Nicodaeus was saying.

"Knock off that 'majesty' stuff," O'Leary said. "Adoranne's the queen. I already told you how I happened to come here."

"Remarkable," Nicodaeus shook his head. "Of course, you had a strong natural affinity for this tricoordinate universe, having lived here until the age of two. Odd that you have no recollection of palace life at all."

"It did seem familiar, in a way. But I thought it was just because I'd invented it. And I caught on to the language in a hurry. I guess it was all there, in my subconscious."

"Of course, and when you began consciously striving to break down the interplane barriers, it was only natural that you should revert to your natural world of origin, thus canceling out at last the Probability Stresses you'd been creating in the other continuum. But I don't think it's ever been done before without equipment. Quite an achievement."

"I still don't see how it works," Lafayette protested. "I just dreamed it up. How could it be real?"

"It was here all along, Lafayette. Your discontent with your drab existence was an expression of the unconscious yearning toward your native clime. As for your belonging—with all the infinite universes to choose from, surely for every man there must be one where he is king."

"But that doesn't explain how I can invent anything from a bathtub to an iguanodon—and find it waiting just around the next bend."

"You created nothing; those things existed—somewhere. You've merely been manipulating them along lines of weakness in the probability fabric. I'm afraid all that will have to come to an end, however, as soon as I've reported in. We can't have anyone—even yourself, your Majesty—mucking about the natural order of things."

O'Leary looked at his watch. "Where's Adoranne?" he inquired. "The party's due to begin any minute."

"She'll be along. Now I have to be going, Lafayette. It's time for my regular Friday evening report." The inspector of continua nodded and hurried away. The orchestra was playing what sounded like a Strauss waltz, except that O'Leary had been assured the number had been composed by someone named Cushman Y. Blatz. He stepped through the tall glass doors to the terrace, sniffed the perfume of flowers on the warm night air. Not a bad place at all, this Artesia—king or no king. And with Adoranne as his intended bride——

There was a sudden rush of feet across the lawn below. O'Leary looked around in time to see Count Alain, dust-streaked and grim-faced, leap the balustrade, naked sword in hand. O'Leary dropped his glass with a crash.

"Hey, you startled me——" he started. Alain sprang to him, jammed the sword point against his new green velvet doublet.

"All right, where is she, you slimy schemer!" he rasped. "One yell, and I'll let you have it. Now speak up—and she'd better be unharmed!"

"Look, you've got the wrong slant on all this," O'Leary protested, backing away. Alain followed relentlessly.

"You're a bold scoundrel," the count snarled. "I take it you've done away with his Majesty—else you'd not be disporting yourself openly, here on his very terrace!"

"Well, we just sort of, ah, sent him away."

"And her Highness!" The sword jabbed harder.

"She's here—she'll be down in a minute! Look, Al old boy, I can explain."

"As I thought; you had her all along. And I, dolt that I was, spent a day and a night on a fool's errand."

"I told you that was a dry run. Did you see what was left of Lod?"

"When thieves fall out . . ." Alain quoted. "You slew him by a trick, I suppose; but you'll have no chance to trick me."

There was a sharp cry from the direction of the open doors. O'Leary looked, saw Adoranne standing in the opening, indescribably lovely in a gown of white, with diamonds in her hair.

"Your Highness!" Count Alain said huskily. "You're safe! And as for this wretch . . ." He tensed his arm, looking O'Leary in the eye.

Adoranne screamed. A dark shadow moved behind Alain; there was a dull clunk! and the young nobleman dropped the sword with a clang and fell against O'Leary, who caught him, letting him down on the flagged pavement. The wide figure of the Red Bull stood grinning a vast, crooked grin.

"I seen duh slob about tuh ram duh iron to yuh, bo," he stated. He ducked his red-maned head at Adoranne. "Hi, yer Highness." He tugged at O'Leary's limp arm. "Look, I waited around like yuh said, and the pickin's was great." The thick red fingers lifted half a dozen gold watches from a baggy side pocket. "T'anks, pal. You and me make a great team. But, look, I got a idear fer a caper dat'll make dis stuff look like chicken feed."

Adoranne gave a long sigh and sagged against the doorframe. O'Leary jumped to her, caught her slender body, lifted her in his arms.

"She's fainted," he announced, in a cracking voice. "Somebody do something!"

"I got to do a fast fade, chum," the Red Bull announced. "How's about we rondyvooze at duh Ax and Dragon at midnight Tuesday? How's about I wear a yeller tulip dis time, OK?" He eased over the balustrade and was gone. People were rushing up now, emitting squeaks as they saw the limp princess.

"I'll take her to her room," O'Leary said. "The poor girl's had a shock." With a fussy chamberlain leading the way and half a dozen ladies-in-waiting clucking alongside, O'Leary puffed up three flights, staggered along the marble-floored corridor and waited while the door was opened. Then he pushed through, made for the wide, canopied bed, with its yellow silk coverlet and eased his burden gently down. Behind him, the door clicked softly. He turned. He was alone in the room with Adoranne. Damn the nitwits! Where were the smelling salts? Probably because he hadn't given his royal invitation, they were all hanging back. Well——

Adoranne's eyes fluttered. "Count Alain . . ." she breathed. "Is he . . . all right?"

O'Leary sat on the edge of the bed. "Sure, he's OK. The Red Bull just cracked him over the head. Are you feeling OK now?"

"Of course, Lafayette. But you—he threatened you with his sword."

"The poor guy still doesn't know the score. That's all right. He was just trying to help you."

"You'll not hold a grudge?" Adoranne's shapely arms reached up around Lafayette's neck and pulled his face down. Her lips were as soft as pink velvet. There were tiny diamond buttons up the front of her silvery dress. Lafayette's hand wandered to them . . .

"Your Majesty," Adoranne murmured.

"Do we have to wait until tomorrow?" O'Leary heard himself saying hoarsely.

"You are the king," Adoranne's hand went to the buttons. They parted easily: one, two . . . a curve of white throat . . . three, four, five . . . a bit of lace . . . six, and a tug at a ribbon, and——

There was a distinct thump! and the lights dimmed to a single bulb glaring fifty feet away over a dark door frame. O'Leary sat up, heard bedsprings squeak under him. "Adoranne?" His hand groped, finding only a coarse blanket stretched over a lumpy mattress.

"Hey, shaddup," a voice growled from six feet away. "Can't a guy get some sleep?"

"Where—where am I?" O'Leary choked out.

"Sleeping it off, hey? I din't see youse when I come in. Yer in the Railroad Men's Y, second floor, a buck for the bed; four bits extra for a shower. But what I says is, who needs it?"

O'Leary stumbled from the bed, picked his way between bunks to the lighted door. He went down the stairs two at a time, pushed through the swinging door to the street, stared at dark shop windows, the blue gleam of mercury vapor lamps on tall steel poles. A few passers-by gave his clothes curious stares. He was back in Colby Corners.

It was an hour later. O'Leary stood on a corner, staring glumly at the gibbous moon hanging above Wienerburger's Gro. and Mkt. Just a little while ago he had seen that moon rise above a garden wall, gleaming through the poplars, reflecting in a fountain below the terrace where he and Nicodaeus had stood waiting for Adoranne. He swallowed an egg a passing goose had laid in his throat. Adoranne . . . and those buttons . . .

He straightened his back. One more try. He *had* to be able to get back. It wasn't fair to get stuck here, now, after all he'd gone through! He squeezed his eyes shut, again evoking the recollection of the garden, the French doors behind him, the music of the Blatz waltz. He sniffed, recalling the scent of jasmine, the fresh fragrance of the garden, hearing the murmur of wind through the trees . . .

There was a clatter of metal, a groaning wow-wow-wow; an engine blattered into life. O'Leary stared dismally at the jalopy parked across the way; it dug off with a squeal of rubber and roared away down the street in a cloud of exhaust fumes. So much for night-blooming jasmine and the wind in the willows.

Something was wrong. Always before, when he hadn't been distracted by something like a dinosaur snapping at his heels, he'd been able to make the shift, if he just tried hard enough. But now—a total blank. It was as though his abilities had suffered a paralytic stroke. He couldn't feel so much as a tentative stir even when he focused every erg of Psychic Energy he possessed.

But there had to be *some* way. If he could only get word to Nicodaeus, tell him——

O'Leary stood stock-still, balancing a fragile idea. Nicodaeus. He had talked to him before, from the phone in the jail. And the number—it had ten digits, he remembered that . . .

He screwed his eyes shut and tried for total recall. The reek of the cell, the chill of the morning air—Artesia was unaccountably cooler than Colby Corners—the white-washed wall. The phone had been an old-fashioned one, with a brass mouthpiece. And the number——

It started with a nine . . . five three four, that was it; then a nine, two oh's, and ended with—was it two eleven? Or one one two? . . .

Lafayette looked along the street. There was a phone booth there, half a block away. He tried his pocket; it yielded a dime. He set off at a run.

The phone booth was small, cramped, of an old-fashioned design, with a folding wooden door. Inside, an ancient instrument with a brass mouthpiece and a hand crank hung crookedly from a wall thick with carved initials and frank anatomical sketches accompanied by phone numbers. He held his breath, dropped the coin, twirled the crank. There was a long silence. Then a click. Then more silence. Then a sharp ping! and a hum.

"Central," a bright voice said tinnily in his ear. "Number, please."

"Uh—nine, five, three, four, nine, oh, oh, two, one one," Lafayette got off breathlessly.

"That number is no longer in service. Please consult your directory."

"Wait!" O'Leary yelled. "I have to talk to you!"

"Yes, sir?"

"I have to get back—back to Artesia," O'Leary gulped, rallying his thoughts. "I was there, you see. I belong there and everything was going swell; then, for no reason—here I was! And now——"

"I'm sorry, sir, where did you say you were calling from?"

"What? Why, from this phone booth—here in Colby Corners, on the corner next to the Schrumph's candy shop—what's that got——"

"An error has been made, sir. Calls from that sector are not authorized——"

"Let me talk to the supervisor!" O'Leary demanded. "It's a matter of life or . . .or exile!"

"Well . . . one moment, please."

O'Leary waited, hearing his heart pound. Half a minute passed. Then a distinguished-sounding voice said, "Yes?"

"Hello! Look, I've been the victim of some sort of mistake; I was perfectly happy there in Artesia——"

"One moment, please," the voice interrupted. Then in an aside: "Operator, this seems to be some sort of eccentric; the call originates in one of the null sectors, I note. Probably an inebriated local, dialing in by mistake. Lucky to get a line, at that. With the circuits as busy as they are, a fifty-year wait isn't uncommon."

"I'm not drunk! I wish I were! " O'Leary yelled. "Somebody listen! I'm King Lafayette the First of Artesia! This is all some terrible mistake! I want to talk to Nicodaeus! He'll tell you! Come to think of it, it's probably all his fault. He went to make his report, and he probably mixed things up and forgot to tell you I belonged there, in spite of having arrived sort of informally."

"Nicodaeus? Yes, I heard of his remarkable report, half an hour ago. You say you were involved?"

"I was there! You can't send me back here! I don't belong here! My little bride is waiting for me, my people demand their king, Yokabump needs a job, and the thought of the foundry——"

"Oh, yes, you must be the fellow Fishnet or

something of the sort; quite a merry chase you led our man. Do you know you've been creating a Probability Stress of .8 for weeks now? A remarkable technique you worked out, but I'm afraid we here at Central can't let it go on. You've caused a rather severe power drain on the Cosmic Energy Sourse. The dinosaur alone——"

"I didn't do that! He was already there!"

"One was, true, but you seem to have brought along another. At any rate, a Suppressor has now been focused on you. It will hold you firmly in place in your present continuum. It will even eliminate all dreaming, so you can look forward to sleep uninterrupted by bothersome fantasies from now on."

"I don't want to sleep uninterrupted by fantasies! I want to go home! Back to Artesia! I belong there, don't you understand?"

"No, my dear fellow; I can understand your desire to return—a rather pleasant, though backward, locus, or so our man states in his report—but we can't have you grasshoppering about all over the continua, now can we? But thank you for your interest, and now goodby——"

"Wait! Call Nicodaeus! He'll confirm what I said!"

"I'm a busy man, Mr. Fishnet; I have a backlog——"

"If you leave me here, there'll be a . . . a Probability Stress! And with the loused-up filing system you've got, it will be forty years before you remember what's causing it. And by then, I'll be a retired draftsman, still subsisting on sardines—and no dreams!"

"Well, I'll just make a check. Hold the line, please; if you ring off, you may never get through again."

O'Leary gripped the receiver, waiting. Through the glass in the door, he saw a fat woman approach along the street, digging in her purse for a coin. She seized the door handle, yanked, then caught sight of O'Leary and gave him an indignant look.

He covered the mouthpiece. "I'll be through in a minute," he muttered, mouthing the words through the glass. The woman snapped her jaw shut and glared at him.

Another minute ticked past. There was no sound on the line but a wavering hum. The fat woman rapped on the glass. O'Leary nodded, made motions indicating that he was waiting for a reply. The woman caught the door handle, pulled it half open. "See here, you, I'm in a hurry."

He jerked the door shut, and braced a foot against it as the invading female shook it furiously.

"Come on," O'Leary muttered. "What's keeping you?"

The fat woman stalked away. O'Leary relaxed. What was that fellow on the line doing? It had been a good five minutes now. What if he never came back! A fifty-year wait, he'd said. Lafayette pictured a pert face with jet-black hair, an impish smile. Never to see her again . . . He blinked. Jet-black hair? But Adoranne was a blonde——

O'Leary turned at a sound. The fat lady was back, a large cop in tow.

"That's him!" He heard the shrill screech

through the door. "Half an hour already he's been sitting there, just to spite me, not even talking. Look at him!"

The cop stooped and peered inside, looking O'Leary up and down, taking in the green doublet, the long yellow hose, the ruff at the neck, the medals, ribbons, gold chain.

"All right, you," the cop said; he hauled at the door. O'Leary braced himself, foot against the panel. The cop set himself, heaved——

The booth seemed to shimmer, faded to a smoky outline, and was gone. O'Leary fell backward off a marble bench beside the graveled walk under towering dark trees.

He scrambled up, looked around at the palace gardens, the tall, lighted windows above the terrace, the colored lights strung around the dancing pavilion. He was back—back in Artesia!

He started across the grass at a run, emerged from a screen of shrubs and skidded to a halt. By a tinkling fountain just ahead Adoranne stood—kissing Count Alain.

O'Leary ducked back out of sight. "Alain, it's all so strange," the princess was saying. "I can't believe he's gone—just like that—without even saying goodby."

"Now, Adoranne, don't fret. I guess he meant well. But after all, he *was* some kind of warlock."

"He was fine, and noble, and brave, and I—I'll never forget him," Adoranne said.

"Certainly; I'm grateful to him for rescuing you—even if he did leave that infernal dragon eating rosebushes in the side garden. When the legend said he'd bring back the thing's hide, I never expected the dragon would still be in it."

"I'm so . . . so glad you're here, Alain." Adoranne looked up into the young count's handsome face. "You won't flit off and leave me all alone, will you?"

"Never, your Highness . . ."

The couple resumed their stroll, hand in hand. As soon as they had passed, O'Leary crept out, crossed to the terrace, went along it to a small door leading to the kitchens. Inside, a startled cook looked up.

"Shhh!" O'Leary cautioned. "I'm traveling incognito." He wound his way past the hot ranges and the tables laden with food, went out by a rear door, took the service stair to the fourth floor. There was no one in sight, here in the servants' wing. He hurried along the corridor, rounded a corner——

A chambermaid in drab gray glanced up from her dusting; O'Leary looked into the tear-reddened eyes of Daphne.

"Oh!" A breath-taking smile took the place of the girl's heart broken expression of a moment before. "Your Majesty!" she breathed.

"Lafayette to you, girl," O'Leary said as he swept her into his arms. "Princess Adoranne is an adorable cutie, and I had an obligation to do what I could for her. But when it got right down to it, it was your face that kept haunting me."

"But—but you're a king, sire, and I'm just——"

"Let's leave the title to Adoranne and Alain. We've got too many things to catch up on to be bothered running the country."

EPILOGUE

Abstract from the log of Nicodaeus, inspector, serial number 786.

Ref: Locus Alpha Nine-three, Plane V-87, Fox 22 1-b. (Artesia)

Subj: Recruitment follow-up on L. O'Leary.

". . . since the double wedding performed the following day, having abdicated his claim to the throne in favor of the Princess Adoranne, subject appears mightily content, living with his bride, the Lady Daphne, in a comfortable apartment in the west palace annex. Communication equipment is still in place in a locked cabinet in the former laboratory of the present reporter. The line will continue to be monitored twenty-four hours daily. Qualified volunteers are in scarce supply, and a number of interesting assignments are waiting. On several occasions, subject has lifted the receiver and listened to the dial tone, but to date, he has not dialed."

Current and Recent Ace Science Fiction Releases of Special Interest, As Selected by the Editor of Destinies

Poul Anderson	ENSIGN FLANDRY	$1.95
	FLANDRY OF TERRA	$1.95
	THE MAN WHO COUNTS	$1.95
James Baen	THE BEST FROM GALAXY, VOL. IV	$1.95
Donald R. Bensen	AND HAVING WRIT	$1.95
Ben Bova	THE BEST FROM ANALOG	$2.25
Arsen Darnay	THE KARMA AFFAIR	$2.25
Gordon R. Dickson	PRO (illustrated)	$1.95
David Drake	HAMMER'S SLAMMERS	$1.95
Randall Garrett	MURDER AND MAGIC (fantasy)	$1.95
Harry Harrison	SKYFALL	$1.95
Keith Laumer	RETIEF AT LARGE	$1.95
	RETIEF UNBOUND	$1.95
Philip Francis Nowlan	ARMAGEDDON 2419 A.D. (revised by Spider Robinson)	$1.95
Jerry Pournelle	EXILES TO GLORY	$1.95
Spider Robinson	CALLAHAN'S CROSSTIME SALOON	$1.75
Thomas J. Ryan	THE ADOLESCENCE OF P-1	$2.25
Fred Saberhagen	BERSERKER MAN	$1.95
	THE HOLMES/DRACULA FILE (fantasy)	$1.95
	LOVE CONQUERS ALL	$1.95
	AN OLD FRIEND OF THE FAMILY (fantasy)	$1.95
	THE ULTIMATE ENEMY	$1.95
Dennis Schmidt	WAY-FARER	$1.75
Bob Shaw	SHIP OF STRANGERS	$1.95
	VERTIGO	$1.95
Charles Sheffield	SIGHT OF PROTEUS	$1.75
Norman Spinrad	THE STAR-SPANGLED FUTURE	$2.25
G. Harry Stine	THE THIRD INDUSTRIAL REVOLUTION (science fact)	$2.25
Ian Watson	MIRACLE VISITORS	$1.95